BAD MOON RISING

"Listen to me, Maguire. Stand down your teams or you will all suffer the consequences. A dozen Judges have been murdered by a rocket attack launched from within this building. The penalty for killing a Judge is death.

Surrender now, all of you, and I'll commute that sentence to life in the cubes. Otherwise I shoot to kill. What's your decision?"

"You're just one man, Dredd."

Riff could hear Dredd's words, utterly implacable. The Judge would kill them all if necessary. Riff willed Conchita to listen to reason, but she was already shaking her head.

"This is our block now. The Justice Department refused to help rescue my daughter, so Oswald Mosley no longer recognises your authority!"

"Wrong answer," Dredd replied. "You just signed your death warrant."

The radio cut to static...

Judge Dredd from Black Flame

#1: DREDD vs DEATH
Gordon Rennie

#2: BAD MOON RISING
David Bishop

More 2000 AD action

ABC Warriors

#1: THE MEDUSA WAR
Pat Mills & Alan Mitchell

JUDGE DREDD

BAD MOON RISING

DAVID BISHOP

BLACK **FLAME**

For John Wagner and Carlos Ezquerra,
the creators of Judge Dredd - where
would British comics be without them?

A Black Flame Publication
www.blackflame.com

First published in 2004 by BL Publishing, Games Workshop Ltd.,
Willow Road, Nottingham NG7 2WS, UK.

Distributed in the US by Simon & Schuster, 1230 Avenue of the
Americas, New York,. NY 10020, USA.

10 9 8 7 6 5 4 3 2 1

Cover illustration by Andy Clarke.

ISBN 1 84416 107 2

A CIP record for this book is available from the British Library.

Printed in the UK by Bookmarque, Surrey, UK.

MEGA-CITY ONE, 2126

PROLOGUE
SEPTEMBER 12, 2126

"Pull over!"

Muriel Staines jumped in her seat, startled by the bellowing voice. Her maroon roadster swerved across John Colby Overzoom before resuming its position in the fast lane, crawling along at half the minimum speed limit for any road in Mega-City One. The ninety-nine year-old motorist squinted at her rear-view mirror, trying to work out who had startled her. It was bad enough having to drive across five sectors in twilight to visit her older sister Grizzelda, especially with the way youngsters tore about the place these days. She didn't need some ninny shouting at her as well.

"Pull over – now!"

The voice was shot through with steely resolve, a bass growl of equal parts rockcrete and suppressed rage. Miss Staines felt sure she had recognised the voice from somewhere but couldn't quite place it. While Muriel searched her memory, the roadster wandered across six eastbound lanes. Normally such a manoeuvre would have caused a horrific crash but this stretch of road was curiously free of traffic.

"Pull over or else I will shoot out your tyres!"

The elderly spinster was the kind of motorist who saw thousands of accidents but never had one herself. The reason was simple: Miss Staines caused accidents, her erratic driving a catastrophic catalyst for chaos and carnage. Muriel had puttered on to John Colby three onramps back, leaving a trail of devastation of which she was blissfully unaware.

"This is your final warning, citizen! Cease and desist driving, or suffer the consequences!"

The mist surrounding Miss Staines's memory cleared and the eldster remembered where she had last heard the voice before. A Judge had come to her block and addressed the Neighbourhood Snooper Society: a collection of elderly busybodies and curtain twitchers Muriel had founded in 2112. The Judge had been a stern-faced fellow, short on patience and terse of phrase. Now what was his name again? Dredger? Drood?

No, it was Dredd – Judge Dredd!

Muriel bit her bottom lip nervously. Why should he be shouting at her? "Oh dear. I hope I haven't done something wrong," she muttered.

Sixty-seven seconds later Muriel was in cuffs, the maroon roadster a crumpled write-off on the overzoom's hard shoulder. Standing over her was Mega-City One's most famous law enforcer. Dredd's motorcycle helmet obscured most of his head and face, so only his surly mouth and jutting jaw line were clearly visible. But his dark mood was all too evident.

"Driving below the legal speed limit – six months," he snarled. "Driving too slowly in the fast lane – six months. Reckless endangerment of other motorists – five years. Careless use of a roadster causing death – twenty counts, each carrying a tariff of twelve years. Failing to observe the commands of a Judge – five years. Total sentence of two hundred and fifty-one years, to be served cumulatively."

A hover-wagon descended from the darkening sky as the overzoom's streetlights flickered into life. It would soon be night. Dredd peered down at his prisoner. "How old are you, citizen?"

Miss Staines was affronted at such impertinence. "A lady never–"

"How old?!"

The eldster sniffed haughtily. "Ninety-nine, if you must know."

The Judge nodded. "I'm disqualifying you from driving for life – just in case. I doubt medical science will keep you alive until your three hundred and fiftieth birthday, but I'm not taking any chances." He nodded to two Judge-Warders who had just emerged from the hover-wagon. "Get her out of here!"

Dredd activated the radio microphone in his helmet as Miss Staines was led away. "Dredd to Control. I've dealt with the perp responsible for the John Colby pile-up. If you haven't got anything else for me, I'm signing off–"

A brief crackle of static in Dredd's ear signified his transmission had been heard by one of the operators in Justice Department's despatch division. Control was populated by hundreds of Judges who sat behind terminals watching the city all day and night. They directed street patrols to crime scenes and potential trouble spots. The Big Meg was home to four hundred million people, crowded into several hundred sectors. Unemployment was endemic and the vast majority of citizens survived on welfare, bored beyond belief. Every one of them a potential criminal.

"Control to Dredd. Sorry but you're needed elsewhere."

The Judge scowled, his pugnacious frown souring further still. "Control, I've been on patrol for twenty-three hours non stop. I need twenty minutes in a sleep machine and a chance to eat. What's so urgent?"

"Sector 87 is severely short-handed and Psi-Division precogs are expecting trouble there tonight. You've been assigned to augment the street patrols in 87. Chief Judge Hershey personally selected you for this job. Report to Sector Chief Emily Caine – she's expecting you."

"Terrif," Dredd growled under his breath. "Anything else I should know?"

"Yes. You're due at roll call in nine minutes."

"It takes half an hour to reach Sector 87 from here."

"Deal with it. Control out." Another crackle of static indicated the conversation was at an end.

Dredd strode to his Lawmaster motorcycle and gunned the engine into life. The fat black tyres squealed in protest as he peeled away from the remains of Muriel Staines's roadster, the bike rapidly accelerating past one hundred and forty kilometres per hour. Dredd had never missed the start of a roll call in his long career as a Judge and he wasn't going to start now.

Misch wasn't like most children in Mega-City One. For a start, her skin was blue and she had mottled yellow spots around her eyes and across the back of her arms. Misch was humanoid, but her alien physiognomy displayed distinct differences from other children. Instead of hair, fat tendrils of excess flesh sprouted from her scalp and hung down from the back of her head. Her eyes were perfectly circular, and they had a nictitating membrane that protected them from the harsh sunlight on this strange world. Her hands had three digits and her mouth was filled with row upon row of sharp incisors. But the alien child had a friendly smile on her face most of the time.

This was not one of those times. Her broodfather, Nyon, was arguing with the creature that lived in the con-apt next door. Misch could hear them shouting at each other outside the front door; the paper-thin walls of the building ensured everyone else could hear the argument too. There were no secrets in Robert Hatch Block. Little more than a hovel, the structure housed three hundred alien families in tiny con-apts originally designed as single person dwellings.

Robert Hatch had been erected to cope with an overflow of newcomers from Alien Town; it was the Big Meg's sector designated for housing extra-terrestrials. The block was made of the cheapest materials available, its components prefabricated elsewhere and then slotted together on site. Robert Hatch has only been designed as a temporary solution to a short-term problem, with a maximum lifespan of eighteen months before it should have been demolished. Eighteen years later, the alien ghetto was still standing, an eyesore in the middle of Sector 87's most prosperous area.

Damp climbed the walls inside and out. The turbolifts had long since ceased working and no repair crew would ever set foot inside the building. Unless the residents were able to fix things themselves, they stayed broken. Paint peeled off the walls, light fittings flickered fitfully and the air conditioning system had years before surrendered. Down some corridors the air had a greasy, noxious taint, while ceilings were stained a sickly green.

Misch listened as her broodfather's guttural voice became harsher and more insistent. He was using Allspeak, the universal language adopted by most aliens when they were talking to each other.

"We have just as much right as you to live here!" Nyon protested.

"Maybe. But can't you do something about the stench from your con-apt? How am I supposed to eat with the smell of rotting flesh infesting my home?"

Misch could not help smiling to herself. Their neighbour was Kehclow, a gaseous lifeform from the Bilal Cluster who best resembled a translucent blue cloud. Misch did not doubt he could smell, but the thought of him having a nose amused her. It would look very out of place on Kehclow, who was seen floating along the corridors tutting to himself most evenings. The alien girl opened the front door a fraction so she could peer out at her broodfather. He did not look happy.

"Kehclow, you know perfectly well that my species are carrion eaters. We can only ingest nutrients from the corpses of animals that have been dead for several weeks. If you can suggest another way we could feed ourselves, I'd be happy to hear it. Otherwise, stop bothering me and my family about things we cannot change!"

Nyon's face was turning purple, a sure sign his temper was fast running out. Misch wished her broodmother was here; she would calm him down with a quiet whisper or two. But she had gone out to the alien shoppera in search of ingredients for their evening meal.

"If the air conditioning system was repaired–" Kehclow began.

"This wouldn't be a problem," Nyon agreed. "If each species was housed separately instead of being intermingled, you wouldn't have to tolerate our ways and we wouldn't have to tolerate yours. If, if, if – you can say 'if' all you want, but it won't change anything! Good evening to you!"

Misch retreated back into the con-apt, not wanting her broodfather to know she had been watching him. But she had heard Kehclow's final comment as Nyon began opening the door. "Vucking vultures…"

Nyon stopped and looked back at his gaseous neighbour. "What did you say?" Misch's broodfather hissed, cold fury in his voice.

"Nothing, nothing," Kehclow replied, hastily retreating down the corridor. "Good morrow to you!"

Nyon stepped into the con-apt and slammed the door behind him. He let slip a string of obscenities in the native tongue of R'qeen before noticing his daughter in the corner playing with her toys. "Misch! I didn't see you there." Nyon shuffled awkwardly. "Don't tell your broodmother what I said, will you?"

She smiled at him, one hand spinning a multi-coloured hover-globe in the air. "Don't worry. I only speak R'qeen here. She says I have to use Allspeak or the human's language when I go outside."

Nyon crouched beside his daughter, stroking the side of her face with one hand. "That's right. If we are going to stay here, we have to make an effort to assimilate some of the culture from this world. That doesn't mean we forget who we are or where we came from – we will always be R'qeen."

Misch smiled and nodded but Something was troubling her: the word that had so angered her broodfather. She had heard it before while playing with offspring from other alien species in the block. "What is a vulture?"

Nyon frowned. "You heard what Kehclow said?"

"I've heard it before. What does it mean?"

He stood up. "It is a bad word. Centuries ago there was a species of animal on this world that fed on carrion, like us. It was called a vulture. The creature was reviled and hunted to extinction. The humans describe anyone who preys on others, especially the helpless, as being vultures. When someone calls you that, they are saying you are no better than an animal. But we are not animals, are we?"

Misch shook her head. Nyon sighed. "I know it is not easy for you, Misch, growing up in this place, apart from most of your family and friends. But things will get better – I promise you." He bent down and held out his arms. "Come."

Misch jumped into her broodfather's arms, burying herself in his warm embrace. It felt like home, even if this strange world did not.

"Who's been assigned to bolster tonight's graveyard shift?"

Sector Chief Emily Caine was sitting behind the desk in her uncluttered office, enjoying the spectacle of her assistant squirming. Behind Caine was a window offering a breathtaking panoramic view of Sector 87. The last glints of sunlight were still colouring the sky but already the buildings, skedways and overzooms were being lit up in a spectacular display of colour and illumination. But Caine had no wish to admire the view. She was having far more fun with her deputy.

Patrick Temple was a weak-willed man who had risen to the rank of deputy Sector Chief by being little use at anything else. Nearly fifty, he had lost most of his hair and years of worry were etched into his nervous face. A failure as a Street Judge, Temple had been shifted sideways to administration where he could do less damage. Successive promotions had nudged him up the chain of command, more by virtue of seniority than expertise.

Caine liked to think of Temple as resembling the scum that floated on the surface of her morning cup of synthi-caff. When the drink was consumed, the scum remained, clinging to the side of the cup. So it was with Temple. Successive Sector Chiefs had come and gone but the deputy remained, never considered good enough for the big chair. At first Caine had considered dispensing with Temple altogether, but he proved an amusing distraction and a useful buffer between herself and the division heads within the sector house. Right now her deputy was reporting on efforts to draft in assistance from outside 87 to fill the gaps in their complement of Street Judges.

"Well, I put in a request to Justice Central for two dozen helmets, ma'am," Temple explained. "But I was told they couldn't spare that many, even bearing in mind the precog prophecy· for tonight..." He trailed off ineffectually.

Grud, what a waste of skin, Caine thought to herself. She smiled broadly at the deputy. "So, how many are we getting?"

"Err, one."

"One?"

"Yes, ma'am." Temple shifted uncomfortably under his superior's gaze. "But he's very good. I've never met the man myself, but I understand he's something of a hero within the department." The deputy consulted the screen of his palm unit for further details. "Numerous citations for bravery and dedication above and beyond the call of duty. Seems to have saved the city single-handedly from several significant threats–"

"And who is this over-achiever coming to join our humble ranks?"

"Dredd. Judge Joe Dredd."

That got Caine's attention. Why him? Of all the helmets they could send, why Dredd? "Really? Well, we are honoured. A living legend in our presence."

Temple nodded enthusiastically. "He's on his way here. Do you want to delay the start of roll call until he arrives?"

Caine snorted disdainfully. "If Dredd can't be bothered to report to a new assignment on time, I fail to see why we should wait for him. Call the graveyard shift together. Roll call begins on time at twenty hundred hours. Dismissed!"

Temple scuttled from the room, already tapping instructions into his palm unit for display on screens spread around each area of the sector house. Once he had gone, Caine went to the spotless bathroom adjacent to her office. Most Judges in the building had to share uni-sex accommodation and cleaning facilities. Being Sector Chief accorded few privileges but Caine felt having her own quarters was one of the most valuable.

She threw some cold water on her face before staring into a mirror. Caine wore the usual Judge's uniform but dispensed with the helmet unless she was going outside the sector house. Her hair was a close-cropped mass of black curls, framing a lean face with piercing, hazel eyes. As she gazed at her reflection, Caine's thoughts kept coming back to the same question – why send Dredd? Did Justice Central know something it wasn't telling her? Was there some detail of the prediction that had not been passed on?

A small speaker set into the wall of her bathroom crackled into life. Deputy Sector Chief Temple cleared his throat before beginning the announcement. "Roll call begins in one minute. Could all members of tonight's graveyard shift please report to roll call now? That is all."

Satisfied with her appearance, Caine pushed aside the doubts raised by Dredd's imminent arrival. She would make sure he was kept on his toes for the next twelve hours – living legend or not. The Sector Chief smiled.

"I'm going to enjoy this," she muttered to herself before striding away.

20:00

Judge Lynn Miller hurried into the briefing room just as Caine reached the podium. Dozens of other law enforcers were already gathered in the large chamber, formed into lines facing a raised platform. Miller slipped into position among the other Judges; there was a conspicuous gap to her left. Deputy Sector Chief Temple was still droning his way through calling the roll to see who was present and correct for the night's graveyard shift. The full complement of Judges for a sector house was three hundred, but only two thirds of them were assigned to street patrol. The rest were ancillary and support staff. Tek-Division looked after all equipment, such as Lawmaster motorcycles and H-Wagons. Med-Division kept the Judges alive and fit for duty, while also providing forensic back up for cracking cases. The Armourer and his staff were responsible for all judicial weaponry, from the standard issue Lawgiver handgun to stumm gas and riot foam. The sector house had its own computer department, Judge-Warders policed the holding cubes and senior staff oversaw each sub-division.

Sector 87 had been through an arduous few months, losing nearly a fifth of its Street Judges. A badge-killer had accounted for more than a dozen before dying in a hail of bullets. Terrorist attacks on the Bloomingmacy's Shoppera by anti-commerce activists had claimed several more lives. In the last hour, Miller's partner Shurlock had been fatally wounded in an antiques heist that had gone spectacularly awry. A dozen perps tried to steal a priceless collection of real paper books from the Jackie Collins Museum of Literature on the corner of Steiner and Waldron. When the heist went bad, the thieves tried to shoot their way out. Shurlock had died thirty minutes earlier in the med-bay. Miller had been changing her blood-stained uniform when the summons for roll call came.

She pushed her shock white hair out of her eyes and looked up at Caine on the podium. The Sector Chief asked Temple for the tally. "Seventy-seven present and correct, ma'am. Five more on life support. We just lost…" Temple paused to consult with his palm unit. "Shurluck."

"Shurlock," Miller muttered under her breath, "you simp."

Caine nodded to her deputy before addressing those assembled. "Seventy-seven Street Judges present from the standard graveyard shift complement of a hundred. Not ideal but there's not much we can do about that now. I personally put in a request to Justice Central for replace-ments and they are sending us one helmet. When he deigns to show his face, I will introduce him. In the meantime, I don't want to hear any grumbling about hav-ing to pull extra shifts to cover for the shortfall. Suck it up, people! You're all here to do a job, so that's what you'll do. Anybody wants to whine about it, they can see me after roll call. But they may find it difficult to ride a Lawmaster with my boot knife up their ass – is that clear?"

Misch was bored. Nyon had gone out to a meeting of the block residents' action group and her broodmother had still not returned. The alien shoppera was two sectors away and it was a convoluted journey just to buy the simplest of ingredients from offworld.

The R'qeen child wiped her blue hand across the con-apt's single window, clearing away the condensation long enough to look down at the busy skedway below. The walls inside Robert Hatch were permanently damp since the air conditioning had given way. The alien girl knew her brood were luckier than most because they lived on the third floor. Her cousins Coya, Aldre and Selmak were stuck up on the twenty-seventh floor, where residents had been forced to smash most of the windows to provide ventilation.

Across the skedway Misch could see two humans skulking in a darkened doorway; they were looking up at her building. Sector 87 was among the city's more affluent areas but vandals had broken many of the street-lights around Robert Hatch; just another symptom of the humans' hatred for the alien residents. A pair of Judges rode past and the humans shrank back into the shadows, one of them clutching a carryall close to itself. What have they got in there, the R'qeen girl wondered? She concentrated hard and reached out with her mind, trying to focus on their thoughts. Misch had found she could sometimes sense what humans were thinking, as if she had a window to see what they felt and imagined. If she did it too often, her head hurt. But it was a useful talent and one that had kept her out of trouble on more than one occasion. She bit her bottom lip and pushed.

Drokking freakshow central!

'Sright. Creeps shouldn't be here!

We'll show them. See how they like a taste of this.

Yeah. Where're we putting that sweet baby?

Downstairs. Near the foundations.

When that goes – these freakin' scum gonna fry.

Hot fat on a stick, man.

You said it.

Let's go!

Misch staggered backwards. There was a searing pain behind her eyes. She tripped over one of her toys and fell to the floor, temporarily blinded by the intensity of the emotions she had experienced. Hatred, raw and vicious, coupled with a hunger for inflicting misery. Something else too – a yearning to see flames burning, red and yellow and white, hot and alive. The alien girl cried out, overwhelmed by these sensations. She knew something terrible was going to happen but she couldn't hold back the blackness any longer. She let it wash over her, chilling her to the bone.

Tek-Division Judge Terry Brady owed his life to Dredd. Ten years earlier the mechanic had been a juve thief for hire, specialising in boosting high performance motor-cycles and hover-cars. It was Dredd who caught Brady hot-wiring a Justice Department H-Wagon to get initiated into Sector 87's leading street gang, the Doug McClure Runners. By rights Brady should still be serving a thirty year stretch in the iso-cubes, but Dredd had offered him a second chance: to join Tek-Division. The department needed new blood and fresh ideas.

At first Brady's rebellious streak almost persuaded him to turn down the offer, until he remembered his time in the juve cubes and decided to get smart. After a lengthy probationary period he emerged as the star pupil of his training class, able to invent unique solutions to prob-lems thanks to a supposedly wasted youth of petty crime. Graduating with honours, Terry had been given the uni-form of a Tek-Judge and offered his chance of placement. It only took him moments to ask for a posting back to Sector 87. That was five years ago and he was rapidly rising through the ranks. But he never forgot the man who had given him a second chance. The Tek-Judge hoped to repay that debt one day.

Brady was just starting the graveyard shift in the sector house's cavernous garage when he heard the familiar roar of an approaching Lawmaster. The motorcycle tore inside the building, tyres protesting as the brakes were slammed on, a thick black skid mark smearing across the floor. Terry ran towards the new arrival who was already dismounting.

"Hey! You shouldn't treat your ride like that! Who the hell do you think you are, anyway? Look after your motorcycle and it'll–"

The Judge turned round and let Brady see the five letter name emblazoned on his badge. "D-Dredd? Judge Dredd?" The abashed mechanic stopped, unprepared for the encounter.

"Roll call. Where do I find it?"

Brady pointed to the nearest turbolift. "One floor up, in the briefing room."

Dredd was already moving. "Thanks!" he shouted over his shoulder.

"You're welcome." The Tek-Judge remembered hearing an earlier announcement. "But roll call started ten minutes ago…"

Caine almost smiled when she heard someone striding briskly towards the briefing room. Good. She would make an example of this latecomer.

"As you may have heard, Psi-Division precogs are predicting trouble for this sector tonight. Frankly, that doesn't require any psychic abilities. There's a full moon tonight and we all know how that brings out the crazies. Coupled with that is the fact we are fast approaching–"

Dredd strode into the room and stopped, ready to report for duty. A few of the other Street Judges acknowledged his presence but the Sector Chief chose to ignore him and carry on with her address.

"We are fast approaching Friday the Thirteenth. According to the superstition, this is a day bedevilled by bad luck. While Justice Department may officially give no credence to such antiquated notions, the reality is that many of our citizens do. As a result, we can expect all manner of madness and stupidity across the sector tonight. The lunatic fringe will be out in force. Case in point: the Mega-City Anti-Superstition Society, also known as M-CASS, is planning a demonstration to prove there is no such thing as bad luck. We've already received reports of thirteen black cats having been stolen from a reserve for endangered domestic animal species. We don't know if these psycho-cube candidates are planning one of their stunts for our sector but, since the society's founder lives here, it seems likely."

Caine stopped and turned to look at Dredd. "Well, it seems our reinforcement has finally arrived. So kind of you to join us."

Dredd saluted crisply. "Excuse my lateness, I was–"

The Sector Chief held up a hand to silence the newcomer. "Spare us the explanations. If you can't make it to roll call on time, at least don't hold us up any further with some weak excuse." Caine stepped down from the podium and strolled towards Dredd, continuing to address the other Judges already assembled. "If there's one thing I cannot tolerate, it is lateness. This indicates a lack of respect not just for my authority, but more importantly a lack of respect for your fellow Judges. I understand some within the department look up to this man as a symbol of justice. Indeed, his volumes on comportment are set texts at the Academy of Law. But that is no excuse for being tardy." She stopped in front of Dredd and sneered at him. "I don't care whether you're a legend or not. While you are assigned to my sector house, you answer to me. Is that clear?"

"Yes, ma'am!" Dredd snapped back.

"Very well. Report to me after roll call and we will discuss the nature of your reprimand. You may now join the ranks of your fellow Judges – that's if you don't consider yourself too good for them."

"No, ma'am!" Dredd moved to fill the empty space beside Miller. Caine walked between the ranks inspecting the Street Judges while continuing with her briefing.

"Now, where was I? Oh yes, the M-CASS. Well, as I was saying before I was interrupted, that is just one of the problems you will face tonight. Sump Industries is hosting the regional finals of its Miss MC-1 Ugly Pageant at the Sid Harmor Hippodrome. So we can expect trouble from anti-ugly activists intent on disrupting the festivities. To add to your fun, Weather Control over this sector has collapsed again. Tek-Division says we can expect temperatures to approach a hundred degrees with humidity in excess of ninety per cent. So, expect a sultry night's work."

The Sector Chief returned to the podium. "Last, but definitely not least, there are reports of more trouble centred on the alien ghetto in Robert Hatch Block – infighting between the various species housed there and threats against the offworlders from xenophobic elements in surrounding blocks. Human residents have called a public meeting to voice their disapproval at having to live next door to families of R'qeen and other offworld species."

"Don't blame them," one of the Street Judges muttered under his breath. "Drokkin' freaks oughta be shipped back into space where they belong–"

"Who said that?!" Caine demanded loudly.

After an awkward silence one of the Street Judges stepped forward; his skull was shaved cleaned while a luxurious brown moustache adorned his top lip. The Sector Chief sighed. "Stammers, I might have known. You've been given one formal warning for inciting xenophobic behaviour. That little remark just earned you another. I will not tolerate bigots in my sector house!"

Stammers stepped back into line, his face flushed red with anger.

"All of you listen up!" Caine snarled. "These creatures may not be human but they have just as much right to live in Mega-City One as anyone else. Until the rebuilding of Alien Town is complete, they will continue to live in this sector and so they deserve our protection just as much as any other citizen. Do I make myself clear?" She turned to her deputy, who was still hovering to one side of the podium. "Temple, I have decided that you will address the public meeting as my representative. Take two Judges along as your escort, in case things get out of hand." Carter glanced back at her troops. "Miller – step forward!"

Judge Miller moved out of line. "Yes, ma'am?"

"You were Shurlock's partner?"

"Yes, ma'am."

"Then you'll need a new one. You can have Dredd, show him the ropes. Once he's settled in, the pair of you will be Deputy Sector Chief Temple's escort for the public meeting."

Miller saluted briskly before stepping back into position. Meanwhile Caine handed the briefing over to Temple. "Hand out the rest of the assignments and fall them out," she said before striding from the room.

Once they had been dismissed, Miller turned to her new partner, offering to shake his hand. "Lynn Miller – we've ridden together before. Ten years back, hotdog run into the Cursed Earth."

The pair began filing out of the briefing room with the other Judges. Dredd stroked his chin thoughtfully. "Been on a few of those... Miller? I once recommended someone called Miller as potential Sector Chief material."

The female Judge nodded. "That was me. Didn't get it. 'Too young' was the official reason."

"And the unofficial reason?"

Miller grimaced. "An incident from my time at the Academy came back to haunt me." Her gaze wandered temporarily to Stammers and his partner before returning to Dredd. "Don't worry about Caine, her bark is worse than her bite. She's just putting you in your place." Miller noticed Dredd regarding her bloodstained uniform. "Look, I need to get changed before we go out."

Dredd nodded. "I'll meet you at the garage in ten."

A heavy fist knocked on the Sector Chief's office door.

"Enter!"

Dredd walked briskly into the room, closing the door behind him before standing to attention in front of Caine's desk. The Sector Chief was reading through reports on a screen in front of her, and ignored Dredd for the moment. Eventually he cleared his throat to get her attention. Caine held up a hand, finishing what she was studying before looking up.

"Yes?"

Dredd grimaced. "You ordered me to report here after roll call, so we could discuss the nature of my reprimand."

Caine smiled. "Of course I did. Just wanted to make sure we both knew where we stood."

"Permission to speak candidly, ma'am."

The Sector Chief arched an eyebrow. "Permission granted."

"I was assigned to your sector house only nine minutes before the beginning of roll call. At that time I was half an hour away by Lawmaster. It was physically impossible for me to–"

"Excuse me for interrupting," Caine said, "but perhaps you didn't hear me earlier. I have no interest in your excuses. And since we're speaking candidly, there's something else you should know. I don't want you here, Dredd."

"Is that a fact?"

"Yes, it is." The Sector Chief stood up and began to

stroll around her office. "I put in a request to Justice Central for at least a dozen replacement Judges. Instead they send me one: you. What I am supposed to make of that, hmm?"

"Resources are stretched to the limit. Few Judges can be spared for reinforcing individual sector houses," Dredd replied. By now Caine was standing behind him.

"You may well be right. But I sense the hand of our Chief Judge at work here," she said. "Of all the Judges who could have been sent, why you?"

"I was available and–"

"At least a dozen other Judges were available. Why you?"

"I don't know," Dredd admitted.

"Really? I can't tell if you're being disingenuous or genuinely ignorant. Either way, it does you no credit." Caine returned to her seat. "I've just been looking through your personnel file. Some very interesting reading, particularly in the sealed section about you and ex-Judge Galen DeMarco."

"Sector Chiefs do not have authorisation to view such data."

Caine smiled. "Let's say I have a few friends in the Chief Judge's office, a fact you would do well to remember." She referred back to the screen on her desk. "According to one report, you had an un-judicial liaison with DeMarco."

"She developed an emotional attachment to me. She subsequently resigned, recognising her feelings were incompatible with being a Judge."

"Well, that's one interpretation." Caine shut down the files before leaning back in her chair, fingers forming a steeple in front of her face. "I've also spoken to a few other former Sector Chiefs who have had experience of your methods, Dredd. Don't think you'll be able to pull the same tricks here."

"What do you mean?"

Caine gestured to the thousands of buildings beyond her office window. "This is my territory, Dredd, and you won't take it away from me. I've heard all about how you turn up, start playing the big man, claiming you are just rooting out corruption whereas all the time you are usurping the authority of those above you in rank."

"I have no interest in usurping anyone," Dredd snarled. "I only care about upholding the Law and–"

"Yes, yes, we all know of your lifelong dedication to the Law. You've made no secret of having turned down the chance to become Chief Judge."

"I felt I could better serve the city–"

"By staying on the streets? Perhaps. But perhaps you prefer the role of kingmaker, choosing the new chief judge and pulling their strings from behind the scenes. It's no coincidence that Hershey's first experience of law enforcement was under you. How far under you, I wonder?"

Dredd slammed a fist on the Sector Chief's desk. "If you're suggesting–"

"I'm not suggesting anything but I seemed to have hit a nerve!" Caine smiled triumphantly. "Now hear this, Dredd. I have no time for grandstanding Judges who only want glory. The sooner you're out of my sector, the better. Do I make myself clear?"

Dredd leaned forwards to confront the Sector Chief. "I don't care what kind of inferiority complex you're nurturing, Caine, or what paranoid delusions you seem to be suffering from. I'm just here to uphold and enforce the Law. But if you repeat any of these baseless allegations outside this office, I will personally ensure you suffer the consequences. Do I make myself clear?"

The Sector Chief stood up abruptly. "You have your orders. Now get out of my face and out of my office." Caine pointed at the door. "Dismissed!"

● ● ●

Miller had just stepped under the shower when two male Judges walked into the ablutions area. In the lead was Stammers, a heavy-set figure in his early forties. He paused to leer at Miller as she soaped herself down. She had an athletic physique toned by more than a decade as a Street Judge, but her generous breasts always attracted too much attention. "Looking good there, Lynn."

"Keep your eyes to yourself, Eustace," she replied, making no attempt to shield herself from his gaze. Unisex showers and changing rooms were standard in sector houses. Since no Judge was permitted to have a sexual or romantic relationship, it had been decided gender segregation was an unnecessary luxury. The idea was fine in principle, but could still create problems with undisciplined officers like Stammers.

"Nobody calls me Eustace!" Stammers raged, his right hand balling into a fist. "You little slitch, I oughta–"

Miller squared up to him, ready to parry any blow and strike back. But Stammers's partner Riley stepped between the two adversaries, keeping them apart. He was the same age as Miller, with a youthful face. "Step back, Stammers! You've already got two formal warnings on your sheet. Start a fight with another Judge and Caine'll have to bounce you out of here!"

Stammers continued to push towards Miller for several seconds before his rage subsided. "I wouldn't waste my effort on the likes of you," he snarled at the naked woman. "Doubt you could handle a real man, anyway."

"If you meet any real men, send them round and I'll find out," Miller replied with a smile.

Riley shepherded his partner away. "Come on, Stammers. We're due on patrol. Now."

Miller blew them a kiss goodbye before returning to her shower. "Stomm for brains," she muttered when they had gone.

· · ·

Lleccas came home to find her broodling unconscious on the floor. The R'qeen woman dropped her bag of groceries and rushed to the child's side. "Misch! Misch! Are you all right?"

The girl stirred in her broodmother's arms. "You're home early…"

"Never mind about that. What happened to you?"

Misch frowned, her head still pounding. "I can't remember. I saw two men across the skedway. They seemed angry. I was trying to reach them–"

"Reach them? What do you mean, reach them?"

The alien child realised she had said too much. She sat up, one hand rubbing her temples where the throbbing pain felt worst. "Sometimes, if I concentrate, I can sense what other people are thinking or feeling."

Lleccas looked hard at her daughter. "Can you tell what I'm thinking?"

"That I'm in trouble?" Misch suggested, smiling weakly.

Lleccas rolled her eyes and gave the child a hug. "How long have you had this gift?" Misch shrugged. "It's called *metema*, the ability to look into the souls of others," Lleccas explained. "My broodmother possessed it, and her broodmother's broodmother had it too. Metema usually skips a generation but I was beginning to think you did not have it."

The child was unsure what to make of this news. "Is metema a good thing?"

"It can be but you must use it sparingly, especially now when you're still so young. Later, when you've grown, you may be able to persuade weaker minds into doing what you want. But this is a powerful gift and should never be used unwisely. Some R'qeen have died from pushing themselves too far. That's why you were unconscious when I came in. It's the body's way of protecting you."

Misch nodded. She thought she understood but it was a lot to take in. At least she wasn't in trouble. Then the alien child recalled what she had seen inside the minds of the two humans. "I think something terrible is going to happen," she whispered.

Dredd strode into the sector house garage to find Miller waiting for him astride her motorcycle. His own bike was nowhere to be seen. "Where's my Lawmaster?" he demanded.

"Just coming!" Tek-Judge Brady emerged from behind a crumpled H-Wagon, pushing Dredd's motorcycle. "I've given it a new set of tyres, recharged the laser cannon and restocked the ammunition panniers. You're all set."

Dredd glared at the mechanic. "And you are?"

"Tek-Judge Terry Brady. Used to be a booster for the Doug McClure Runners, until you set me straight."

Dredd took the Lawmaster from Brady and mounted it. "Thanks for the assist. Good to know I've got a few friends in this place."

"Anything you need, just let me know," the Tek-Judge added eagerly.

Dredd nodded before turning to Miller. "Ready?"

She gunned her engine into life. "Let's go!" she replied and peeled out of the garage. Dredd followed, accelerating quickly to catch up with her. Once they were riding side by side she activated her helmet radio. "Looks like you've got a fan in the garage!"

"Unlike Sector Chief Caine," Dredd replied.

"She's twitchy," Miller said. "Rumours of a reorganisation have been floating around for weeks. Scuttlebutt is Caine's going to be shifted sideways into administration or become warden of a work camp in the Cursed Earth."

"Why? She's still in her forties, physically active..."

"That's the question everyone's asking. Caine's under pressure and she's been looking for someone to take it out on. You're it."

"Terrif." Dredd switched channels. "Dredd to Control. I am starting graveyard shift in Sector 87 with Judge Miller. Anything for us?"

"Control to Dredd. Nothing at this time. Begin street patrol."

Riff Maltin had always dreamed of seeing his name in lights. He wanted to be famous more than anything else, with the possible exception of being rich like those billionaires living on the exclusive Ridley Estate. If he had to choose between the two, Riff favoured being rich while he was alive and famous in death. Ideally, he wanted to be rich and famous simultaneously but figured one would tend to beget the other. He had opted for finding fame first and letting the credits roll in later. There was no need to be greedy, after all.

There was only one major problem stopping his quest for fame; Riff Maltin had few obvious talents. He couldn't sing, couldn't act, and was useless at popular spectator sports like skysurfing or shuggy. He couldn't write, couldn't dance, and didn't have any unique or even unusual physical characteristics that might help him stand out from the crowd.

Of course, you could buy a distinguishing feature. Everybody in the Big Meg remembered the case of Citizen Snork, a fame-hungry teenager who paid to have his nose enlarged to an enormous size. It led to all sorts of trouble and strife, but it did achieve Snork's goal of grabbing the headlines. Riff contemplated a similar route but quickly realised the impediment to such a path – he wasn't wealthy enough to finance such an endeavour. It was just another example of how riches and fame went hand in hand.

Riff was despairing of his quest for the immortality of fame when he saw something intriguing on the tri-D. He had just been watching the grand final of the house cleaning competition *Mop Idol* when a newsflash cut into

the broadcast. It showed an on-the-spot report from a
street journalist in an attempt to free alien superfiend
Judge Death from captivity. Sadly for the journalist, she
died live on air, having wandered into the crossfire
between Judges and the Death cultists trying to free their
figurehead.

Afterwards, the tri-D invited anyone willing to take up
this dangerous occupation to audition for the job. There was
no pay on offer, just the chance to make a name for yourself – if you survived long enough. Riff was already dialling
the auditions number before the programming returned to
the window cleaning eliminator section of *Mop Idol*. Finally,
among the millions of channels offering an inane selection
of trivia masquerading as entertainment, here was a chance
for Riff to find the fame he so desperately wanted!

At the audition, Maltin's naked ambition and raw enthusiasm won him a tryout, despite his lack of experience or
expertise. After thirty minutes of training he was sent to the
stores department to collect all the essentials for life as a
street reporter: a badge with the words NEWS MEDIA on it,
a handheld microphone and a hovercam. This last item was
a small silver globe fitted with a camera, a transmitter and
a tiny hover-engine to keep it floating two metres off the
ground. Riff asked what special privileges the NEWS
MEDIA badge earned him.

"None," replied the bored droid handing over his equipment at Channel 27. "But it does contain a homing beacon."

"Great! So, if I should be kidnapped or get lost while on
the streets, you'll be able to alert the Judges to where I am?"

"Yeah, right," the robot replied. "The homing beacon is
so the hovercam always stays within five metres of the
badge. If you get kidnapped or lost, we'll be able to get
our equipment back. Trust me, the hovercam is worth a
lot more to Channel 27 than you are."

This news had perturbed Riff temporarily, but he soon
pushed such worries aside. He was ready for glory. The

channel's news editor had heard a whisper about trouble being expected in Sector 87. Maltin got the first zoom available and positioned himself just a few blocks from the sector house. If something bad was going down, it would be the Judges who responded. Riff planned to follow them to the scene of the crime. Wherever that might be. Quite how he was going to keep up with them on foot was another matter, but the would-be journalist decided to worry about that later.

In the meantime he decided to grab some vox pops from the locals to assess the mood on the pedways and skedways. Riff had never heard the term until his audition for the street reporter job. "Vox pops – vox populi, you dolt!" the news editor had snarled. The blank look on Maltin's face had obviously shown he needed more of an explanation. "It's Latin. Means the voice of the people. Man on the street interviews. Ever seen one of them?"

Riff checked his reflection in the metal surface of his hovercam. His black hair was slicked down close to the scalp, his eyebrows were bushy and luxurious and pimples surrounded his thin-lipped mouth. Maltin looked like a simp and he knew it. But that will be my secret weapon, he told himself fervently, I'll be able to get the stories nobody else can, because I don't fit the glamorous image most citizens have of the news media. Satisfied with his rationalisation, he took a firm grip on the microphone and approached the nearest man on the street.

"Good evening, my name's Riff Maltin and you're live on–"

"Drokk off, spugface!" The burly citizen shoved Riff aside and kept walking. Maltin picked himself up and decided to try again. A grey-haired eldster was approaching on a Zimmer-Skimmer, her kindly face offering more hope.

"Excuse me, madam, but I'm a street–"

The handbag connected brutally against the side of
Riff's head, sending him sprawling. "Keep away from me!
I'm a granny with attitude and I ain't taking any stomm.
You hear me, sonny?"

Maltin nodded weakly as she zoomed over him. Once
she was gone he sat up. Never judge by appearances, he
told himself. Getting back to his feet, he saw a middle-
aged woman walking towards him. She was twitching
and mumbling to herself. There was a line of drool hanging from her mouth. In normal circumstances Riff would
have stepped aside and let her pass, or even crossed the
skedway to avoid her. But after two rejections he was
determined to get an interview, no matter what. The
would-be journalist stepped into the woman's path and
rested one hand gently on her shoulder.

"Excuse me, citizen. May I have a moment of your
time?"

It was only then Riff noticed the kitchen laser she was
clutching.

"Alot of construction underway in this sector," Dredd
noted as he and Miller passed a building site. The half-
formed tower was illuminated by massive arc lights
suspended from industrial hover pods. A cluster of tall
metal droids was slotting together the framework for a
new citi-block. Each robot stood nearly twenty metres
tall, equivalent to a six-storey building. Their human
controllers were visible in glasseen domes positioned
inside each droid's chest.

"Part of a sector-wide rebuilding programme," Miller
told Dredd via their helmet radios. "We got hit pretty
hard by a meteor shower last year, damaged more than
a third of all structures. Construction company called
Summerbee Industries picked up most of the contracts
by under-bidding their competitors. The deals were all
sanctioned by Justice Central."

"They're using Heavy Metal Kids," Dredd noted, gesturing at the building droids. "I thought they had been superseded by more reliable models."

"That's how Summerbee undercut the opposition," his partner responded. Their exchange was cut short by a crackle of static.

"Control to all units, Sector 87. Report of a female fut-sie running amok near the corner of Merrison and Currie!"

"Miller to Control. Dredd and I'll take it, we're less than a minute away!"

"Look, lady, I just wanted a few quotes. Nothing complex. You don't need to overreact like this. Just say no and I'll go away..." Riff swallowed hard, a task not made easier by the Q-Tel Kitchen Laser held at his throat. Try as he might, Maltin couldn't help recalling the tri-D advertising slogan for the product. Apparently it sliced, diced and julienned vegetables in seconds, whatever the drokk "julienning" was. Riff made a silent pledge to find out if he ever got away from this crazed citizen.

"Cut you up... It's the only way... Only way to be sure... This is tomorrow calling, see... Slice and dice, twice as nice... Meat, meat, dead meat... hanging from the branches of the petrified forest," the woman replied.

Riff felt the woman's drool running down the back of his neck. She had been sniffing at his scalp for more than a minute while swiping backwards and forwards just in front of his neck. "Fascinating, really quite fascinating. You could probably have a lucrative career as a writer coming up with bon mots like that. Have you ever thought of sending them to a publisher?"

The woman just gurgled, her spare hand creeping down inside Riff's u-fronts to clasp his testicles. Riff lost the power of speech momentarily, such was his surprise.

He only regained the ability to talk when he saw the two Judges roaring towards him on Lawmasters. "Sweet drokking Jovus, thank you," the fledgeling reporter whispered.

"Praise be his name," the woman responded, squeezing tightly on Maltin's scrotum. He winced, tears of agony brimming in his eyes.

The two motorcycles stopped at a safe distance and both Judges dismounted. They had Lawgivers in their hands but were not yet taking aim. The male law enforcer took the lead, walking slowly towards Riff and the gibbering citizen. "Citizen! Drop that weapon and step away from the simp!"

"Hey! I'm not a simp!" Riff protested. "I'm a journalist!"

"Whatever," the Judge responded. "Do as I say and nobody gets hurt."

"Cuts and peels, but it never says hello... Cuts and peels, but it never says hello... See what it does to flesh..." The woman released Riff's testicles and flung out her arm. Burnt into her arm were the number four and the word REALITY. "Needs to cut more now... Needs to cut this one all up..."

Maltin could hear the female Judge calling in the case to Control. "Definite case of future shock. Woman seems to be obsessed with her kitchen laser. Futsie is holding another citizen hostage." After a few moments the Judge nodded and then joined her colleague. "Med-wagon's on the way. If it gets here in time, that'll take her to the psycho-cubes."

Riff didn't like the sound of that. If it gets here in time? What if the med-wagon *didn't* get here in time? What would happen to him? His first day on the job was not going well so far. His only compensation was that the hovercam had been capturing all of this and transmitting it back to Channel 27. If he did die in the next few minutes, the broadcast might still grant him a fleeting moment of fame in the day's news summary.

"Cuts and peels," the futsie muttered. "Juliennes too, they were right about that... Right about that... My husband, he didn't know what juliennes was. Tried to tell me it was a clear broth, the fool – so I showed him... Slice and dice, slice and dice... He's in shreds all over now..."

"You have ten seconds to drop the weapon and step away from the citizen," the male Judge commanded. Both law enforcers raised their handguns and took aim at what little they could see of the futsie. "Ten. Nine."

"All over the kitchen... Tasty little shreds... That showed him..." The crazed woman was pressing herself against Maltin's back, grinding her groin against his buttocks. On any other occasion he would have been flattered and all too willing to return her attentions. But the presence of the hot kitchen laser at his throat was hampering any sexual desires he might have felt.

"Eight," the Judge continued. "Seven." He stepped sideways to get a better shooting angle and Riff was able to read the name badge: DREDD. The reporter would have felt reassured but his attention was taken by something happening behind the two Judges. "Six."

A heavy vibration ran through the pedway, like an earth tremor. "Five." But it was followed by another, then another, each tremor greater in magnitude than the last. "Four." As the tremors grew closer, so did a thunderous sound, rockcrete protesting as tonnes of metal thudded into it. "Three."

It was the female Judge who turned first to see what was causing the cacophony. "Dredd!" she hissed to her partner.

"Not now, Miller. Two."

"Dredd, you better see this!"

"Stay where you are citizen," Dredd warned before glancing over his shoulder. One of the Heavy Metal Kid robots from the construction site was marching towards them, massive metal arms flailing in the night air as its mighty feet crunched into the pedway. In the glasseen dome the body of the controller was slumped forwards, either dead or unconscious. Either way, the construction droid was out of control. "Drokk!"

"Exactly," Miller agreed. "You stay here – I'll stop this!"

"No, wait–" Dredd began, but his partner was already running back to her Lawmaster. She gunned the engine into life and sent her motorcycle spinning round in a tight half-circle until it faced the rogue robot.

"Bike cannon!" Miller unleashed a fusillade of fire-power that ripped apart the metal just below one of the mechanoid's knee joints. The Judge shouted a new command to her motorcycle's voice responsive computer control system. "Laser cutter!" A beam of red light sliced through the air, searing across the section made vulner-able by the previous attack. As the Heavy Metal Kid lurched forwards at Miller, its crippled leg tore apart, sending the droid tumbling sideways, arms still flailing. It crashed through a multistorey hover pod car park, howl-ing impotently at the air.

Dredd turned back to the futsie and her captive. "One," the Judge announced and shot the distracted woman through the shoulder. Her arm went limp and the kitchen laser dropped to the pedway, turning itself off. Riff threw himself to safety, not wanting to be near the futsie for another moment. She staggered backwards and collapsed into a crumpled heap, still muttering strange phrases and threats. The Judge activated his helmet radio.

"Dredd to Control – futsie is down, but Med-Wagon still required. Citizen is unhurt."

"Control to Dredd – that's a roj."

"Miller is dealing with a rogue construction droid..." Dredd paused to watch his partner in action. She had cracked open the control dome of the fallen robot and was deactivating its remaining systems. "But she seems to have that under control. Better send a clean-up squad down here."

"Noted."

"And get in touch with the boss at Summerbee Industries. It was their droid that ran amok. Tell them they'll have to answer to me."

"Rog that. Control out."

Miller had finished with the Heavy Metal Kid and was strolling back to join Dredd. "Our metal friend is out of action. Controller's still groggy but said the systems just went haywire. Lie detector backs him up."

"Like I said – unreliable."

Miller admired Dredd's handiwork with the futsie. "How'd you–?"

"Waited until the rampaging robot distracted her," he explained.

"Worked out well then." She smiled before addressing the citizen still cowering on the ground. "What's your name?"

"Riff. Riff Maltin." The reporter stood up, trying to assume a more relaxed guise. "I'm a street journalist for Channel 27."

"Not a very good one," Dredd commented, pointing at the silver globe floating nearby. "You haven't taken the lens cap off your hovercam."

"Oh!" Riff checked his equipment and realised the lawman was right.

Miller managed to suppress her laughter. "What were you doing here?"

"My news editor wanted some vox pops. You know, the voice of the–"

"We know," Dredd growled. "Next time I suggest you choose your interview subjects more carefully."

By now the Med-WΔ29

agon had arrived and the wounded futsie was being strapped on to a hover-stretcher before being taken away for treatment. The two Judges turned and began walking back to their motorcycles. Riff scampered after them.

"Err, your honours, I was wondering if–"

Dredd and Miller stopped, exchanged a glance and then turned back to face Maltin. "You were wondering what?" Miller asked tersely.

"If you'd be willing to help me recreate the incredible spectacle that just took place here. It would make for amazing tri-D viewing and I'm sure it wouldn't be too much trouble to just… to just…" The remorseless gaze of the law enforcers brought Riff's suggestion to a shuddering halt. "No, I guess not. How about an exclusive interview where you talk about what just happened?"

Dredd and Miller resumed striding to their Lawmasters. "We better get back to the sector house," the female Judge said. "We're supposed to be escorting Deputy Temple to this public meeting."

"Just a quick quote, perhaps?" Riff was jumping up and down, trying to pluck the lens cap off his hovercam. By the time he had finally succeeded, the Judges were already riding away into the distance. "I'll take that as a no, shall I?" Maltin's shoulders sagged.

Not a great start to my quest for fame, Riff thought bleakly. Then he remembered the carnage caused by the collapsing mechanoid and hurried towards the smoking remains of the car park. "Still, not a completely wasted opportunity."

21:00

The Leni Riefenstahl Assembly Rooms were only a few minutes' walk from Sector House 87 but Temple insisted on travelling by H-Wagon, accompanied by Dredd and Miller.

"How would it look if I arrived at a public meeting on foot? Hardly the image the Justice Department wishes to project to our citizens, is it?" he explained fussily. Dredd scowled a little more than usual while Miller kept her own counsel. She had no wish to antagonise a senior officer, even one so inept as Temple. He was a disgrace to the uniform of a Street Judge: prissy and pedantic with an over-developed sense of his own importance. A weak chin, flabby cheeks and beady, little eyes did not improve his appearance. It was a wonder Temple had survived this long, Miller thought to herself.

They arrived just as the public meeting was starting. Rather than take an unobtrusive position at the back of the room, Temple insisted on striding up the centre aisle and sitting with the other dignitaries on the raised dais at the front. Dredd had been obliged to follow but whispered to Miller to stay out of sight. He pointed at the building's closed circuit security cameras. "Find out where those images go and route them through to the PSU for processing."

It had been a simple task for Miller to follow the wiring to a control room near the building's main entrance and arrange for the signal to be shared with the

Public Surveillance Unit. Located inside the towering Statue of Judgement, the PSU maintained the Justice Department's vast network of security cameras and alarm systems across the Big Meg; both overt and covert. Hundreds of operators monitored the output from these to identify crimes in progress and anticipate future law-breaking. Coupled with the efforts of Psi-Division's precogs, the PSU's bleeding edge technology gave the Judges a powerful head start towards keeping the city and its citizens under control.

Once the signal had been rerouted through PSU, Miller returned to the main assembly room to watch the public meeting for herself. It had been called by a self-appointed committee of concerned busybodies, the Sector 87 Citizens for Collective Responsibility. The leader of the group was a middle-aged woman with blue-rinsed hair, Carolla O'Hare. She was addressing the meeting, peering over her horn-rimmed glasses at the gathered throng.

"I have nothing personally against these extra-terrestrials being allowed to stay within Mega-City One, as long as they stay in their place. The Judges permitted them to have residences in the sector known as Alien Town; fine, so be it. But what I do object to is having these, these... creatures... living in the block next to my own. Property values in Sector 87 have dropped dramatically since Robert Hatch Block was given over to housing these creatures from outer space. What I want to know is when will these beings be leaving? Deputy Sector Chief Temple, perhaps you could answer that question for us?"

The matronly speaker invited Temple to take his turn at the microphone. While he went through an elaborate ritual of being coaxed forward, Miller scanned the gathered crowd. Most wore the usual assortment of synthetic clothing, a few of the more affluent flaunting their wealth with designer kneepads from outlets like Tommi Illfinger

and the Gyp. But most noticeable was the high proportion of citizens wearing camouflage and Citi-Def insignia.
Each citi-block had its own defence unit, a volunteer
reserve called in to support the Judges against only the
most dangerous threats, such as an invasion.

Citi-Def squads could be a useful resource at times,
but in Miller's experience they tended to attract gun
nuts and those with extremist tendencies. Getting such
a militia force to stand down had often proved prob-
lematic and many questioned the wisdom of retaining
this throwback to the days of global conflicts like the
Apocalypse War. Others felt it was a useful diversion
that kept the more right-wing elements within each citi-
block occupied.

Miller surveyed the crowd more closely. Two particular Citi-Def squads were heavily represented; they were
from Oswald Mosley and Enoch Powell Blocks. Both
had caused trouble in the past with their xenophobic
tendencies, mostly due to a personality clash between
their respective leaders. It now seemed Oswald Mosley
and Enoch Powell had found a common enemy – the
residents of the alien ghetto at Robert Hatch. Miller's
attention returned to the dais as Temple began to address
the gathering.

"My fellow citizens," he began to murmurings of
dissent. "First let me thank you for the invitation to
speak here today. I offer apologies from Sector Chief
Caine, who would have attended herself but for more
urgent matters." Temple smiled weakly and continued. "I
would like to reassure you that the problems surrounding
Robert Hatch Block are among our highest priorities. The
rebuilding of Alien Town continues apace and we are
hopeful its residents will soon be returned to their own
sector."

"When?" a woman shouted from the crowd.

"The exact timing of this remains uncertain. However–"

"When? When are you getting these bug-eyed monsters out of our sector?" The heckler stood up and pointed accusingly at the Sector Chief. She was a small woman with swarthy skin, thick black hair and fierce features. The insignia of Oswald Mosley Citi-Def was displayed proudly on her shoulder. "You've been giving us promises and false hope for years, Temple, but you never deliver. We want to know when you will!" Those around her nodded in agreement, and murmured their approval.

"Perhaps you could identify yourself?" Temple asked.

"You know me. You all do! My name is Conchita Maguire and my husband died fighting aliens to protect this city. Now those same scum live alongside us and you say we should all try to get along!"

Temple nodded at her. "Ahh, Ms Maguire, I should have recognised your voice. Your husband died after picking a fight with an alien who was legally visiting his family in this sector."

"He was protecting this city!" she screamed back at him. "Anyone who says otherwise is a liar!"

"Be that as it may, the residents of Robert Hatch have as much right–"

"Rights? Don't talk to us about rights, Temple!" Maguire snarled back. "You Judges are all too willing to step forward and protect these creatures' rights. What about ours? The right for our children to play freely without fear of being molested or worse by these freaks? The right to breathe air that hasn't already been breathed by these monsters? The right to live out our lives without continually fearing that these things will murder us all in our beds and claim this sector, this city, as their own?"

By now those around Maguire were up on their feet too, cheering her on. Temple did his best to calm them down but was unsuccessful. "Please, please, if you'll just listen to me," he pleaded in vain.

"We've listened enough," Maguire cried out. She picked up a small girl from the chair beside her and held the child in the air. The girl had an ugly bruise around her left eye. "This is my daughter, Kasey. She got this black eye when she fell over, running away after being scared by one of those freaks at the shoppera. Should our children be put in danger like this?"

Miller's helmet radio crackled into life. "Dredd to Miller, you hear me?"

"Loud and clear. You going to step in?"

"Only if Temple can't get them back under control."

"I'm standing ready to back you up."

"Roj that – Dredd out."

Nyon returned home from his action group meeting to find Lleccas and Misch waiting for him. "What is it? What's wrong?" he asked, concerned by the look in their eyes. Lleccas told him about their broodling having metema. Nyon gave his daughter a hug, delighted for her. But he could sense something was still troubling Misch. "You should be happy – some of the greatest among the R'qeen have possessed this gift."

She nodded as tears welled in her sad, little eyes. Misch explained about what she had sensed in the minds of the two humans earlier. "They wanted to hurt us all," she said.

Nyon brushed the tears from his broodling's face. "They are afraid of us, because we are different. Beings of all kinds fear that which they do not know nor understand. Before I came to this world I feared humans. But there are many among them that are kind and generous. They may not understand our ways but they are willing to learn."

"But what about all I saw in their minds? They wanted to burn us!"

"Many beings have hate in their hearts. Some may even think about hurting us and those like us. But very few ever act upon such impulses," Nyon whispered soothingly. "You're safe here with your broodmother and me. We will always look after you. You believe that, don't you?"

Misch managed a weak smile and Nyon hugged her again, the proudest of broodfathers. "Everything will be all right," he said, rocking her gently.

But Nyon was wrong. Lleccas had walked to the doorway of their con-apt, sniffing at the air. "I smell something strange," she said quietly.

"Probably Kehclow boiling a Joshua cactus again," Nyon replied. "You know how he likes to inhale the fumes."

"No, it's something else," Lleccas said urgently. "It's smoke. Acrid, burning... I smell fire!"

Temple was still ineffectually trying to bring the meeting at the Leni Riefenstahl Assembly Rooms to order. "Please, you must understand that my hands are tied in this matter. The alien ghetto, sorry, the alien settlers in Robert Hatch Block are perfectly entitled to-"

The deputy Sector Chief's nasal, whining voice was cut short by a kneepad slapping against the side of his head. "Who threw that?" Temple demanded to know but mocking laughter was the surly crowd's only response. He blushed crimson with rage and embarrassment before storming off the dais. "I've never been so insulted in all my days as a Judge!"

Maguire was leading a chant, aided by her brothers in arms from the Oswald Mosley Citi-Def. She had taken to standing on her chair and shaking her fists in the air, exhorting those around her to join in. "Alien scum out, human beings in! Alien scum out, human beings in!"

A single gunshot echoed round the room, sending nearly everyone present diving for the floor. Dredd was standing on the dais. A wisp of smoke curled from the end of his Lawgiver. "You've all had your say – now it's my turn."

"Hey, who gives you the right to–" Maguire began to protest, climbing back to her feet. Dredd silenced her with a glare. The rest of the audience stayed silent as the lawman surveyed them.

"That's better," he said eventually. "First of all, you should know that we've been transmitting closed circuit camera footage of this meeting to PSU. Facial recognition software says forty of you have outstanding warrants against your names. There's an H-Wagon waiting outside. Turn yourselves in quietly or suffer the consequences. That includes the individual who threw the kneepad at Deputy Sector Chief Temple. Secondly, we know the identity of each and every person present here. If any one of you gets involved in anti-alien violence or related crime, you will be severely punished. Thirdly, you will disperse quietly and return to your homes. Otherwise I will not hesitate to fill this room with riot foam and leave you all here overnight to cool down. Do I make myself clear?"

There were some murmurings and a shuffling of feet, but none of the citizens dared to contradict Dredd. At the back of the chamber Miller smiled despite herself. He might be getting on in years but Dredd possessed a real presence, a gravitas the likes of which Temple could never hope to have.

Just as Dredd was bringing the meeting to a close a juve ran past Miller and into the assembly room. "Fire!" the kid shouted. "There's a fire at Robert Hatch! The aliens are burning!"

The blaze had started in the basement, just as Misch had foreseen. It quickly spread, smoke and flames escaping into the ventilation shafts running the height of the building.

Within minutes the fumes were choking the corridors on most floors, while tongues of fire licked at the walls and danced across ceilings. The defunct turbolift shaft was a breathing tube for the inferno, drawing air in from above to feed itself.

All citi-blocks were required to have smoke alarms and thermostat warning systems to alert residents to danger. All citi-blocks were required to have more than sufficient fire escapes so everyone inside could get out in time. All citi-blocks were required to have sprinkler systems and flame retarding sprays to keep signs of fire in check. Robert Hatch Block had all of these – but almost none of them were working. Years of neglect and anti-alien prejudice finally found their target.

Nyon made sure Lleccas and Misch got out before preparing to go back for others. He realised how lucky they were to be housed so close to ground level. Getting down the smoke-clogged stairs had been difficult enough for them – what must it be like for those ten or twenty storeys up? Just as fortunate was his sibling Keno and her brood. The family of four had been visiting friends in Alien Town when the blaze started. They returned to find Robert Hatch on fire and Nyon's brood huddled outside.

Nyon looked at the upper levels of the building. The fire was clearly visible against the night sky, smoke and flames billowing out of most windows. The R'qeen tore a strip of fabric from his tunic and tied it around his face as a filter mask. Where were the Judges? Why hadn't Weather Control responded to the fire, and doused the sector with rain to help slow the progress of the blaze?

Nyon hurried into the lobby of Robert Hatch and back up the stairs. If nothing else, he might be able to help his immediate neighbours to escape. Nyon touched a three-fingered hand to the front door of the con-apt nearest the stairwell. It was cold, so the R'qeen hammered on the surface, shouting in Allspeak. "Gruchar, can you hear me? It's Nyon. You have to get out, the block's on fire!"

No response. "Gruchar, are you there? It's Nyon! Can you reach the door?" Still no response. Nyon leaned back and kicked at the door. The weak lock collapsed inwards with little resistance.

Inside, the arthropod from Andromeda IV was slumped against a white-hot wall, gasping for breath. Steam was rising from Gruchar's back where the alien was being cooked by the heat behind it. Gagging on the stench of frying skin, Nyon dragged Gruchar out into the corridor. "Can you make it down the stairs?" The arthropod nodded and began dragging itself away. Nyon moved onto the next doorway and found it open, the tiny room beyond empty. Next was Kehclow's con-apt. The door was ajar but the room was filled with flames. The gaseous entity was trapped on the other side of the blaze, pinned into a corner.

"Kehclow, come out. We've got to go!" Nyon shouted.

"I can't pass through the flames!"

"Why not?"

"Beings from the Bilal Cluster are flammable..."

Nyon looked around desperately. "Can you get to the window?"

"I had it sealed to stop myself sleep-floating. It's welded shut."

"Not for long," the R'qeen vowed. He ran into his own con-apt and retrieved an Aurillian Hope Crystal the size of his fist. Nyon hurried back to Kehclow who was fast running out of air in which to hover. The R'qeen hurled the crystal at the only window in the room but it bounced off uselessly.

"I had them specially reinforced," Kehclow explained, "to keep out burglars. I didn't trust anyone else here." The cloud folded in on itself. "I should have trusted you. Goodbye, Nyon." Flames licked up into

the air, engulfing the gaseous entity. Kehclow died
screaming.

Nyon stumbled out of the con-apt. By now the fire had
spread into the corridor and was crawling up the walls. If
he wanted to get out alive, the R'qeen would have to run
through flames.

Riff Maltin was basking in the glory of his "construction
droid running amok" exclusive when he heard about the
fire. Channel 27's news editor had called the fledgeling
reporter and offered him a permanent job, communicating
via the small replay monitor on the hovercam. "Good
work, Maltin. Keep feeding us visuals like that and you'll
be famous within a week."

Riff had glowed at this praise but it was short-lived.
"What we really need," the news director continued, "are
some good human interest stories. Tug at the heartstrings
stuff, show us the face of tragedy and terror."

Maltin was about to respond when a crowd of citizens
poured out of nearby Oswald Mosley Block and began
running down the skedway. "What's the rush?" Riff
shouted after them.

"Fire at Robert Hatch!" one of the citizens responded.
"Get your mushmallows, we're going to watch those
alien freaks burn!"

"Yeah! Anyone here like barbecued vulture?" another
of them joked.

Maltin turned back to his boss. "Sorry, but it sounds
like a story–"

"Go!" the news editor commanded.

By the time Dredd and Miller arrived, Robert Hatch was a
charred and blackened husk, burnt out from the fifth floor
upwards. The smell of burning flesh and charred rubble
hung in the air. A cloud of smoke created a haze around
the streetlights nearby that still worked. A few fires still

illuminated the middle levels of the citi-block but everything above that was ominously dark and lifeless.
H-Wagons with water cannons had been brought in to
extinguish the blaze but the response was too late to save
most of the building's alien residents. A crowd of rubber-
neckers had gathered around the smoking remains, held
back by a Justice Department cordon. For those outside
the barriers there was a carnival atmosphere, with plenty
of laughing and anti-alien jokes doing the rounds.

"What do you call a vulture from Robert Hatch?" one
of the bystanders shouted out.

"Well done!" replied another, to collective laughter.

Inside the cordon was another matter. H-Wagons with
red crosses on their sides were clustered around the
building as Med-Judges tried to help those lucky enough
to escape the blaze. Their job was made harder by the
rich variety of alien species that had resided inside Robert
Hatch. Treatments appropriate for human burn victims
could hardly be applied to creatures with chitinous skins,
a hundred legs or no corporeal existence.

A pair of Tek-Judges was emerging from the burnt out
remains of the building. Dredd suggested Miller talk to
the Judges manning the barriers to see if they had heard
anyone bragging about involvement with the blaze, while
he quizzed the two fire investigators. Dredd waited until
the Tek-Judges had removed their breathing apparatus
before approaching them. The elder of the pair went into
a coughing fit, trying to gasp in the old night air.

"Dredd – I'm on assignment to 87 for this graveyard
shift."

The other Tek-Judge was a young black woman.
"Kendrick." She indicated her partner, a heavy-set man
in his forties still coughing heartily. "This wheezing bag
of blubber is Osman."

Dredd jerked a thumb towards the remains of Robert
Hatch. "Where did it start?"

"Basement. Could have been electrical. Whole block was a deathtrap waiting to happen. All the fire safety systems were broken or disabled. We'll be pulling charred remains out of there for hours," Kendrick said grimly.

"Could be electrical, you said. Are you thinking there's another possibility?"

Osman had recovered enough breath to answer. He gestured at the jeering crowd beyond the perimeter. "The aliens in this ghetto weren't exactly the most popular residents in the sector. There is no shortage of people wanting to torch this place."

Dredd nodded. "You found anything to back that up?"

Kendrick shrugged. "No obvious accelerants. If it was arson, it'll be almost impossible to prove and harder to trace." Osman began coughing again. Flecks of blood stained his chin. "Right now I need to get my partner some clean air," she said. "So if you don't mind..."

Dredd stood aside. As he did so, the Judge noticed a cluster of alien survivors gathered around a tall, blue-skinned creature. It seemed to be the dominant presence. Perhaps it could help identify how and why the fire began.

Miller found Stammers and Riley together at the barricades, talking with some of the bystanders. Stammers shared a joke with those beyond the cordon. "You'd think the vultures would be happy about the fire. Now they don't have to bother cooking their next victims!" Stammers howled with laughter at his own jest, not bothering to hide his amusement, even when Miller made her presence known. "Well, well, if it isn't the luscious Lynn. How's life with Old Stony Face, Miller? Can he still get it up?" Stammers formed his thumb and forefinger into a circle before thrusting his daystick back and forth through the gap.

Don't rise to the bait, Miller told herself. Don't give this drokker the satisfaction. She turned to Riley instead, pulling him away from the cordon. Once they were out of Stammer's hearing, she took off her helmet and asked Riley if anyone in the crowd had tried to grab the credit for the fire.

"Not that I've heard, but Stammers talks enough for five people."

"All of it trash," Miller commented. "How can you stand having that jerk as your partner?"

"Somebody else turned me down, remember?" Riley looked at her intently. "That can still change, if you want it to."

She shook her head. "I left all that back at the Academy. It was a mistake, one that nearly cost me my badge."

"But that was different. We were–"

"No!" Miller realised she was shouting and dropped her voice before speaking again. "Look, keep your ears open, okay? Dredd thinks this could be arson, so anything you hear that's relevant, pass it on."

"Whatever. Far as I'm concerned, the ETs got what they deserved." Riley returned to his partner, leaving Miller silently fuming. Most of the time Riley was a good Judge, but his attitude to the city's alien residents sickened her to the stomach. She noticed Dredd approaching.

"Riley heard anything?"

"Nothing useful," she replied, surveying the crowd. "But if it was arson, I'm betting our firestarter is among the crowd. They'd want to see the show."

"Agreed." Dredd looked at the survivors again. "How's your Allspeak?"

"Why did the humans do this? What do they hope to gain from our misery?" Nyon asked.

Less than a hundred residents had made it out of Robert Hatch alive, from a total population of more than a thousand. A third of the survivors were still being tended to by the Med-Judges. The rest were gathered around the R'qeen male, huddled under blankets for warmth. A few of them clutched whatever possessions they had carried out of the burning building. Nyon had been the block representative for his species on the action group. Now he was emerging as a leader for all the survivors.

"Perhaps it was an accident?" Gruchar ventured. The arthropod always thought the best of everyone – a common trait among its kind.

Nyon's sibling Keno agreed with this. "We all knew about the problems with the turbolifts and the fire escapes," she said, hugging her three broodlings.

But Nyon shook his head, anger darkening his blue skin to indigo. "My broodling Misch has the gift of metema. She saw into the minds of those responsible for this atrocity."

"Misch has metema?" Keno asked Lleccas.

"We only discovered–" But the R'qeen female was interrupted by her pairling. Nyon was still convinced by his own theory about how the fire started.

"This was deliberate!" he thundered at the other survivors.

"What was deliberate?" Miller and Dredd strode towards the survivors, the female Judge fielded the question while her partner observed.

"This fire. You humans started it!" Nyon replied.

"You have proof of this?"

The R'qeen leader was going to respond but Lleccas stopped him, gently applying pressure to his arm. Nyon looked into her eyes and saw her concern. Then he turned to the Judge. "Nothing that you would believe."

"Try us."

Nyon shook his head. "We look after our own. We will see justice done."

Dredd stepped towards the R'qeen. "We cannot let you or anyone else take the Law into your own hands."

"If you believe you have been wronged," Miller said, "let us take up your case. While you live here, you are one of us and we look after our own too."

Nyon pointed at the charred, smoking citi-block. "Like you looked after everyone who lived inside this building? Where were your promises then? Hundreds of our kind burned alive while you humans watched, laughed and cheered!"

Lleccas spoke up for the first time. "Why do you humans attack us? We have done nothing wrong. All of us here are refugees. We may have different ways from yours but that is no reason to fear us. To hate us."

Miller hung her head, ashamed. "Not all humans are alike," she said.

Dredd looked around the rest of the survivors. "Unless you help us find those responsible for this crime, they may escape punishment. Is that what you want? You may not trust us, but we are your best hope."

Nyon picked up Misch and hugged her. "Then we have no hope."

Dredd stomped away from the survivors. Miller ran to catch up with him. "For the love of Grud, will nobody see sense?" he muttered darkly.

"You can't blame them for being suspicious," she said. "Humans haven't given them much reason to trust us."

Dredd nodded unhappily at the truth of the remark. "Until we get feedback from the PSU and the forensic team, there's not much we can do here. I'll call the sector House. No doubt Caine has a new assignment ready for us by now."

Miller noticed a silver hovercam floating at the edge of the cordon. She went over to investigate and found Riff Maltin leaning over a barricade for a better view. "What are you doing here?"

"Where the news is, I follow!" he replied. "Quite a blaze. I only caught the end of it but it was still good footage. Any hot tips you can give me? Cause of the fire, how many fatalities, that kind of thing?"

"Hundreds have just died in that building!"

"Yeah, what a break – and on my first day too!" Riff smiled happily. Miller clamped one hand over the lens of his hovercam, and at the same time· her other hand grabbed him by the throat.

"Xenophobes call the R'qeen 'vultures' because they feed on rotting flesh, but stomm like you are the real vultures, feeding on pain and misery!" She threw Maltin to the ground. "Now get out of my sight, you little drokker, before I run you in!"

Riff protested to the bystanders around him. "Judicial brutality! You all saw that, you're all my witnesses. Judicial brutality!"

Miller glared at the crowd, which shrunk back. The citizens nervously hid their faces in the darkness. "Anybody here just see anything?" Miller demanded, but nobody spoke up. "Thought not." She sneered down at Maltin, and let the hovercam float free again. "I'd think twice before you shout judicial brutality, Maltin. The Justice Department does not look kindly upon citizens who make false accusations against its law enforcers."

"Miller!" Dredd was shouting to her from his Lawmaster. "We're needed elsewhere!" She nodded and strode back to her motorcycle.

"Where are we going?"

"You wouldn't believe me if I told you," Dredd scowled.

"Try me."

"It seems we're providing extra security for an ugly pageant at Sid Harmor Hippodrome."

Miller smiled despite herself. "Grud on a greenie – what next?"

22:00

Carla Prins would have been considered one of the world's greatest beauties if she had been born at any other time in any other city on the planet. She had the physique and stunning good looks that would reduce most men to gibbering wrecks and sends bitter shards of envy and hatred through the soul of any woman she encountered. Carla was tall and slim, every part of her body in perfect proportion. The crowning glory was her face, with luscious lips, a cute upturned nose and eyes that hinted at pleasures beyond imagining. By rights Carla should have been celebrated and adored.

But Carla had been born in Mega-City One just three days after Otto Sump appeared on *Sob Story*. Sump was perhaps the ugliest man alive, with a face so hideous he had been fired from his job as rat scarer after protests by animal rights campaigners. Otto had then appeared on the tri-D hit show *Sob Story*, pleading his case before the Big Meg's viewers. The response was overwhelming and within days Sump became a billionaire thanks to all the donations he received. He was a cause célébre. He used this new-found wealth to launch a series of ever more bizarre business ventures, that cashed in on the citizens' mania for crazes.

In a metropolis where fewer than one in seven people had a job, boredom was a universal problem. The populace responded by embracing whatever outlandish concept caught its fancy. And millions of them joined in with every single fad. Sump Industries responded to that demand, most famously with its line of Get Ugly cosmetics. Such was the impact of Otto's first tri-D appearance that thousands of citizens wanted to replicate his appalling visage. Beautiful was out, ugly was in. The more pitiful your face, the more popular you were. Overnight the fashion industry was revolutionised: distorted noses, pus-riddled skin and unsightly facial hair became all the rage.

Otto had since died but his influence remained. Sump Industries continued his crusade to celebrate the foulest of features, smells and sights. The centrepiece of this campaign was the Miss Mega-City Ugly Pageant, an annual event staged at Sid Harmor Hippodrome to find the ugliest looking woman in the Big Meg. Unsightly juves from all sectors of the city competed against each other for the prestigious title and a lifetime supply of Sump Industries products like Pimple-On, Skank-Breath-U-Like and I Can't Believe It's Not Pus.

For Carla Prins, being one of the world's greatest beauties was of no use in such a city. Her incredible good looks and flawless skin had been the source of shame and humiliation all her life. At school, the other students had taunted Carla, calling her cruel nicknames like Spotless and Pretty. Each night she cried herself to sleep, praying for a pimple or cold sore to form on her face. But every morning the horror staring back at her in the mirror was the same; she was beautiful and there was nothing she could do about it. Too poor to afford any of the products that might artificially render her ugly, Carla retreated into herself and became ugly on the inside instead.

She made contact with other beautiful women and formed a pressure group – Pretty People Opposed to Ugly Stereotypes. PPOTUS developed its own constitution, registered as a political activist alliance and staged demonstrations. At first these were low-key affairs: they disrupted the ugly products department at Bloomingmacy's or painted the moustaches off billboard posters of ugly supermodels such as Caitlin Lichen and Sofia Dull.

But tonight PPOTUS was going for maximum exposure at the Miss Mega-City Ugly Pageant. Carla and three of her fellow activists had acquired media credentials for the event and had secreted themselves among the audience. The rest of the group was staging a rowdy protest outside. The plan was to storm the catwalk during the symphony of suppurating skin and wart-encrusted limbs that was the swimsuit competition. But the members of PPOTUS hadn't counted on Judges Dredd and Miller being assigned to provide extra security for the event.

"You can't do this to me! I have a legitimate right to display my feelings," she shouted. Carla and her trio of fellow protesters had stripped naked and charged on to the stage just as the result of the swimsuit final was being announced. The four women had handcuffed themselves to the winner, Prunella Fernandez, a jaundiced fattie from Sector 66 with a gloriously malformed chin and half her nose missing. Fernandez shrieked in horror at having such beautiful people standing besude her. Her pitiful cries alerted the two Judges.

"It's not displaying your feelings that's illegal," Dredd replied, pulling a small laser-cutter from one of the pouches on his utility belt. "It's the rest of you."

The angry crowd began shouting and screaming at the protesters, demanding that their perfectly formed features and immaculate bone structure be banished from the building. Miller took off her helmet and held it in front of Carla's flawless face, to shield it from the audience's gaze. "Say another word and I'll add inciting a riot to your list of crimes," Miller shouted at Carla, struggling to be heard above the howls of the audience.

"These contests demean women everywhere," Carla cried out. "We shouldn't be forced to conform to ugly stereotypes, and to debase ourselves for the benefit of companies like Sump Industries."

"And stripping naked in front of all these people isn't debasing yourself?" Dredd asked while slicing through the protesters' handcuffs.

"This is a legitimate act of outrage. All those who condone pro-ugly attitudes must be confronted by the truth!" one of Carla's fellow activists yelled.

A squad of back-up Judges arrived to haul away the protesters from PPOTUS. Dredd jerked a thumb at the exit. "Get 'em out of here! I've seen enough of their truths for one night!"

Carla was still shouting at the contestants as she was dragged away. "Don't be stooges of the ugly industry! Embrace your inner beauty. Don't be defined by your pimples and imperfections!"

Miller shook her head as the last protester was removed. "You'd think they'd learn to cope with being beautiful. Why inflict their troubles on others?"

Dredd shrugged. "Misery loves company." The helmet radios of both Judges crackled into life. "Speaking of which…"

"Control to Dredd and Miller. You finished with the Ugly Pageant?"

"That's a roj."

"You better get back to Robert Hatch. Things are getting out of hand."

Dredd scowled. "Aren't there Judges already on site?"

"Stammers and Riley," Control replied. "They need back-up. Control out."

Miller sighed. "I'm not surprised. Those two."

"Tell me on the way," Dredd said, already striding towards the exit.

. . .

Riff decided to stay close to the burnt-out shell of Robert Hatch. The fire might have been extinguished but he was hopeful of catching some good footage of charred remains being pulled from the building. His decision proved critical in what followed. Most of the bystanders had dispersed and gone back to their own blocks. With Weather Control offline, Sector 87 was sweltering in an unusual humidity. The ambient temperature had dropped since dusk but was still well above the norm for this time of year. All in all, it was a hot and sticky night.

As the crowd thinned out, Riff sidled across to Riley and Stammers. The two Judges were still maintaining a cordon but their attention was on the huddled survivors being treated at the scene. "Wasting good resources on offworlders again," Stammers sneered to his partner. "They should send them all back to where they came from, and get them out from under our feet."

Riley nodded his agreement. "My brother told me the vultures used to keep the dead in charnel pits before eating them. Now those freaks are living here, taking up homes that decent humans could be using." He spat on the ground. "Peace treaty or no peace treaty, they shouldn't be here. Danny'd still be alive…"

Riff introduced himself to the two Judges. "How'd the fire start?"

Riley shrugged. "We're still waiting on forensics from the Tek-Judges."

Stammers laughed. "It was arson and you know it! Somebody went in there and did a little fire starting. Know what I mean?"

"We don't have proof of that–"

"Give it time. Then they'll want us to find whoever started the fire and arrest them. If you ask me, I think we oughta give whoever did this a medal!"

"Well, that's definitely one point of view," Riff said noncommittally.

Riley pointed at the blackened front entrance to Robert Hatch. "Come on, Stammers. Let's see if the Tek-Judges are finished inside."

His partner followed Riley away from the cordon, still grumbling. "These freaks can bring out their own dead, that's what I say."

Riff waited until the two Judges had gone inside before slipping under the barricade. The reporter edged towards the survivors, his hovercam floating behind him. Riff was not fluent in Allspeak but knew enough to make himself understood. "Excuse me, I'm a reporter for Channel 27. Is there anyone here who can speak English?"

An R'qeen male stepped forward, replying in halting words of English. "I can, a little. My name is Nyon. What do you want of us?"

Maltin was taken aback by how tall and imposing the R'qeen was; Nyon towered over him. He had seen the species on tri-D before but never in the flesh. "I just need to ask you some questions, if that's all right?"

"Ask your questions, human."

"I've been told this fire was deliberately started, probably by some anti-alien faction here in Sector 87. How do you feel about that?"

Nyon's three-fingered hands began clenching into fists and unclenching again, his head leaning forward to hiss at Riff. "We will not stand by and see our kind butchered by those who would cast us out!"

"Are you saying you will retaliate?"

"We will lay our dead to rest – then we shall see."

Riff nodded. He could sense the alien's anger bubbling below the surface. It would be dangerous to provoke this creature further, but it might also make good viewing. "I've just recorded some comments by one of the Judges responsible for investigating this terrible fire. Perhaps I could show them to you, see if you have anything to add?"

Nyon agreed, so Riff grabbed his hovercam and scrolled backwards through its most recent recordings. After carefully selecting what to replay, the journalist turned the silver globe so Nyon could see the monitor screen.

"It was arson and you know it!" Stammers announced to the camera. "Somebody went in there and did a little fire starting, know what I mean?" Riff then pushed the sequence forward a few seconds to another comment by Stammers. "If you ask me, I think we oughta give whoever did this a medal!"

The other survivors had crowded forward to watch the playback. They reacted with horror and anger towards the Judge's comments. Nyon pushed the hovercam aside and grabbed Riff by the throat, lifting the reporter into the air. "Where are they? Where are the ones who said this?"

Riff shook his head weakly, gasping out an answer. "Inside... The Judges went inside."

Nyon threw the reporter aside and stormed towards the entrance of the block, followed by the other aliens. Riley and Stammers were just emerging from the smoke-stained lobby, brushing themselves down.

"Forget it," Stammers announced. "I ain't touching them. Hell, the vultures will probably want to eat what's left of their families anyway..." His voice trailed off as he registered the crowd of angry aliens surrounding the entrance.

Riley was first to call for back-up. Stammers had already drawn his daystick and was pointing it at the survivors. "Just move away and nobody needs to get hurt," he commanded.

Nyon stepped forward to confront the Judge. "Many of our kind died inside that inferno," the R'qeen spat back. "Is that not enough hurt for you?"

"Now look, I didn't mean anything by it," Stammers began.

"Perhaps you were busy thinking about the medal you are going to award to whoever is responsible for this fire?"

"What medal? What are you talking about?"

Nyon pointed at Riff, who was still recovering on the ground nearby. "He showed us what you said. You want to see us all dead, don't you?"

"Now I never said that..." Stammers protested.

"How do we know you didn't start the fire?" Nyon demanded, sniffing at the law enforcer. "I can smell your fear, human. What are you afraid of?"

Stammers glanced back at his partner. "Where the hell is that back-up?"

Dredd and Miller were speeding from the ugly pageant back towards Robert Hatch, but a traffic jam on the Arthur Hayes Underpass forced them into a detour. Dredd used his helmet radio to quiz his new partner about Stammers and Riley. "You weren't surprised they were in trouble. Why not?"

Miller didn't reply straight away.

"Well?"

"Riley and I were at the Academy together," she said. "He was Roll of Honor material but had a blind spot when it came to offworlders. His older brother died in the colony wars on R'qeen when we were out on our first hot-dog run. Riley and his brother had been very close, so when he got news of what had happened..."

"He blames all aliens for what happened to his brother?"

"Especially the R'qeen. As for Stammers..." Her voice trailed off, but Dredd would not let the matter lie.

"I'm not SJS, Miller; I'm not conducting any covert investigations despite what Caine might believe. I'm just here for a graveyard shift."

She nodded. "I know, but talking about another Judge like this, it makes me uncomfortable."

"Then get over it. We're partners. What you tell me goes no further."

"All right," Miller said. "Stammers is bad news. Not corrupt as such, but extreme in his views and prone to using excessive force, especially where offworlders are involved. If you're on his side, there's nothing in the world he wouldn't do to protect you. If you're not, watch your back."

Dredd considered this. "And Stammers has taken Riley under his wing?"

Miller nodded. "Caine put them together, the worst possible combination. Riley's becoming more and more like his partner. Sometimes I still see traces of the friend I knew at the Academy, but…" The duo was back on a direct route to the alien ghetto. Miller switched frequencies on her helmet radio and called Control. "Dredd and I will be back at Robert Hatch within sixty seconds."

"Roj that – the sooner, the better!"

Miller acknowledged the message and activated her motorcycle's siren. The device was not often used but was a good way of driving off minor lawbreakers who preferred to avoid the Judges. Dredd followed her example and the duo rode down an off-ramp towards the smoking remains of the alien ghetto.

Who struck the first blow was never clear. Nyon had been looming over Stammers, intimidating the lawman with his superior height. But the Street Judge would not back down, his daystick drawn and ready for action. Riley had tried to persuade his partner to avoid the confrontation but Stammers refused to budge. "No bug-eyed monster is pushing me around," he hissed.

"What did you call me?" Nyon demanded, one arm ready to lash out.

"You're a no-good, blue-skinned, stomm-eating son of a Grud-alone-knows-what. The sooner you drokkers get off my planet the better!"

Within seconds the pair were sprawled on the ground. Stammers was clubbing the R'qeen repeatedly with his daystick. The alien tried to defend himself, pushing his long fingers inside the Judge's helmet, gouging at Stammers's eyes. Riley tried to pull the combatants apart but Nyon caught him a glancing blow with an elbow. Riley lashed out with the butt of his Lawgiver, pounding it against the side of the R'qeen's head. The rest of the aliens gathered round the brawl in a circle, urging their leader on against the two humans.

Riff skirted around the edges of the melee, content to send his hovercam in to capture footage. The reporter transmitted a running commentary of the scrap. "Live and exclusive here on Channel 27, a grudge match between the aliens burnt out of their home at Robert Hatch Block and two Judges trying to bring peace to this troubled area of Sector 87. The leader of the aliens has accused the lawmen of starting the fire that gutted this once noble building, causing the deaths of hundreds of residents. The two Judges were outraged and now the conflict has escalated into this: a knockdown brawl in front of the still smoking structure!"

The sound of approaching sirens cut through the air. The alien spectators parted to reveal the combatants, so that all three fighters were clearly visible in the headlights of the two Lawmasters. Nyon and Stammers were too intent on throttling each other to notice the new arrivals. Riley hammered at the R'qeen's head with his Lawgiver.

"What the drokk is going on here?" Dredd demanded. The Judge climbed off his bike and strode through the gap in the spectators, followed by Miller.

Riley looked up and quickly holstered his handgun. "Dredd!" He stepped back from the tangle of limbs and anger on the ground. "This vulture accused us of starting the fire. When we tried to arrest him for slander, he resisted and we were forced to subdue him."

"Is that right?" Dredd snarled. Stammers and Nyon were still grappling with each other. "Miller, will you do the honours?"

She drew her Lawgiver and fired once into the air. The alien spectators drew further away, and the shot finally got the attention of Stammers and Nyon. They stopped fighting and rolled away from each other before getting to their feet. When questioned, Stammers repeated the same story as Riley. Nyon told a very different tale, recounting how the reporter from Channel 27 had shown him Stammers's xenophobic comments.

It was Miller who saw Riff trying to creep away. "Maltin!" she shouted, stopping the reporter in his tracks. "I might have known you'd be where there was trouble. Is your hovercam working now?"

Dredd and Miller reviewed the footage from Riff's camera before discussing what to do. "I'll deal with this," Dredd told his partner. "I'm only here for one night. You have to work alongside these two for months or even years to come. If they want to blame someone, better they blame me."

Miller reluctantly agreed. The pair returned to the main gathering. Stammers and Riley were sporting bruises and scrapes but Nyon looked much worse. The skin across his left cheek was split, the pupil of one eye appeared bloody and he was nursing his right arm. An R'qeen female and child helped tend his wounds as best they could.

"I've reviewed this incident and there is clear evidence of provocation by Judge Stammers," Dredd announced. "I will be recommending a reprimand be placed on this officer's permanent record. In view of the circumstances, I will let this R'qeen male go with a verbal warning. But if I see him fighting again, I will consider initiating deportation proceedings." Stammers was outraged. And the aliens were less than impressed; they abused Dredd in their native tongues.

"Last but not least, Riff Maltin." The reporter had been enjoying the show, but his face fell as he was included in Dredd's judgement. "I suspect you provoked this conflict

just to create news for your broadcast. If I find you using
similar tactics in future, you will be spending the next year
in the cubes. Do I make myself clear?" Riff nodded hurriedly before making himself scarce, relieved to have
escaped incarceration.

"You've got no authority to put a reprimand on our
records," Stammers sneered. "I know Caine – she'll never
let it stand. You're wasting your time."

"Maybe," Dredd agreed. "I can only recommend you get
a reprimand. But I want that on record, even if Caine does
choose to protect the likes of you."

"It sounds like I've arrived at just the right moment," a
woman's voice interjected. The four Judges turned to see
Sector Chief Caine walking towards them. "I heard someone called for back-up and decided to visit the scene for
myself. Now, who is protecting whom, exactly?"

Conchita Maguire switched off the tri-D in her cramped
con-apt. Channel 27 had been broadcasting coverage of
events at Robert Hatch, thanks to the presence of Riff
Maltin and his hovercam. But after Dredd's intervention
the channel switched its focus to the finale of the ugly
pageant. Conchita felt no need to see some sow-faced juve
showered with gifts and adulation.

After the public meeting at the Leni Riefenstahl Assembly Rooms had broken up, Conchita had brought her
daughter home to Oswald Mosley Block. The single
mother's heart sank every time she walked into this con-
apt. How was a family of four meant to live in just three
tiny rooms? Conchita was forced to share a bedroom with
her eight-year-old daughter Kasey, while her two sons slept
in the largest room, which also served as kitchen and din-
ing area. The smallest room was the bathroom, a space
barely large enough for the toilet and the tiniest of shower
cubicles. If you wanted to dry yourself, you had to step outside into the hallway.

On the rare occasions Conchita lured a colleague from the Oswald Mosley Citi-Def back to her bed, she always turned the lights off so they couldn't see the dismal limitations of the con-apt for themselves. In the morning, the faces of her lovers reminded the single mother of how just shabby and hopeless her existence appeared to others. The Maguire family home was a dump, the taint of sweat and despair stained every surface.

Trapped on welfare and starved of adult company, Conchita had devoted herself to the block's Citi-Def squad. Membership was usually an all-male affair, but Conchita had proved herself the equal of any man in shooting, fighting and her utter hatred of all outsiders. She despised their rivals in Enoch Powell with a passion that frightened others. If you believed the rumours – and Conchita did little to dispel them – she had killed two men from Norman Tebbitt during the madness of Block Mania more than twenty years ago.

But her greatest hatred was for offworlders. They represented everything that was wrong with this city. How could the Big Meg provide a home for alien scum when decent citizens like her had to get by in this hovel? How could the Judges betray the valiant struggle of warriors like herself during the Apocalypse War, defending the city from Sov-Block invaders, only to allow freaks like the R'qeen and their kin to settle in Sector 87? Conchita hated aliens with a passion that made her blood boil. She would happily die in a nuclear holocaust if she could take all the aliens with her to hell; it'd be worth it. Sometimes she seriously considered taking a machine gun from the Citi-Def armoury and running amok in Alien Town, taking out as many of the offworlders as possible before the Judges gunned her down.

There was one ray of hope that kept her sane. For the past month decorating droids had been refurbishing the top floor of Oswald Mosley Block. Half a dozen spacious new con-apts were being created and the Maguire family was at the top of the list for relocation. Moving day was coming soon and then everything would be different, Conchita promised herself. Maybe then she could learn to stop hating so much.

Conchita had rejoiced in the carnage at Robert Hatch but had not dared visit the scene of the blaze herself. Her anti-alien sentiments were well known and she would be a prime suspect unless she could prove otherwise. To make sure of her alibi, she had deliberately drawn atten- tion to herself at the public meeting. Judge Dredd himself had seen her and Deputy Sector Chief Temple had singled her out from among those attending. Nobody could blame the fire on her.

"They'll be home soon, go back to bed," Conchita said brusquely.

"When's soon?"

"It doesn't matter! Go back to bed."

But the child ventured closer to her mother. "Why did you lie tonight?"

"What?"

"In that big room full of people. Why did you tell that man I fell over? That isn't how I hurt my face."

Conchita pulled back a hand, ready to slap her daughter. "I warned you, Kasey! We don't tell outsiders what happens inside these walls. Remember?"

The girl shrank back, shielding her face from fresh blows. "I remember," she whimpered.

Conchita closed her eyes. What has gotten into me, she wondered. Why am I so angry that I hit my own daughter? Conchita crouched beside Kasey and gave her a hug. "I'm sorry, my darling. I didn't mean to frighten you."

Kasey was sobbing quietly, sniffing and snivelling.

"For Grud's sake, Kasey, stop crying!"

But the girl kept on sobbing.

Conchita could feel anger growing inside her again. Why did the child always have to do this? Why did she have to antagonise her? "Did you hear me? I said stop crying!"

Kasey's hands began shaking in fear. A dribble of mucus hung from each of her nostrils; Urine soaking the front of her night-gown, dripping down on the floor. Conchita lost control of her temper shouting with frustration as she lashed out. It was only the return of Dermot and Ramone that stopped her raining blows down on Kasey's head and arms. The little girl ran into the bedroom as her mother began mopping the mess from the floor.

Dermot winced in disgust. "Jovus, don't tell me she's done it again! We've got to sleep in here!"

Ramone jabbed his twin brother in the ribs with an elbow. "Save it. We've got good news for you!"

Conchita smiled at her boys. "I know, it was on Channel 27. Did anyone see you go into the basement?"

Dermot shook his head. "No way. We planted that thing more than an hour ahead of time, then went to the shoppera like you said. When the device went off, we were being cautioned for defacing a plastic tree."

"Yeah, it was sweet. Just like clockwork," Ramone agreed.

Caine listened while the Street Judges gave their differing accounts of what had taken place outside Robert Hatch. Dredd restated his belief Stammers should receive an official reprimand for conduct unbecoming of a Judge. Caine asked Miller for her opinion.

"Why me?"

The Sector Chief smiled. "With all due respect to Dredd, he has only been assigned to 87 for a few hours. You have been here much longer and have worked alongside Judges Stammers and Riley. Do believe they should be reprimanded as Dredd suggests?"

Miller shifted uncomfortably under the accused officers' gaze. "Dredd believed only Stammers should be punished."

"But surely Riley is just as culpable. If he failed to report his partner's failure, is he not just as complicit?"

Miller nodded unhappily.

"Well," Caine demanded, "should Riley and Stammers be punished?"

"Yes," Miller replied, aware of the growing hatred etched on their faces.

The Sector Chief folded her arms. "I disagree. Stammers's comments were personal opinions obviously made in the heat of the moment, when he was unaware that the hovercam was recording him. While his attitude does him no credit, I shall not punish a Judge for having opinions. As long as Stammers continues to enforce the Law equally for all residents of this sector, I am prepared to overlook this lapse in judgement. The same applies to his partner. As for you, Miller, you would do well to think twice before accusing fellow Judges in future. I doubt such actions will encourage them to help you in future."

Dredd cleared his throat. "Permission to speak, ma'am."

"I was wondering when you were going to stick your helmet in," Caine said. "You've only been here since eight and already you are finding faults with my Judges. What exactly is your agenda here, Dredd?"

"I have no agenda. My first and only ambition is upholding the Law."

The Sector Chief laughed. "We both know that is far from being the truth."

"If you don't believe me, use a birdie." Dredd retrieved the palm-sized lie detector unit from his utility belt.

Caine shook her head. "Another of your grandstand gestures? I think not. Fooling a birdie might impress younger Judges but that doesn't convince me."

Miller pointed at Nyon and the other offworlders. "What do we do about these survivors?" she asked Caine. "They can't spend the night out here. It might be warm enough but Tek-Judges say the building will probably collapse before morning. The fire has left it structurally unsound."

The Sector Chief turned to Dredd. "You seem to be full of ideas for how to improve performance here. What do you suggest we do?"

"House them in temporary accommodation overnight. Some citi-blocks in this sector have spare capacity. Displaced Persons can find new homes for these unfortunates in the morning."

"Finally, something we agree on!" Caine said, her voice heavy with sarcasm. "Stammers and Riley, since you have such a close relationship with the aliens, I suggest you help them into temporary accommodation. The refurbishment projects at Enoch Powell and Oswald Mosley are nearly complete. Take the aliens there for tonight." The two Street Judges saluted and bustled Nyon and the other survivors away.

Dredd stepped towards Caine. "Could I have a word with you in private?"

She smiled broadly. "Why in private, Dredd? I have no guilty secrets. Perhaps there is something you wish to conceal from your partner?"

"Of course not!"

"Then let us speak freely. I encourage a lively debate," Caine said.

"Very well. I believe you are making a grave error. From what I saw at the public meeting earlier, both Oswald Mosley and Enoch Powell are focal points for anti-alien activists, especially from within their Citi-Def squads. Moving these offworlders into those blocks is an act of folly, bound to provoke reprisals."

"Really?" The Sector Chief turned to Miller. "Do you agree with your partner's assessment?"

"I would suggest there are less volatile places the aliens can be sent."

Caine leaned closer to Miller. "Are you dancing to his tune already? That doesn't say much for your powers of judgement or your loyalty."

"You asked for my opinion, ma'am. I gave it to you," Miller replied. "This is not about loyalty, it is about common sense."

"Indeed?" Caine turned back to Dredd. "Well done. It seems you have gained one ally for your little crusade. But remember this, it was you who suggested the aliens be shifted into citi-blocks temporarily. If this goes wrong, I will make sure the decision leads directly back to you."

"But–" Dredd began.

"Silence!" Caine snarled. "I have nothing further to say on the matter. Now get back on patrol. This graveyard shift is short-handed as it is. We need Judges visible on the skedways, not arguing with their superiors. Dismissed!"

23:00

Dredd and Miller accelerated away from Robert Hatch on their Lawmasters, both remaining silent for several minutes. Miller had expected her partner to rant and rave about Caine's behaviour but he kept his own counsel. She was about to ask for his opinion when Control got in touch. "PSU has finished analysing the crowd from the meeting at Leni Riefenstahl. All civilians present were residents of Sector 87. More than twenty of them have convictions for crimes against aliens, mostly xenophobic abuse and threats. PSU has backtracked their movements to before the meeting and has monitored them since it ended. No one has been within sight of Robert Hatch for more than twenty-four hours," Control reported.

"Among those with convictions, how many have affiliations with their block's Citi-Def squad?" Dredd asked.

"Hold for that," was the reply. A few moments later the radio crackled back into life. "More than half. In fact ten of those all belong to the same squad."

"Oswald Mosley?" Miller interjected.

"Yeah, how did you–"

"Call it an educated guess," she replied. "I made several of those arrests. A citizen named Conchita Maguire is the ringleader."

"That's a roj. But she was at the meeting," Control noted. "No way she could have been involved with the arson attack."

"Tek-Division is convinced it's arson then?" Dredd asked.

"Preliminary report lists the blaze as suspicious, yes. Tek-Judges Kendrick and Osman are analysing samples from the scene now. They estimate having a final report ready within an hour or two."

"Dredd to Control, standby for a moment." He switched channels so that only Miller could hear his transmission. "The presence of all those anti-alien activists at that public meeting when Robert Hatch caught fire – it's too much of a coincidence."

"You think they used it to establish their alibis?" she replied.

"That would be the smart move," Dredd agreed. He reactivated the link to Control. "I have another request for PSU. We need a list of all Sector 87 residents with convictions for crimes against aliens who weren't at the public meeting. How long will that take?"

"At least an hour," Control said.

"Also, we need a name and residential address for the boss of Summerbee Industries. Get back to us – Dredd out!"

Tarragon Rey did not believe in bad luck. He did not believe in good luck either, not any form of good fortune, happenstance or kismet. To him all such notions were the sort of superstitious nonsense that should have been left behind in the twenty-first century. For Grud's sake, this was 2126! Surely the human race should be beyond blaming its own errors and missed opportunities on the fates, the stars or any other random scapegoat.

Rey's view stemmed from the bizarre death of his mentor, the celebrated thinker and skysurfer, Osvaldo Carlos. Carlos liked to muse on the nature of human existence while soaring high above Mega-City One. He began to ponder the way so many people credited responsibility for their own flaws and foibles on random elements.

After spending five days and nights atop his surfboard half a kilometre over the city, Carlos had a brainwave. All superstition was self-delusion and only those who foreswore such foolishness could hope to achieve true nirvana.

Carlos told another skysurfer of his vision and convinced them of the truth behind this belief. Soon word spread of a messiah in the sky, preaching a new gospel of accountability and modernist rationalism. Rey had only been seventeen years old at the time, an impressionable juve who fell under the spell of this charismatic speaker. But it was the manner of Carlos's freakish demise that convinced Rey this doctrine was worth demonstrating to all those still trapped on the ground, trapped with their witless beliefs and fears. Few men are killed by a number thirteen hoverbus carrying thirteen mirrors at 13:13 in the afternoon on Friday the Thirteenth. The fact that the hoverbus was operated by The Black Cat Pet Transportation Agency was just coincidence, nothing more.

So Tarragon Rey gave up skysurfing as a hobby and devoted the rest of his life to exploding the myths of superstition. His first step had been forming M-CASS, the Mega-City Anti-Superstition Society. For its emblem the group chose an image of Mama Cass, an obscure and obese singer from one hundred and fifty years before who had choked to death on a ham sandwich. Her passing had little to do with superstition, Rey once admitted, but her name fitted the initials perfectly.

For the past decade M-CASS had been staging events across the Big Meg to prove its case against the belief in luck of any kind. The society had always staged these extravaganzas on Friday the Thirteenth, the ultimate bad luck day in the minds of most people. If Rey and his fellow members could defuse any notion that this random date held any special terrors, then eliminating irrational worries about breaking of mirrors or spilling of salt would be easy.

The last series of events had not gone well. For a start, shouting the name "Macbeth!" at actors had proved to be rather limited as a visual spectacle. Driving a hover pod through thirteen large mirrors had seemed a good idea in principle, but the practicalities of it were rather painful. The driver and all the passengers had been cut to ribbons by the shards of glass and had only got as far as the eighth mirror before crashing to a halt. Channel 27 dubbed the fatalities as "Bad Luck Plagues Anti-Superstition Loons,", not exactly the publicity that M-CASS had been seeking.

But Rey believed this time was going to be different. This time everyone would see luck, good or bad, was just a myth. Stealing thirteen black cats had proved easy; the home for endangered domestic animal species had little funding to spend on security. Getting the felines lined up on one side of Anton Diffring Overzoom was another matter. The cats insisted on doing whatever they wanted, and not what Rey desired. Whenever he had most of them together, two would immediately wander off, another would start licking its backside and the rest would just glare at him with withering contempt.

Finally, he resorted to stuffing them back into their carrying cages and lining these up along the side of the overzoom. Rey had planned to release the cats at midnight but a call from one of the society members posted on lookout back along the overzoom hastened his hand. "Pair of Judges on their way," the society's treasurer warned. "PSU cameras must have spotted you."

Rey dismissed this suggestion. "We chose this part of the overzoom because it isn't covered by a camera tower."

"Maybe a spy-in-the-sky hovercam?"

"No, I don't think so." Rey had tried to keep watch for the roving devices but coping with the cats had taken most of his attention. He glanced around but could see no sign of a silver globe floating nearby.

"Must just be bad luck then," the treasurer suggested.
"Oh! Sorry!"

"Don't say bad luck," Rey fumed. "There's no such
thing!"

"Well, that 'no such thing' will be beside you in less
than a minute."

Rey looked at his watch – still more than half an hour
until midnight. But the Judges would surely see him and
intercede. It was now or never. Rey ran along the line of
cages, pulling up the flaps and tipping the cats out on to
the edge of the overzoom. "Go, you so-called talismen of
misfortune. Show the people of Mega-City One there is
no such thing as bad luck!"

"Control to all units, Sector 87! Major collision is taking
place on the Anton Diffring Overzoom, between exits 13
and 13a. More than a dozen vehicles already involved
with more impacting by the second!"

Dredd and Miller were passing exit 12 when they
received the bulletin. "Dredd and Miller responding!"

Misch did not like the two humans herding them into the
hoverbus. Lleccas was helping Nyon into a seat while
Misch waited outside. The humans had hurt her broodfather. They wanted to hurt him again, given the chance.
She didn't need metema to sense that, it was obvious. But
she couldn't understand why they hated offworlders like
herself so much. What was wrong with them? Without
thinking about the consequences, Misch closed her eyes
and reached into the mind of Judge Eustace Stammers.

*The little boy heard his mother crying out. She was in
pain, he had to help her. He pushed against the door but
couldn't open it. He reached up and turned the handle,
opening the door a fraction. Inside, he could see her on the
bed, pinned underneath a monster. It had blue skin and
yellow markings. It kept pushing against her, straining*

and sweating. Another monster was standing nearby, touching itself and muttering in words beyond under- standing. The boy could see his mother's face contorted strangely. She was urging the monster on, telling it to go faster. She reached down between her legs and–

The boy screamed at them to stop, to leave his mother alone. She shouted at him to get out of the room. The monster standing up pushed the boy out and slammed the door shut. The boy hammered at the door with his tiny fists but got no response. He then collapsed to the floor, sobbing.

Later the monsters left, gurgling in satisfaction and leaving a handful of credits by the front door. The boy's mother came out and began beating him. She screamed at him never to interrupt her again when she had visitors. The little boy had never understood the words scrawled across the front door to their tiny con-apt before, but now he did: ALIEN WHORE.

Misch snapped back out of the trance to find Stammers standing over her, one hand clutching at his helmet. "You little slitch," he snarled. "I know what your kind can do. Stay out of my mind or else!" The Judge drew back a fist, ready to lash out at the R'qeen broodling until Riley intervened.

"Stammers! For Grud's sake, leave her alone. Haven't you gotten us into enough trouble for one night?"

"She was poking around in my head," Stammers protested. "I could feel it. She's got no right to–"

"She's just a kid," Riley replied. "Get her in the bus and let's go."

Stammers picked up the R'qeen broodling and held her in front of his face. She could smell his shame and anger, sensed his frustration. "You tell anyone what you just saw," he hissed in Allspeak, "and I'll kill your parents. Then I'll do to you what your kind did to my mother. You understand me?"

Misch nodded, too afraid to speak.

Satisfied, the Judge pushed her into the hoverbus and slammed the door. "That's the last one. Get them moving!" he shouted to the robot driver, banging a fist against the side of the vehicle. "We'll follow you."

There were more than a hundred vehicles smashed into each other when Dredd and Miller reached the back of the impact zone. Control had shut down the section of the overzoom immediately behind them, rerouting traffic down off-ramps and emergency exits to other routes. The resulting traffic chaos was likely to bring much of the sector to a standstill for the rest of the night. Fortunately, "Judges-Only" bypasses would keep some paths open for 87's law enforcers, but everybody else was being advised to stay home and avoid making any unnecessary journeys.

The citizens caught up in the carnage on Anton Diffring Overzoom were not so fortunate. A handful of those in the first few pods and roadsters that collided had managed to stumble away from their vehicles to the safety of the hard shoulder. Meanwhile more and more travellers slammed into the back of the metal melee, most dying on impact. Within a minute of Tarragon Rey opening the cat cages, fifty-three people were dead or dying. Then things got worse.

Once all five lanes were blocked by the crash, drivers swerved on to the hard shoulder to avoid a collision. Those who had sought refuge there were run down, adding to the death toll. Vehicles that tried to avoid the pedestrians either thudded into the side of the impact zone or rebounded against the side railing and were flipped over the top, falling the equivalent of fifteen storeys to Soren Linsted Skedway below that started another pile-up.

By the time Dredd and Miller reached the scene the death toll was over a thousand on Anton Diffring and still rising. Judging by the sounds of metal crushing into metal and the screams drifting up from the skedway below, a similar number of deaths were occurring down below.

"Grud, what started this?" Miller wondered. She switched off the engine of her Lawmaster and dismounted, stepping into a dark, crimson stream of blood and oil that rolled from the pile-up. The sounds of the wounded punctuated the night air with cries of pain and fitful screams for help mixed. A blur of black fur passed the Judges as a cat ran past them, away from the bloody carnage. A second feline followed it, then a third. "Cats? Why would cats–"

Dredd left his Lawmaster and joined her. "M-CASS. At roll call Caine said the anti-superstition society had abducted thirteen black cats."

"But what are they doing here?"

"We can worry about the cause of this later," Dredd replied. "Let's concentrate on the effects." He activated his helmet radio while still assessing the carnage. "Dredd to Control, am at the Anton Diffring crash site. Estimate hundreds dead, many more injured and/or trapped in the wreckage. Expect similar below us on Soren Linsted Skedway. We need a fleet of med-wagons and an H-Wagon overhead loaded with fire-fighting capability. Better add some riot foam as well, in case things get out of hand."

Miller waited until Dredd signed off before asking about the riot foam. "I'd have thought that's the last thing we'll need – the survivors are in shock."

"Maybe. But if my suspicions are correct, things could get ugly and fast."

One by one, the survivors began to emerge from the wreckage. Most were bloodied, many badly injured, but all were glassy-eyed and shivering despite the humidity. "What happened? What could have caused this?" they asked the Judges.

Another cat crept out from a gap between two crushed roadsters, its black fur matted with blood. Dredd pointed at the animal. "I suspect someone released thirteen black cats into the path of the oncoming traffic."

"But why? What possible reason could they have for–"

"I did it!" a lone voice announced proudly. It came from the edge of the fast lane, where a man's arm protruded from beneath a jumble of twisted metal and glasseen. Miller held the growing crowd of survivors back while Dredd pulled back the ruptured remains of a roadster to reveal the instigator.

"Tarragon Rey," Dredd muttered. He grabbed the M-CASS leader and pulled him clear, paying little heed to Rey's protests about having a sprained ankle, cuts and bruises. Dredd dragged Rey to his feet and forced him to look at the pile-up. "See this? Hundreds dead, perhaps thousands by morning. Lives ruined, families torn apart, people left in pain and misery – and for what? What were you trying to achieve?"

The M-CASS leader shrugged. "I was just proving that having a black cat cross your path wasn't proof of good luck. I didn't mean for all of this–"

Dredd shook Rey as if he was a puppet, trying to rattle some sense into his brain. "Have you any conception of the human cost for this demonstration of yours?"

But Rey remained undeterred. "Sacrifices must be made if progress is to be achieved. Superstitions belong to centuries past. We must drag ourselves into the twenty-second century!"

Dredd looked over his shoulder at the crowd gathering behind Miller. "See all those people? They're the lucky ones: they survived. Right now they're looking for somebody to blame. What do you think would happen if I told them you caused all of this, just to prove some deluded belief?"

The M-CASS leader's face hardened. "You wouldn't explain it to them properly. The fact that you call the beliefs of the great Osvaldo Carlos 'deluded' proves my point. Let me speak to them."

Dredd almost smiled. "Perhaps you're right. You speak to them." He stepped behind Rey and pulled the culprit's wrists together before snapping a pair of handcuffs around them. "Are you sure you want to do this, Rey? They may not share your more enlightened viewpoint."

"I insist! Once I make them see the sense of this, they will thank me."

"Have it your way, creep," Dredd replied. He pushed the prisoner towards the survivors. "Listen up! This man has something he wants to tell you."

Rey cleared his throat and began shouting to the gathered crowd of bloodied and bruised motorists.

Dredd retreated to the side of the overzoom, taking Miller with him. "Dredd, what exactly are you doing?" she asked.

"He insisted on having the chance to explain his actions to the survivors."

"But they'll tear him apart once they find out."

"Don't worry, I've got riot foam standing by."

Now The crowd was becoming restive and angry, as it realised the implications of what Rey was saying. Fists began to clench and faces hardened into rage and murderous fury. Within thirty seconds Rey was sprinting away from the pile-up towards the nearest off-ramp, pursued by an angry mob. Miller called in the H-Wagon with riot foam before turning back to her partner. "You wanted Rey to feel the same terror as those who died in this crash, didn't you?"

Dredd nodded. "Chances are he'll spend the rest of his life in either the iso-cubes or the psycho-cubes, depending on how Psi-Division judge his mental state at the time he caused the crash. Either way, it'll never bring back his victims. But at least he'll remember this moment of pure terror that will stay with him. It isn't justice, but it's a start."

Evan Yablonsky had been a news editor at Channel 27 for nine years, having fought his way up from cadet reporter. His ruthless advance on the ladder of promotion marked him out as a man willing to do almost anything to get ahead, a quality underlined by his determination to run the stories other tri-D news channels would never touch. It was Yablonsky who pioneered the audition process for prospective journalists, along with the "all aspects" waiver those auditioning had to sign. If they unearthed a scoop and survived their first night on the skedways and pedways of the Big Meg, they were offered a job. If they died or were incarcerated for going too far, Channel 27 retained culpable deniability and avoided any financial responsibility for the consequences.

The anonymous news hotline was another of Yablonsky's innovations. Citizens could call in with information about anything. The Dish-Dirt-Today line (known as DDT in the office) had proved a valuable source of leads. Everything from the neighbour that had let their goldfish licence lapse to the serial killer down the corridor was good news for Channel 27. It was most useful as a conduit for the city's criminal organisations if they wanted to stitch up their opposition. A call tipped off Channel 27, then Yablonsky passed this information to the Judges and claimed the reward for any wanted perps captured as a result. It was a sweet deal all round.

So when the DDT vidphone began ringing, the news editor did not hesitate to answer, even when it was an audio-only call. The voice was heavily distorted too, undoubtedly by some electronic means. Yablonsky set the auto-trace programme running more from habit than any expectation of it identifying where the call originated. Whoever was going to this much trouble to mask their identity was not going to give themselves away that easily.

"I have a hot tip for you," the caller said, the words sounding harsh and metallic. The news editor could not even determine the gender of the voice, so heavy was the distortion.

"Tell me more," Yablonsky drawled in his Texas City accent. He had grown up in the Lone Star city-state before moving to the Big Meg as a juve.

"The fire at the Robert Hatch. It was arson."

The news editor sighed. That was old news and he said so.

But the caller was not done yet. "The device used to start the fire, it could only have come from one of two sources – a Citi-Def squad or the Judges."

"Prove it."

"Tek-Division will find traces of a chemical compound called Lucir-74 near the seat of the fire. That compound is used exclusively for incendiary devices issued by the Justice Department to Citi-Def squads."

"Jovus drokk," Yablonsky gasped. "How do you know this?"

But the DDT line was already dead.

Yablonsky sat by the hotline for another thirty seconds, his mind still racing through the implications of what he had just heard. If it was accurate – and that was a big if right now – then there was a major scandal brewing. Could someone within the Justice Department have deliberately torched Robert Hatch and roasted most of the alien residents inside? Why would they do that? It was more likely the work of a rogue Citi-Def squad. Sector 87 had more than its fair share of those, several with strong anti-alien elements.

The news editor hurried back to his own desk, trying to decide who to call first. He needed at least one source to corroborate the story before running it. Channel 27

might be at the edge of what was acceptable for broadcast in Mega-City One but even he balked at accusing the
Justice Department of using arson to commit mass
murder without any evidence to back it up. It was time
to call an old friend inside Tek-Division. But first Yablonsky
needed to get his street journalists close into the action.
He hit the transmit button on his communications system.
"All Channel 27 reporters call in. I need to know your
positions. Now!"

Miller and Dredd stayed beside the Anton Diffring pile-up
until clean-up squads were able to cut a path through the
carnage. As Med-Judges began the grisly job of removing
corpses and severed body parts from the crushed metal,
the pair rode through the gap on their Lawmasters. Once
clear of the wreckage, Dredd called Control for progress
on his previous enquiries.

"Kendrick says she's found the residue of an unusual
chemical compound among the samples taken from the
basement of Robert Hatch. Something called Lucir-74."

"I've heard of that," Miller said.

Dredd nodded his agreement. "What else, Control?"

"PSU has cross-checked all current Sector 87 residents
with anti-alien convictions against all those who
attended the public meeting at Leni Riefenstahl. Only
three such residents were not at the meeting out of more
than two hundred."

"That's some turnout," Dredd noted. "Who are the
three and what are their locations?"

"Roberto Conti, currently in traction at St Peter Root
Hospital after losing a fight with an alien last week,"
Control replied. "Also out of the running is Huston Wark,
resident at a hospice for those with terminal cases of Jigsaw
Disease. The only other candidate is a juve called Benoit
Roth. He was arrested six hours ago and is sitting in a
holding cell at Sector House 87."

"I'm the one who arrested the little punk," Miller said. "He's too fond of wall-scrawling anti-alien slogans for his own good."

"What about the boss at Summerbee Industries?" Dredd asked Control. "Anything further on him?"

"That's a roj. Werner Summerbee resides at number fifteen, Ridley Estate, but lives most of the year in tax exile on the Moon. Returned to Mega-City One this morning, according to spaceport records, but is only here for another twenty-four hours."

"Thanks, Control. Dredd out."

A watch-post platform jutted from the side of the overzoom ahead of them. Dredd began to slow down as they approached it and motioned for Miller to join him. Once they were stationary Dredd switched off his engine and helmet radio, his partner following suit. From this high platform they could look out over the sector, at a million lights glowing in the darkness. The full moon was rising in the distance, appearing unusually large as it cleared the horizon. But both Judges had others things on their minds.

"Lucir-74. That's a compound in incendiary bullets, isn't it?" Miller asked.

Dredd nodded. "And in some explosives issued to Citi-Def squads."

"Backs up our alibi theory, but doesn't get us any closer to knowing who planted it," she commented. "The device used to start the fire could have been planted hours or even days earlier but—"

"But that would have made it more susceptible to discovery," Dredd said. "Much more likely to have been put in place within an hour or two of the fire starting, cutting down the risk of detection. So it probably wasn't anybody at the public meeting."

Miller scowled. "There's another possibility. It could have been a Judge."

"Perhaps, but we're hardly inconspicuous. Even the likes of Stammers isn't stupid enough to be seen planting such a device." Dredd stroked his chin. "No, I suspect someone else was used, a go-between, somebody whose name wouldn't show up as an obvious suspect with PSU."

"So we're back to square one?"

"For the moment." Dredd looked out at the city, deep in thought. "There's something else going on here, Miller. Something below the surface."

"Like what?"

"I don't know," he admitted. "Just a suspicion, nagging at me."

Miller smiled. "I thought you were double-zero rated, no discernible psychic abilities."

"Gut instinct has its uses too. The precogs were expecting trouble–"

"Haven't we had enough already?"

Dredd shook his head. "Nothing more than you'd expect with a full moon and Friday the Thirteenth starting in a few minutes. Precogs wouldn't issue a sector-wide warning without serious concerns. Whatever's coming, we've only seen the leading edge of it." His shoulders slumped momentarily, exhaustion evident on his features.

"When was the last time you got any rest?" Miller asked.

"More than twenty-seven hours ago."

"Then we should get back to the sector house. Control can spare you for ten minutes on a sleep machine." Miller reactivated her helmet radio. "What about Summerbee? Do you want me to see him about that rogue droid?"

"He can wait. Right now we–"

"Control to all units! There's a hundred members of a doomsday cult on the roof of Maurice Waldron Block. Can anyone respond?"

"That's just below the next off-ramp," Miller noted.

"Guess that sleep machine will have to wait for me," Dredd said before signalling Control they would take the call.

00:00
FRIDAY, SEPTEMBER 13, 2126

Sharona Moore was disappointed. For five years she had been leading a cult of eschatologists, watching for the signs and portents that indicated the end of the world. Her team of researchers had scoured all the ancient texts for clues: the Book of Revelations from the Bible, the prophecies of French visionary Nostradamus and the collected horoscopes of fabled Brit-Cit astrologer Russell Grant. From these diverse sources had emerged fragments of evidence, all of them pointing to this time and this place.

Revelations spoke of a full moon rising on the last night, while Nostradamus wrote of the apocalypse enveloping the city of the one Magi (Mega-City One was the accepted modern interpretation of this sixteenth century text). Russell Grant suggested Friday the Thirteenth would bring disaster for all those under the star sign of Libra. Grant also suggested there was a chance for new romance and the day's lucky colour would be blue, but the researchers dismissed these elements of the prophecy as droll fripperies inserted to satisfy the low brow culture prevalent back in the year 2004. Every member of Sharona's cult had been born under the star sign Libra, confirming the truth of the flamboyant soothsayer's vision. In fact, all members were the product of conceptions fuelled by festive season inebriation, but they preferred not to discuss this.

So it had come to pass that one day, one date and one time stood out from all the years of contemplation and

interpretation – Friday, September thirteenth, 2126 AD.
As this day began, a mighty calamity would decimate
Mega-City One and the creator of all things would come
down and rescue all those (and only those) who were
ready to accept deliverance. At least, that was how
Sharona saw it. If pressed, she was willing to admit the
exact year was never stipulated and the presence of blue
as a lucky colour still worried her. And how could there
be a chance for new romance to blossom if the world was
going to end?

But Sharona had put those doubts aside and gathered
her followers. The cult was a hundred strong, mostly
adults with a smattering of juves. Sharona had gathered
them to herself with charismatic speeches, a litany of salvation for a select few and free memberships for anyone
born between September twenty-fifth and October first.
Setting up her own cult had proved surprisingly easy. The
Justice Department favoured a policy of religious tolerance,
so long as the religion frowned upon all forms of law-
breaking. Once the Sect of the Last Redemption was
registered with the necessary authorities, Sharona was free
to hold meetings, predict the end of the world and organise
pre-apocalypse fund-raising sales of baked goods.

The cult members were now gathered atop Maurice
Waldron Block, waiting for the end of the world. All were
resplendent in their purple and gold robes, specially
purchased for Judgement Day from the proceeds of
baked goods sales. Everyone had said their goodbyes to
the non-believers in their immediate family and friends.
It wasn't easy to mentally prepare yourself for salvation,
knowing so many were not be spared the full horrors of
the apocalypse, but Sharona counselled her followers not
to fret. The creator might take pity on associate members
and upgrade them to full redemption status.

So the one hundred waited, their hands linked
together. They recited a fervent prayer over and over

again as the moment of destiny approached. "Creator of all things, hallowed be thyself. Thy kingdom is nearly come, thy will be done, in the Big Meg as it is wherever you hang out. Give us this day our ticket off this stommhole and forgive us our hoverbus passes. Lead us not into a cul-de-sac but deliver us from bad stuff. For thine is the kingdom and the glory and stuff like that, now and forever and a day. All right?"

Sharona smiled – she was fond of the prayer, it struck just the right note of reverence and informality in her opinion. You could be too drokking pious, you know?

It was ten minutes after midnight when the prayers began to falter. Everyone still believed the end was nigh, but they were starting to get a little impatient. A half-hearted chorus of "Why are we waiting?" was stifled by a harsh glance from Sharona.

"Do not goad the Creator!" she shouted. "If, in his or her infinite wisdom, he or she chooses to be a little late, that does not mean we should be any less respectful of our saviour."

By quarter past it was obvious something had gone awry. Sharona did her best to conceal the disappointment from her followers. "Perhaps we have misinterpreted the signs and portents," she allowed.

"But you seemed so sure," her main disciple insisted. Gunther Beck had been the first to join the cult, admitting to Sharona his life was a barren, soulless existence since his mother died two years earlier. The fact he believed in her, had a small personal fortune and was also eager to pleasure her with oral sex had in no way influenced Sharona's decision to make Gunther a disciple. Well, the belief and the credits had perhaps played a small part in the decision, but the erotic encounters were just a bonus.

"Well, everybody makes mistakes," she admitted. The cultists groaned, some mumbling that they had been duped, others wondering about how they could get their old jobs back. Sharona realised events would spiral out of her control unless she exerted some authority.

"Everyone, listen to me. I am experiencing a vision!" She fell to her knees and pointed at the full moon overhead. "I can now clearly see what we must do. If the apocalypse will not come to us, then we must go to the apocalypse!"

"Err, Sharona, you're not making much sense," Gunther whispered.

"It's simple. The Creator will only save us if we deliver ourselves to him!"

"And how do we do that?"

"By killing ourselves, of course!"

Riff Maltin had been wondering where his next story would come from when the call came through from Channel 27's news editor. Yablonsky wanted all his correspondents to investigate anti-alien sentiment in the sector's Citi-Def squads. Riff had glowed inwardly with pride at being referred to as a correspondent. But there was no time to savour the moment. Yablonsky was already handing out assignments, sending his best reporters to those blocks with the most rabid Citi-Def squads. Riff knew he couldn't leave this to chance.

"I want Oswald Mosley!" he shouted when the news editor paused.

"Why?"

"Call it a hunch," Maltin replied.

"Fine, whatever. The new boy's going to Oswald Mosley. Next..."

Riff had more than a hunch backing his request. He had returned to Robert Hatch after Dredd left and witnessed the survivors being loaded into hoverbuses. Creeping closer, he had overheard Judge Stammers directing the driver droid to deliver its cargo of aliens to Oswald Mosley. Riff had already seen what strong feelings the offworlders aroused. The residents of Mosley had a reputation for being notoriously anti-alien. The arrival of their new neighbours was bound to cause more trouble and that meant news.

Riff caught the midnight zoom train across Sector 87, luckily avoiding the traffic caused by the Anton Diffring pile-up. As a result the roving reporter reached his destination ahead of the hoverbus. He approached Oswald Mosley with some trepidation. It was a typical citi-block, one hundred storeys of con-apts and support facilities providing homes to sixty thousand residents. Residents could be born, live their whole lives and die without ever leaving the building. It contained shops, recreation areas and a medical centre. None of that worried Riff. But the scrawl emblazoned across the entrance to the block: ALIEN SCUM STAY OUT! attracted his attention. If the Judges were planning to relocate survivors from Robert Hatch to here, there wouldn't just be trouble – there was going to be a riot.

Riff smiled. Why was he worrying? A riot was exactly what he wanted. Grud knows, it would make good viewing on tri-D. It wouldn't be long before the hoverbus arrived. Now was his chance to alert the residents to what was coming, and stir them up a little. Maltin remembered the lecture Yablonsky had given him at the audition. "You can't always break the news. Sometimes you have to manufacture it – by any means necessary."

The reporter hurried into the block's entrance, encountering a surly juve inside picking his nose. "Do you know who runs the Citi-Def squad here?"

Ramone Maguire peered at the stranger. "Why do you want to know?"

"My name's Riff Maltin, I'm a reporter for Channel 27." He gestured at the hovercam just above his right shoulder to prove his identity. "I've got news about a threat to the security of this block and its residents."

Ramone shrugged. "You want my mom: Conchita Maguire, con-apt 729. But she won't be happy about you waking her up at this time of night."

"She'll thank me when she hears what I know."

"Have it your way." The juve jerked his head towards a phone on the wall. "You can call her from there. But I'm telling you, she won't be happy."

Riff soon discovered the juve had not been exaggerating. It took several minutes of cursing and swearing before Conchita calmed down enough to hear what Maltin was trying to tell her. "Offworlders? Coming here?"

"Yes." Riff heard the telltale hiss of a hoverbus stopping outside the entrance. "I think their transportation has just arrived outside."

"Those freaks aren't coming into my block!" the fiery Maguire vowed and slammed down the phone.

Riff smiled, the reason he had been sent to Oswald Mosley long forgotten. He could smell trouble and it was coming at his command.

Dredd and Miller screeched to a halt outside Maurice Waldron Block. A crowd of bystanders had formed around the building, many of them pointing upwards and discussing previous suicide jumps they had witnessed. Up above, a line of people could be seen standing on the edge of the roof, their figures silhouetted against the full moon overhead.

"One of us will have to stay here on crowd control until back-up arrives," Miller observed, frowning at the ghouls gathered on the ground. "If the cult members do decide to turn themselves into street pizza, we don't want them taking out the bystanders as well."

"Agreed," Dredd growled. "You stay here. I'll go up."

"Hey! Why do you get to go?"

"Trust me. I've dealt with more leapers than you. I'll get these punks down, one way or another."

"Have it your own way," Miller said. "I'll contact the block maintenance droid, make sure countermeasures are available if the worst happens."

"That's a roj." Dredd dismounted from his Lawmaster and strode into Maurice Waldron, checking he had a full clip of ammunition loaded.

Miller watched him go in before looking up into the air again. "Drokking full moon, always brings out the crazies," she muttered.

On the roof Sharona Moore had convinced her acolytes that suicide was definitely the way to nirvana. "Just before we reach the ground the Creator will reach down and scoop out our souls, preserving us for all eternity," she announced with a smile.

All one hundred of the cult members were standing in a line along the edge of the roof, gazing out across the city. To Sharona's left, Gunther was having second thoughts. "Are you sure you've got the prophecy right this time, my darling?" he whispered from the side of his mouth. "I don't mean to question your wisdom, but earlier you were saying the entire world was coming to an end. Now you think it's just us who have to die."

"Do you doubt me, Gunther?" Sharona asked.

"Well, frankly, yes."

"Can't say I blame you," a gruff voice interjected. Sharona and her disciples swung round to see Judge Dredd emerging from the rooftop access door. "Seen a lot of religious types in my time and few of them have got any proof to support their claims of divine guidance."

"Unbeliever!" Sharona shouted, pointing an accusing finger at Dredd. "You know nothing of what you speak!"

"Maybe, but it doesn't sound like you've got a hotline to Grud yourself, or whoever you believe in."

"We believe in the Creator of all things," Gunther said, trying to be helpful.

"Uh-huh. This creator says it's a good night to fall a hundred storeys before going face-first into a rockcrete grave, does he?"

"The Creator does not have a gender," Sharona snapped. "They are beyond such worldly concerns as gender and sex."

"I know the feeling," Dredd replied. "Well, off you go."

"Sorry?"

"Jump. I'm not stopping you."

Sharona was perplexed. "If you're not going to stop us, why did you come up here?"

"Justice Department requires I try to talk you out of it, but I can't be bothered tonight. I haven't eaten in fifteen hours, I haven't slept in nearly twice that time and I couldn't give a flying drokk whether you jump or not." Dredd put his Lawgiver back into its holster. "Makes no difference to me."

"Oh. Err, okay." Sharona turned back to her disciples. "Well, if everybody's ready, we'll go on a count of three. One–"

"There's just one thing," Dredd said.

Sharona sighed in exasperation. "And what's that?"

"I can't let you take all these people with you."

"Why not?"

"You want to kill yourself, be my guest – one less kook to put in the cubes. But taking all these citizens with you, now that's mass murder."

Sharona frowned. "You can't be serious."

"Try me," Dredd growled.

"These people have agreed to follow me wherever I go. If that means jumping to their deaths, they will do so."

"I'm not convinced."

"You're not convinced?"

"No," Dredd said, shaking his head. "The citizen on your right, for a start. He didn't seem too sure when I came up the stairs. Since he's standing next to you, I'm guessing he's probably one of your assistants. Now, if you can't convince your assistants that suicide is a bright idea, well…"

Sharona glared at Dredd malevolently. "Have you quite finished?"

The Judge nodded.

"Fine. Then I shall prove how wrong you are. I will step off this roof and fall to my death. And all my acolytes will follow me. Now, if you don't mind."

"Go right ahead. Turn yourself into street pizza. No skin off my chin."

Sharona rolled her eyes before readying herself. "On my mark. One. Two. Three!" She stepped off the roof and began falling.

It was then Dredd realised all the cultists were tied together. Once Sharona went over the side, the others followed, whether they wanted to or not. Dredd began running towards the edge of the roof but was too late to grab the last of the sect members before they were dragged over. Instead he dived off the roof after them.

By the time Stammers and Riley reached Oswald Mosley, more than a hundred residents had blocked the entrance to the building. The two Judges had been called off escort duty to help with the aftermath of the Anton Diffring pile-up. They were now faced with another angry mob – only this one hadn't been immobilised with a bombardment of riot foam. The protesters had surrounded the hoverbus filled with aliens and were trying to tip the vehicle over.

"Terrif," Stammers muttered darkly. "As if this night couldn't get any worse." He fired six shots into the air. Most of the crowd scattered, falling back to the block's entrance. But a hardcore of two dozen remained around the hoverbus, all wearing flak jackets and helmets marked with CITI-DEF insignia. At the front and in the centre of this group was a woman with a face like thunder. She marched towards the two Judges.

"How dare you fire upon us! These are decent, law-abiding citizens staging a non-violent protest!" the woman snarled with venomous fury.

"Trying to turn over a hoverbus? Not exactly a page from the passive resistance handbook, is it?" Stammers replied sarcastically. "Anyway, we didn't fire on you. Those were warning shoots. What's your name, citizen?"

"Conchita Maguire, leader of Oswald Mosley Citi-Def."

"Well, you're not setting much of an example," Riley observed. "You're supposed to welcome and protect new residents – not attack them."

"So it's true! You intend to bring these alien scum inside our building!"

Stammers decided to take a more placatory approach. "Look, lady, I ain't any happier than you about this. But the situation is just temporary. Tomorrow morning they'll probably be moved to another facility."

"Temporary – that's an interesting word," Conchita said. "I had a friend in Robert Hatch who was temporarily moved out to make way for the vultures and all the other freaks. How many years did that temporary measure last?"

"Citizen, you can bitch and moan all you like. That ain't changing the fact these aliens are being housed here for the night," Riley replied.

"Where?" Conchita demanded. "Every con-apt in this building is already full beyond capacity. Where do you intend to put these, these, things?" She spat on the ground between the two Judges to underline her hatred.

Stammers smiled. He'd tried being nice but that didn't get him anywhere. He was fast losing patience. Time to put an end to this. "I'm told the top floor refurbishment is nearly done. The aliens can spend the night up there. We'll move them out in the morning."

That was when Conchita lost it. She could see her one dream, her last hope disappearing before her eyes. If the aliens shifted into the new home meant for her family, would the monsters ever move out again? She would remain trapped in her con-apt for Grud knew how many more months or years! Even if they were relocated, she wasn't sure she could stand to live where the aliens had been. It would be like sharing her body with them.

The red mist descended and Maguire went into a frenzy, running towards the hoverbus and throwing herself at the doors. One fist smashed through the glasseen, tearing the skin off her knuckles in the process. "I'm gonna kill you! I'm gonna kill you all!" she kept screaming, over and over. The rest of the Citi-Def squad took up her chant, banging their fists against the side of the hoverbus. Inside, the alien passengers cowered back from the windows, huddling against each other, terror and anger in their eyes. Meanwhile the rest of the residents were cheering the Citi-Def squad on.

The two Judges exchanged a glance.

"Stumm gas?" Stammers asked his partner.

"Stumm gas," Riley replied, already reaching for a canister of the paralysing liquid attached to his utility belt. The Judges pulled the pins simultaneously and rolled the smoking tubes towards the hoverbus, before pulling down the respirators on their helmets.

Stammers stepped away from his motorcycle and drew out his daystick. "Let's bust some heads!"

Dredd dived headfirst from the roof of Maurice Waldron Block, streamlining his body shape so he fell faster than the cultists below him. Sharona Moore and her ninety-nine disciples were tumbling slowly through the air like a human charm bracelet, each member tied to another at the wrist. Maurice Waldron was a hundred storeys high, giving the leapers plenty of time to scream for help as they fell towards the pedway below. Dredd activated his helmet radio.

"Miller, can you hear me?"

"Yes. Dredd, the cult kooks have just jumped off the roof!"

"I know. I jumped after them."

"You did what?!"

"I jumped after them. Are the block safety measures fully functional?"

"Yes," Miller replied. "I can control them from the onboard computer on my Lawmaster. Do you want me to deploy them?"

"Not yet."

"Why the drokk not?"

"I want to arrest these creeps on the way down," Dredd said.

"Well, I estimate you've got another sixty storeys and half a minute left."

"Roj that. I'll keep this channel open!" By now Dredd had caught up with the last of the cult members, a gibbering woman. Being at the end of the human chain, only one of her wrists was tied to another disciple. Her purple and gold gown was flapping around her face, revealing that she was otherwise naked. "You're under arrest," Dredd announced, "Attempted suicide, disturbing the peace and gross indecency. Six months for each charge, eighteen months in all."

"Are you crazy?" the woman screamed. "We'll all be dead in a minute!"

"If that happens, I'll let you off the attempted suicide," Dredd replied, handcuffing himself to her free wrist. "But the other charges still stand."

"You are crazy!" his prisoner replied.

Dredd ignored her and shouted so the other leapers could hear him. "You're all under arrest for attempted suicide and disturbing the peace! Come along quietly or there will be trouble!"

Misch had watched as the two Judges attacked the protesters outside the hoverbus. She felt waves of hatred and anger surging from the crowd but this turned to terror when the stumm gas canisters began billowing clouds of paralysing smoke into the air. Some of the gas seeped into the hoverbus through a broken window. The arthropod Gruchar began spewing green bile into the air while a family from Wolfren were sent into a frenzy of howling and tears. Misch was grateful for the R'qeen respiratory bypass system. The gas made her a little dizzy but that was the limit of its effects.

Among those caught in the conflict was a human Misch could recall seeing outside their old home. He was followed everywhere by a floating silver globe that seemed to be watching what was happening. The human threw himself against the doors of the hoverbus, begging to be let inside. He was clubbed to the ground by one of the Judges. It was the man with the moustache whose mind she had reached into. He was grinning, enjoying every second of this carnage.

Once the gas had cleared, the broodling could see the battered and bleeding bodies of the protesters scattered around the entrance of the building. Most of the others had retreated inside and shut the doors. But the two Judges overrode the electronic locks and drove the residents back up the stairs or into the lifts. Only when a path had been cleared into Oswald Mosley did the aliens dare venture from the hoverbus.

Nyon was first out, leading his family into the block lobby. Lleccas had fashioned a sling for his shattered arm. Misch clung on to her broodmother's arm, not wanting to be separated. She had grown to know their old home but this one was new and strange. The R'qeen girl could feel a seething resentment all around them, as if the building itself was willing them to go. The others slowly emerged from the hoverbus and joined them inside the block. In all there were half a dozen families: four R'qeen, one from Wolfren and Gruchar. Keno and her brood were one of the other R'qeen families.

The Judges reappeared down the staircase. "Turbolifts are stuck on the seventy-second floor. Residents have jammed them." It was the human with the moustache again. He seemed grimly satisfied with the situation. "You'll have to go up the stairs."

"How far?" Nyon asked.

"You're on the top. A hundred storeys up."

"But some here have injuries from the fire. Others are still suffering the effects of your gas. You can't expect them to climb a hundred flights of stairs."

The Judge leaned close to Nyon's face. "I don't care if it takes you all night, vulture. Get moving!"

Misch could feel her broodfather struggling to control his anger, a great mass of red and black boiling inside him. Eventually he walked past the human towards the stairs.

"Wait!" the Judge commanded. "Riley, you better take the lead. We've dealt with the worst of the troublemakers but they might still be planning another protest. I'll cover the flank. Okay, let's move!"

On the ground Miller's hand hovered over her Lawmaster's on-board computer while she watched Dredd and the hundred cultists plunging towards her. "For the love of Grud, you're running out of time!" she shouted into her helmet radio. "When do you want me to engage the countermeasures?"

"They're all under arrest," Dredd responded. "Engage now!"

Miller slammed her fist down on the computer screen. Wall panels two storeys up from the ground slid backwards into the building and several giant nets spat outwards, forming themselves into huge hammocks on all four sides of the block. Less than a second later Sharona and the other cult members plunged into the suicide nets, their fall slowed and halted within moments. Dredd was last to hit the netting, landing astride the nearly naked woman, his crotch jamming into her face.

The deployment of the building's safety measures brought a groan of collective disappointment from the bystanders but they soon began applauding Dredd's daring manoeuvre. Underneath him the scantily clad woman was struggling to make herself heard. "I can't breathe," she gasped. Dredd uncuffed himself from her wrist and clambered off her face.

"My apologies, citizen."

"Are you all right?" Miller shouted up to her partner.

Dredd gave her the thumbs up before swinging himself over the side of the net and dropping to the ground below. "Dredd to Control. We need catch wagons outside Maurice Waldron to collect a hundred religious kooks; twelve months each in the psycho cubes."

"What about me?" the nearly naked woman asked from atop the pile of cult members.

"Correction, Control," Dredd said. "Ninety-nine kooks at twelve months each and one simp who wants an extra six months."

In the nets Sharona overheard the request. "You can't do that! You've denied us our religious right to worship as we see fit."

Miller jerked a thumb at the bystanders who were now drifting away. "Religious tolerance stops when you endanger the lives of others."

Gunther was squeezed next to his leader in the nets. "You know, the signs and portents may have been right about the date of the apocalypse. We may have simply interpreted the wrong year from the prophecies."

Sharona smiled at him. "You mean the end of the world might be happening at midnight between June twelfth and thirteenth next year?"

"Maybe."

"Maybe," Sharona agreed before calling down to Dredd. "Excuse me, Judge. How long did you say our sentence was?"

"Twelve months for everybody except the woman who was cuffed to me – eighteen months for her. Why?"

"It's just we might have miscounted the date for the apocalypse. Same time next year, what do you say?"

Conchita Maguire had been one of the lucky ones during the brawl outside Oswald Mosley. Her sons had pulled her away from the worst of the stumm gas and bundled her inside before the Judges laid into the others with daysticks. Conchita wanted to fight alongside her fellow squad members but Ramone and Dermot would not let her. "We'll get our chance," Ramone said. "But you choose the time and the place, not them."

He was smart, that boy, Conchita had to admit. She decided on a tactical retreat, leading her sons and those squad members that had escaped the gas up to the seventy-second floor. Once there they disabled all the turbolifts, knowing the Judges would have to bring the aliens up the stairs. Conchita returned to the family con-apt to get changed, her squad uniform splashed with blood from the melee.

Inside 729 she found Kasey snivelling by the bedroom door, a red cloth wrapped round her left foot. "Please don't be angry," the girl said.

"What have you done now?" Conchita demanded.

"I didn't mean to," Kasey stammered. "It just happened. You were gone so long and I got thirsty…"

Conchita went to the icebox. Broken glasseen was splintered across the floor. Bloody footprints led away from an orange stain of Gloomy-D synthi-juice. "You cut yourself?"

Kirsty nodded, heavy tears brimming in her frightened eyes. "I didn't mean to get blood on the floor..."

A fist hammered against the con-apt's front door. "Conchita! Paul called from twenty-two: they're on their way up now!"

"Get everyone gathered by the stairs. I'll be right there."

"Gotcha!"

Conchita glared at her daughter, the anger rising inside once more. "Why can't you be more like Ramone or Dermot? They're ready to defend this block from the aliens and all you can do is make another mess."

Kirsty's bottom lip began to wobble. "But I didn't–"

Conchita advanced on her daughter, one hand clenching into a fist. "You have to be punished. I warned you before – learn to clean up your own messes or suffer the consequences."

Kirsty closed her eyes, whimpering in terror.

Miller pushed the last of the cult members into the back of a catch wagon. Dredd shut the door, then banged his fist on it. "Okay, take 'em back to the sector house for processing." The vehicle rolled away from Maurice Waldron Block, leaving the two Judges behind.

"Want me to catch the paperwork on that lot?" Miller offered. "You look like you could do with that sleep machine session about now."

"You might be right," Dredd replied. "It's–"

Their helmet radios crackled into life. "Control to all units, east side of Sector 87. Garbled reports of a confront between Judges and the Oswald Mosley Citi-Def. Can anyone respond?"

Dredd was about to climb on his Lawmaster but Miller stopped him. "That's the other side of the sector. By the time we get there it will all be over. We're not the only ones on this graveyard shift, you know." Within seconds several Judges much nearer were responding to the incident. Sector Chief Caine called Control to announce she would lead the back-up team. "See what I mean? Come on, let's get back to the sector house."

"All right," Dredd reluctantly agreed. "But you go on ahead. I've got to put in a call to an old friend – in private."

His partner smiled. "Got a guilty secret you're trying to hide?"

"I don't have any guilty secrets," Dredd responded humourlessly. "The less you know about what I'm going to do, the better your future in Sector 87."

"I can take a hint," Miller said, climbing on to her Lawmaster and gunning its powerful engine into life. "See you back at the sector house."

Once she was gone Dredd activated his helmet radio. "Control, put me through to Chief Judge Hershey's office. I need to speak with her – Urgently!"

At first, Riley thought the chanting must be from a resident's tri-D set, the noise drifting down the emergency stairwell in Oswald Mosley Block. That would be a code violation, section 56b of the noise pollution regs: minimum sentence of three months, with a month added for each decibel of noise above the legal limit. Judging by the cacophony, the perp responsible was facing three years in the cubes, maybe more. Street Judges had discretion when it came to sentencing, but mandatory minimums set the bench mark.

Riley enjoyed being a Judge, the feeling of making a difference. The lives of every human being in this sector were a little better because Riley was on the job. He didn't count offworlders as citizens. To him they were a mistake. Justice Central should never have granted these things the right to stay in the Big Meg. It was our city, not theirs. Good men and woman had died to defeat alien species like the R'qeen; now vultures could become citizens! Well, they might be legal aliens, but they would always be scum to Riley.

Besides being able to help people, there was another aspect of the job Riley found even more satisfying – administering the firm spank of authority. He liked the power, liked knowing he could take charge of almost any situation, that he could determine the fate of other people's lives, even whether they lived or died. It was a trip and no mistake. But you had to be careful. All that power could be intoxicating. Riley had seen what happened to Judges who got addicted to the buzz, and got caught. Not me, he vowed.

When he reached the sixty-ninth floor, Riley realised the noise was not coming from one of the con-apts. Looking up he could see dozens of residents three storeys above, chanting the same phrases over and over. "One, two, three, four, kick the aliens out the door! Five, six, seven, eight, keep the scum from our top floor!" Riley drew his Lawgiver and called down to his partner via helmet radio.

"Stammers, we've got a problem up here. I think the residents are planning another protest against the aliens."

"Keep going. Control says back-up is on its way."

"You sure?"

"Do it, Riley! If the residents want another taste of my daystick, I'm more than happy to administer it to them. Stammers out!"

Riley looked back at the aliens climbing the stairs below him. They looked exhausted, easy meat for any citizens carrying a grudge. Riley almost felt sorry for them, until he remembered what had happened to Danny. "Drokk 'em," he whispered and resumed his progress up the stairs.

Conchita Maguire and her sons were blocking the seventy-second floor landing, along with dozens of other residents. Dermot and Ramone had gone from door to door, rousing their neighbours and spreading news of the aliens taking up residence in the penthouse con-apts. It didn't take much provocation to draw citizens out of their beds.

Conchita stepped in front of Riley when the Judge reached the landing. The aliens were still climbing the stairs behind him. "They're not going any further," she said. "Send 'em back where they belong. Not here with decent citizens."

"Step aside or I'll arrest all of you for disturbing the peace," Riley warned.

"We're making a legitimate protest," Dermot replied. "Try to arrest one of us and you'll have a riot on your hands. Is that what you want?"

"I've been cracking skulls since before you were born, juve. You want a piece of me? Bring it on," Riley said.

Dermot began towards the Judge but Conchita stopped him. "No, that's exactly what he wants. Don't give him an excuse."

"What's the problem?" Stammers bellowed up the stairwell from the floor below. "What's happening?"

Riley was about to answer when he heard a familiar noise from beyond the crowd of residents. "Residents won't let us past. Looks like we've got a stand-off, but that's about to change."

Conchita smiled. "Why? You backing down?"

"No, you are!" a woman shouted from behind the residents. They swivelled round to see a dozen Judges emerging from the turbolifts, all heavily armed. Standing at the front of them was Sector Chief Caine, a small electronic key held in her left hand. "Judicial override. Nice work jamming the circuits but Tek-Judges soon found a way to bypass your efforts." Caine drew her

Lawgiver and aimed it at the residents gathered on the landing. "Now, you've all got five seconds to stand aside or else we take you down. Permanently."

"What do we do?" Ramone asked his mother. The other residents were all looking to her for guidance, unsure how to react.

"Stand aside," she hissed, her voice shaking with anger.

"But we can't–"

"Stand aside!" Conchita screamed at her eldest son, shoving him against a wall. She glared at the other citizens. "You heard me!" They all moved away from the stair-well, creating a gap for the aliens.

Caine told Riley and Stammers to transport the new-comers the rest of the way up Oswald Mosley in turbolifts. "I think they've been through enough for one night, don't you?" The rest of the Judges began ushering residents back to their own con-apts, the confrontation defused for now.

The Sector Chief was about to talk with the protest ringleaders when her helmet radio crackled into life. "Control to Caine. Message for you from the Chief Judge's office."

"At this time of night?" she wondered outloud, before responding to the call. Caine listened intently, her face becoming a scowl. Once the call was finished she resumed her conversation with Control. "Where is Judge Dredd now?"

"En route to your position at Oswald Mosley. Should be outside soon."

Caine nodded grimly. "Good. Tell him to wait for me in the lobby. I'll see him once I've dealt with the situation here."

Dredd had despaired of getting a reply from the Chief Judge's office, so he decided to confront Caine instead.

When he arrived at Oswald Mosley Block a clean-up squad and half a dozen Med-Judges were dealing with the aftermath from the earlier brawl. Dredd saw Maltin slumped against a pillar nursing a head wound, his hovercam dutifully shooting every moment of Riff's agony. "You were outside Robert Hatch," Dredd recalled. "I warned you to stay out of trouble."

The reporter shrugged. "Can I help it if trouble follows me around?" A Med-Judge began examining Riff's skull, pushing aside hair matted with blood to examine the wound. "Hey, careful!"

"Stop your griping, citizen," the physician retorted. After a cursory study of the contusion he handed Riff a rapi-heal patch. "Stick this on it. Should be good as new by morning." The Med-Judge was already moving to the next injury.

"What about the pain? Give me something for the pain," Riff pleaded.

"Get over it," the physician replied. "Feel better now?"

"Oh yeah. Just terrif!"

Dredd nudged Maltin with his boot. "What happened here?"

"Difficult to say," Riff admitted. "Residents tried to stop two Judges taking the aliens inside. Thirty seconds later the place was awash with stumm gas and one of your colleagues was trying to reshape my head with his daystick."

"Who was it?"

"I don't know, I was too busy bleeding to get a look at his badge. But he had a big moustache and a way with a beating, know what I mean?"

Dredd's helmet radio demanded his attention. "Control to Dredd. Sector Chief Caine requests that you wait for her in the lobby of Oswald Mosley. She should be with you presently."

"Roj that. Dredd out." He looked at Riff thoughtfully. "Stick around. I've got more questions for you."

01:00

Misch had only known about her gift for a few hours, but she was already beginning to think metema was as much a curse as a blessing. Being able to read the thoughts and feelings of others whenever you wanted was a good thing. But the emotions around her now were so strong, so overwhelming, it was all she could do to keep them out of her head. The woman who had been stopping them from going any further was the worst. Her anger and hatred was so palpable she appeared as a red blur on Misch's thoughts. Some of the others were almost as angry, but none with such power or conviction. Being the target of such hostility left the R'qeen child quivering with fear.

The Judges had begun moving the Robert Hatch Block survivors into the turbolifts, but there wasn't enough room for everyone to travel to the top floor at the same time. Nyon volunteered his family to stay behind and wait for the next turbolift. Misch wished her broodfather hadn't been so generous, but it was typical of him to put others first. That was his way and she loved him for that.

Misch had been holding on tightly to her brood-mother's hand, not wanting to be left behind when their turn came. Then a fresh mind caught her attention. There was a girl nearby, not far from her in age. She was so sad, sadder than anyone Misch had ever met before. The R'qeen child let go of her broodmother's hand to look for this girl. Perhaps she could make her happy.

"Don't go far," Lleccas said. "The turbolift will be back for us soon."

Misch nodded dutifully to her broodmother before wandering away. She knew the sad girl was close by, but where? Misch closed her eyes and let the emotions draw her near. The unhappiness called to her, clearer than any voice. She felt her way round a corner and reached out with her mind.

Can you hear me?

The other girl was frightened by the thoughts suddenly appearing in her head. *Who are you? What do you want?*

Misch tried to think a smile of reassurance. *I don't want to hurt you,* she thought. *I just want to know why you are so unhappy.*

I–I can't–

The R'qeen child received a mental flash of a clenched fist. *Somebody hurts you? Hits you?*

How do you know that? Can you see that in my head?

Misch had stopped at a doorway. She was very close to the girl now. *I can sense what others think and feel. Don't be afraid. My name is Misch.*

The door opened a fraction and a small, frightened voice spoke from inside. "I'm Kasey," the girl said.

Misch opened her eyes. Through the gap in the doorway she could see a little of Kasey's face. It was mottled with black, purple and yellow, but Misch knew those were not the usual markings of a human child. "Hello Kasey." The R'qeen broodling was startled to realise she was speaking the human's language, despite never having learned it. This must be another aspect of metema. She would have to ask her broodmother about it later.

"Do you want to play?" Kasey asked, biting her bottom lip hopefully.

Misch smiled. "Yes please!"

Miller was delivering Sharona Moore and her disciples to the desk sergeant at Sector House 87 for processing when a thought occurred to her. What if the incendiary device that gutted Robert Hatch had come from within the Justice Department? She and Dredd had assumed it must have been taken from a Citi-Def squad's armoury, but these could not be easily accessed without judicial authority. The device might have been stolen from the sector house, or more likely from the panniers on a Judge's Lawmaster. It was a long shot, but still worth investigating. Miller took a turbolift down to the Armoury in the lowest sub-basement of the sector house. The storehouse of ammunition and weaponry appeared deserted until the night droid appeared from behind a crate of Lawgivers.

"Armourer not around?" Miller asked.

"At one in the morning? You jest," the robot replied impatiently. The mechanoid announced it was busy with the overnight stocktake. "Can I help you with anything?"

"There was a suspicious fire at Robert Hatch a few hours back. Tek-Division detected Lucir-74 among the chemical compounds left as a residue. I was wondering if any incendiary devices have been stolen or reported missing in the last, say, seventy-two hours?"

"Nope," the droid said without hesitation.

"How can you be so sure? You didn't check the computer."

"No need." The robot tapped the side of its head unit. "I have a direct link to the system in here. Plus I undertake a full and thorough stocktake of the armoury's entire inventory every night at this hour – assuming nobody disturbs me. Nothing comes in or out of here without my knowing about it."

Why did department droids always have to be officious, Miller wondered? Just once she'd like to encounter a robot that didn't consider itself a cut above its masters. "Well, it was just a hunch," she said, beginning to leave.

"The only recent change in our stocks of incendiary

devices was last night when a colleague of yours collected one for a demonstration. It's due for return at dawn. Other than that, nothing to report."

"Right." Miller smiled and continued towards the door. She stopped on her way out, calling back to the droid. "Tell you what, give me the name of the Judge and I'll remind them about returning the device."

"It was Stammers. Judge Eustace Stammers."

Stammers was standing inside the turbolift, glaring at the two remaining aliens on the seventy-second floor of Oswald Mosley. "Are you coming or not?"

Lleccas shook her head. "It's our broodling. She's missing!"

Stammers sighed, not bothering to mask his exasperation. You'd think these vultures would have enough sense to keep a firm grip on the creepy little creatures they spawned. "Then find her, for Grud's sake! I ain't holding these doors open all night," he growled in Allspeak.

"Why don't you help us?" the male R'qeen asked, nursing one of its arms. "What if something has happened to Misch?"

"Just one less of you freaks for me to worry about," Stammers said with a cruel smile. "I'll give you two minutes to find her. After that you make your own way to the top of this dump." The R'qeen looked ready to attack Stammers but was dragged away by its mate. It was only after the aliens had gone Stammers realised the male was the same one he had fought outside Robert Hatch. Damn vultures all looked the same.

Sector Chief Caine was lecturing Conchita in front of the citizen's sons. "What sort of example are you setting for these juves? Children learn how to hate and who to hate from their parents."

"They don't have parents, they just have me. Their father was killed by a vulture years ago. It was Judges like you who let his murderer get away."

"Don't call them vultures!" Caine growled. "The R'qeen may be carrion eaters but they are also residents of this sector. They have as much right to live in this block as you do, citizen."

Conchita shook her head. "Those con-apts on the top floor, they were being refurbished for families like mine. Decent families, human families. Not the bug-eyed monsters you've put up there!"

"This is a temporary measure until–"

"Cut the stomm, lady!" Dermot said. "We know what's going on here!"

"Yeah," his brother added. "You want us out so you can fill the building with these freaks! Your kind makes me sick. Drokking vulture lover!"

Caine glared at both juves before regarding their mother. "Congratulations. I see you've done a good job teaching these two to hate."

Conchita pulled back a fist, ready to strike, but stopped herself. Instead she smiled at the Sector Chief. "Nice try." The smile drained from her face as two R'qeen approached. "What are those things still doing on this floor?"

"Excuse me," Nyon said, his English heavy with accent. "We are looking for our – how do you say – our child?"

"Your broodling?" Caine asked.

"Yes, our broodling, Misch. She has wandered off…"

The Sector Chief activated her helmet radio. "Caine to all units in Oswald Mosley. There is a…" She stopped, having noticed movement over Conchita's shoulder. "Cancel that. All units return to what you were doing. Caine out." She stepped past Conchita and pushed open the door of con-apt 729. Inside an R'qeen child was playing with a human girl. "Is that your broodling?"

Lleccas rushed forward and grabbed her daughter. "Misch, what were you doing?" she whispered in R'qeen. "We didn't know where you were. Your broodfather and I have been searching for you."

"This is Kasey. She was sad, she didn't have anyone to play with," Misch replied in her native tongue.

"That's all very well but you should have told us where you were going. We were so worried about you!"

"I'm sorry." Misch waved goodbye to Kasey, who shyly waved back.

Conchita watched with horror and then anger as the two R'qeen females walked out of her con-apt and down the corridor to the turbolifts with Nyon. "I'll deal with you soon," she hissed at her daughter before closing the con-apt door. "Was there anything else?" Conchita asked Caine.

"Yes. I notice your daughter has bruises on her face and arms."

"She's a very clumsy child, always hurting herself."

"I wonder if she would say the same thing – especially if tested against a lie detector?" Caine reached into a pouch on her utility belt and pulled out the palm-sized birdie unit.

"You come near my daughter with that thing and I'll show you the meaning of hate," Conchita warned.

"Is that a threat, citizen?"

"That's a promise!"

Caine held up the lie detector to show Conchita. The display was green. "It seems you're telling the truth – for once." By now the rest of the Judges had finished returning the other residents to their con-apts and were gathering in the corridor. "All units return to patrol. Nothing more to do here." Soon it was just Caine left facing the Maguires.

The Sector Chief stepped closer to Conchita. "I'll be keeping an eye on you. If there's any more trouble in

Oswald Mosley tonight, I'll hold you personally responsible. That's a promise, by the way, not a threat."

"You brought the aliens here. When they step out of line – and their kind always do – you'll be the one responsible," Conchita replied before leading her sons into their con-apt.

Caine stood outside the door listening, but heard no sounds from inside. Satisfied, she went to the turbolifts. It was now time to deal with Dredd.

"She's gone," Dermot said, his right ear pressed against the con-apt's front door. Conchita nodded, one hand clamped over her daughter's mouth.

"Good. Take your brother down to the juve hall. Once the Judges have left the building, I want you to contact our friends. We'll need help if we're going to get rid of the scum on the top floor."

Once Dermot and Ramone had gone, Conchita released her daughter. Kasey tried to hide herself in a corner, but there was no escaping the disgust in her mother's eyes. "I can't believe what I just saw," Conchita began. "A child of mine communing with one of those... those creatures. What possessed you?"

"She seemed nice," Kasey whimpered.

"Do you know what their kind do? They kill other animals and let the flesh rot until it is putrid. Only then do they eat it. The vultures are carrion eaters, the lowest of the low. They carry diseases and bacteria everywhere. And you let one in here. We should burn everything that monster touched!"

"Misch isn't a monster!" Kasey protested. "She's my friend!"

Conchita slowly undid the belt from her waist. Clasping the buckle firmly, she looped the belt several times around her fist but left half the strap hanging free. "Scum like that will never be our friends, Kasey. I've told you that before but it seems you weren't listening. So now I'm going to beat that lesson into you."

Dredd had been waiting in the lobby of Oswald Mosley for nearly ten minutes before Caine stepped from the turbolift, carrying her helmet under her arm. "Good, you're here," she said. "I understand you wanted to see me–"

"What happened up there?" Dredd demanded.

Caine sighed. "Going to be like that, is it? Very well. There was a confrontation between the residents and the new arrivals. The conflict has been defused and all involved given a verbal warning. I doubt we will see any more trouble from Oswald Mosley tonight."

"Then you're living in a dream!" Dredd replied. "This place is an explosion waiting to happen. Putting the aliens here, even temporarily, was a colossal misjudgement. I guarantee this place will be in flames before dawn."

"Well, thank you for that outburst – I'll take it under advisement. Was there anything else?" the Sector Chief asked.

"That street reporter for Channel 27, Riff Maltin. His credentials should be withdrawn. He seems more interested in creating news by provoking anti-alien hatred than simply reporting what happens."

Caine shook her head. "I've seen no evidence to confirm such an allegation, Request denied. What else?"

"Have you suspended Stammers and Riley yet?"

"Why should I?"

Dredd jerked a thumb at the scene outside the lobby. "They caused that chaos. Those two are out of control, especially Stammers."

"Is that right?" Caine asked.

"Yes!"

She smiled. "For somebody who's just arrived at this sector, you seem very quick to pass judgement on your

fellow law enforcers. I wonder what they would have to
say about you?"

"What do you mean?"

"I wonder how they would feel about you calling the
Chief Judge's office to complain about this sector's
performance."

"I have requested an urgent meeting with the Chief
Judge, but that is all. How do you know about that?"

"I told you before, Dredd, you're not the only one with
friends in high places. Don't expect the Chief Judge to
respond to your request anytime soon. By the way, it may
be some hours before she receives it." The smile faded
from Caine's features as she stepped closer to Dredd.
"If you've got a problem with somebody under my
command, you bring it to me first."

"What if you're the problem?"

"The procedure remains the same," Caine replied.
"While you're under my command, you have to respect
my authority and the chain of command."

Dredd shook his head. "This sector is a pressure cooker
waiting to blow and you keep turning up the heat, Caine.
Putting these aliens here is just the latest in a long line of
bad calls you've made. No wonder Justice Central is
getting ready to take you off active duty. You're a liabil-
ity. The sooner they get you away from the streets, the
better," he snarled.

"Keep this up and I'll be more than happy to have a
formal warning put on your permanent record," Caine
hissed back.

"Be my guest," Dredd replied. "What I want to know is
how the likes of you got to be Sector Chief in the first
place. Your record suggests you used to be a good Judge
until your ego got the–"

"My ego?" Caine burst out laughing. "That's rich
coming from the king of the grandstanders, the legendary
Judge Dredd, who has to be the star of every incident he

attends. Frankly, I'm amazed you deign to help us mere mortals!"

Dredd began striding to his Lawmaster, Caine following him. "Don't you dare walk away from me! I haven't dismissed you yet!"

Dredd stopped, turning back to face Caine. "Then dismiss me. I've got better things to do than be lectured by the likes of you."

"That's it! Now you've gone too far!" Caine pulled on her helmet and activated its radio. "Sector Chief Caine to Control, I wish to lodge a complaint against Judge Dredd. The charge is gross insubordination."

"Control to Caine, not sure we heard you right."

"I want a formal warning placed on Dredd's permanent record and a hearing held within twenty-four hours. Is that clear enough for you?"

"Roj that. Control out."

Caine smiled at Dredd. "Happy now?"

"Ecstatic."

Caine mounted her Lawmaster motorcycle. "Try to go over my head again and I'll have your badge for breakfast." She offered one final comment before accelerating away. "Now you're dismissed!"

Dredd looked around but Maltin was nowhere to be seen.

Miller completed her paperwork for the suicidal cult members while pondering what the armoury droid had told her. Stammers was an ultra-violent xenophobe but even he would stop short of committing arson, wouldn't he? She couldn't believe Riley would be a part to such an atrocity, even with his feelings about aliens. Yet there was no record of either Judge being involved with any incendiary device demonstration. Something didn't add up.

Where was Dredd, she wondered. He should have been back at the sector house by now. Miller considered calling him with the new information she had gleaned, but thought better of it. Any such call would be broadcast via Control and the content was bound to reach one of her two suspects. Better to leave him a message and investigate further on her own. Miller recorded a vidmessage for Dredd and took it to the garage where Tek-Judge Brady was refuelling her Lawmaster.

"Could you give this to Dredd when he comes in next?"

The mechanic was bemused by the request. "Why not just–"

Miller laid a hand on Brady's shoulder. "Let's just say it's for his ears only and leave it at that."

"Okay, if you say so. Your bike will be ready in a minute."

Miller called Control. "Can you give me a current position for Judges Stammers and Riley?"

"That's a roj. Both are leaving Oswald Mosley now, en route for the Sector 87 dust zone. You want to be connected to them?"

"No thanks, it's nothing urgent. Miller out." The dust zone was one of several areas in the city devoted to industrial factories and warehouses. Many had been abandoned following the shift in production to cheaper labour markets like Indo-City. As a result dust zones were favourite haunts for fugitives and criminals. Perhaps Stammers and Riley planned to pick up some easy collars there, but Miller wasn't so sure. She collected her Lawmaster from Brady and rode out into the sultry night air.

"Miller to Control, am going off-radio to follow a lead."

"Roj that. Call back in when you're ready to receive messages again."

Lleccas was stunned when she saw her family's new accommodation. It was only supposed to be for one night, but already she was hoping they never had to leave. After the crumbling edifice that had been their old block, the top floor of Oswald Mosley was grander than any Lleccas had seen on this world. The emergency stairs curled up the centre of the circular building, surrounded by the turbolifts. Around these was a wide corridor, subtly lit with glass panels in the ceiling revealing the night sky overhead.

Doorways opened from the circular hallway on to six luxurious con-apts, each set against the outer wall of the building. In the middle of each con-apt was a communal living area with plush, comfortable furniture and warm lighting. Instead of an external wall the room had glasseen picture windows from floor to ceiling, affording a dramatic view of the full moon hanging in the air over Sector 87. Further rooms ran off the main space, offering sleeping quarters for at least half a dozen residents along with cooking and cleaning facilities. A few rooms remained unfinished but the con-apt was still a palace compared to the damp, fetid, decaying hovel that had been Robert Hatch.

Lleccas was blinking back tears as she went from room to room. "All of this!!! for us?" she stammered in amazement to Nyon.

Her pairling nodded sadly. "Yes, but this is just for tonight. No doubt we will be returned to our appointed place in the morning."

Lleccas knew he was right but she was still determined to enjoy this rare treat, no matter how brief it might be. "Misch, which room do you want?"

The R'qeen child emerged from one of the bedrooms, dragging a blanket and cushions out into the main space. "I want to sleep here, so I can watch the sun rise," she said. "Is that allowed?"

Nyon could not help smiling at his broodling's enthusiasm. "Yes, that's allowed. Now, let's get some rest. It's been a long night and we don't know when the Judges will come for us in the morning."

Misch was already settled into a well-padded chair facing the windows. "Goodnight," she said, wrapping blankets around herself.

Lleccas and Nyon kissed their broodling before retiring to the main bedroom and quietly closed the door behind them. Lleccas sighed as Nyon drew her into his embrace, careful not to brush against his injured limb. For the first time in too long, she felt safe again.

When Kasey regained consciousness all she felt was pain. The left side of her body throbbed. She had turned into the corner to keep the worst of the beating off her face and body, and had offered her left side to the belt her mother wielded. She was now paying the price for it: her left arm was all but useless, her left leg a mass of lumps, bruises already crowding both limbs. Angry red weals crisscrossed her skin where the fabric of her clothes did not reach.

Kasey did not know how long she had been in the darkness. A light still seeped from beneath the door of the bedroom she shared with her mother, but Kasey was not going back in there tonight. She had to get away. The little girl was not the brightest of children but none of the other children she knew in Oswald Mosley seemed to have marks like her. She never heard anyone else crying themselves to sleep at night. But where could she go?

Kasey, are you all right?

The voice in her head made the girl jump. She concentrated, trying to reply by only saying the words in her thoughts. *Misch, is that you?*

Yes. Are you hurting?

Kasey nodded before realising her friend could not see her. *Yes,* she thought. *My mom hit me with her belt. She said I had to be punished.*

Show me, Misch asked.

So Kasey recalled a little of the beating before the memory was too much to bear. *See?*

Why does she do that? My broodmother would never hurt me.

I think she hates me. She hates you too.

I know.

Kasey waited but no more words came into her head. *Misch? Are you still there?*

Yes, the R'qeen girl replied. *I was just thinking. Would you like to come up and stay with me? We have plenty of rooms...*

Could I?

Yes! It'll be an adventure!

Kasey shook her head. *No, you'll get in trouble. Your mom might get angry and punish you too.*

Not if we hide you.

All right, the human girl decided. *But how do I find you?*

Just concentrate on my voice. It will bring you to me.

Kasey stood and began walking slowly towards Misch's words.

Miller rode her Lawmaster into the dust zone, headlights turned off to avoid attracting too much attention. The full moon overhead might bring out the kooks but it also provided enough light to see where she was going. Even so, Miller kept to a low speed, not wanting to ride into a chem pool and find herself sinking into the acid-laced liquids. She activated the heat sensors on her Lawmaster's computer, scanning the surrounding area for movement. The hotter an object was, the brighter it appeared on screen.

Two dull red shapes were moving ahead of her from the east. A bright white shape was converging on them from the west. The computer identified it as a Lawmaster, the heat from its engine and exhaust emissions all too characteristic. Miller shut down her own motorcycle and continued ahead on foot, Lawgiver drawn. Perhaps Stammers and Riley had split up to hunt perps in the dust zone. That would explain why only one Lawmaster was evident; the other could be several klicks away, out of the computer's sensor range.

Another thought occurred to Miller, one that gave her hope for Riley's future. Perhaps only Stammers was involved with the arson attack? He could not have placed the incendiary device that torched Robert Hatch, but Stammers might have supplied it to someone else. A gruff voice in the distance brought Miller to a halt. She dropped to a crouch and moved sideways to take cover behind an abandoned roadster.

Ahead was a clearing illuminated by the moon; eerie blue light bathed the empty space. Two figures sauntered into view, their faces obscured by hooded clothing. Miller pulled tiny binoculars from her utility belt to get a better look at the pair. Despite keeping their faces hidden, both were obviously juves, neither of them eighteen yet. They looked about, seemingly expecting someone else to be present. "Hey, we're here! You can come out now!" one of the juves shouted. A Judge walked into the clearing from the opposite side.

"Keep your voices down," Stammers said, his gruff voice recognisable now Miller could hear him properly. "We don't need an audience."

The taller juve pulled back his hood and laughed. "It's gone midnight, lawman! There's nobody here but us." Miller didn't recognise his face.

"Even so," Stammers replied. "No need to take unnecessary chances. You did well at Robert Hatch."

"Yeah, and how did you repay us? By helping those bug-eyed freaks move into the top floor of our building!"

Miller smiled. That narrowed down the number of places where these juves lived considerably. Keep talking bigmouth, she thought.

"Sector Chief's orders. Nothing I could do about that," Stammers said.

"Well, we need your help to get them back out. Or else," the second juve said, pulling back his hood to reveal similar features to his partner in crime. Miller decided the pair must be brothers.

"Or else what?" Stammers sneered. He stepped towards the juves, Lawgiver held casually in one hand. "You boys shouldn't try making threats. You haven't had the practise to carry them off."

"Or else we tell your Sector Chief what you've been up to behind her back," the second juve said, trying not to be intimidated by the Judge. "Caine will rip you if she ever finds out."

"Then we'll have to make sure that never happens," Stammers said. "What can I do to help you?"

The two juves smiled at each other. "That's better, lawman," the taller one said. "Give us the codes to unlock the Citi-Def armoury in the basement of our block. We need those weapons to take on the vultures."

"Anything else?"

"Keep the rest of the Judges away from Oswald Mosley until dawn. It'll all be over by then," the other juve said cockily.

Stammers began laughing at them. "You two ought to be on tri-D..."

"Why you laughing at us, lawman?" the elder juve demanded.

"Did you honestly think I'd kow-tow to punks like you?" Stammers's Lawgiver spat twice, death punching holes through the protesting juve's head. The Judge turned to the other juve, ready to shoot again. "Now it's your time, stomm for brains." Another shot and both juves were dead on the ground, their bodies still twitching.

. . .

Kasey closed the front door of the con-apt quietly behind her. She did not often venture outside during the day without Ramone, Dermot or her mother to accompany her. Sneaking out in the middle of the night would provoke severe punishment if she was caught.

Kasey, are you all right? Misch's voice was inside the human girl's head, guiding her forwards.

Yes, Kasey thought. *Now where do I go?*

Turn right and walk to the turbolifts.

Kasey followed Misch's instructions, her progress hampered by the severe contusions down her left side. Her leg was already stiffening up, making it difficult to walk. Kasey staggered sideways as she approached the turbolifts, her shoulder brushing against a doorbell pad outside a neighbour's con-apt. She hurried on as best she could but the door to 721 behind her opened before the turbolift arrived.

"What the drokk do you want at this hour? Haven't I had enough disturbances for one night?" Kurt Sivell glared up and down the corridor, one hand trying to rub the sleep from his eyes, a gown wrapped round his ample girth. An immigrant from Euro-Cit, Sivell had little time for the Citi-Def squad, calling them power-crazed tin-pot tyrants. He was surprised to see Kasey by the turbolifts.

"Was that you, juve?"

Kasey nodded. "Sorry, it was an accident."

"Well, don't do it again," he replied, wandering towards her. "Where are you going at this time of night?"

Misch, what do I say? Kasey asked in her mind.

Tell him you're going to see a friend, the R'qeen broodling suggested.

Sivell was unconvinced by this explanation. "Does you mother know about this? Perhaps I should call her–"

"It was her idea! She says the further I am away from those things on the top floor, the better," Kasey replied at Misch's prompting.

"Quite right too." Despite being an immigrant himself, Sivell wanted no truck with offworlders. Mankind had enough problems learning to get along with itself. There was no need to throw aliens into the mix as well, in his opinion. "Well, your turbolift is ready. Off you go."

Kasey smiled at her neighbour before stepping into the turbolift. Without thinking, she pressed the button for the top floor and the doors began to close. "Goodbye," she said and waved with her good hand.

Sivell returned the wave and waddled back towards his con-apt. Only when the doors had closed did he look back to see where the turbolift stopped next. To his surprise, it was going up instead of down. He must mention that to Conchita in the morning. Right now he needed sleep and no disturbances. A good dose of Double-Doze ought to do the trick.

Miller could not believe what she had witnessed. Shocked from the first shots, she was too late to stop the second juve being executed. She held back, watching to see what Stammers would do next. He holstered his Lawgiver and began dragging one of the corpses towards a chem pit. The body slid down into the acidic liquid, bubbles and acrid smoke rising from the surface as the juve dissolved. Stammers went back for the second body. Miller waited until he had his hands full before emerging from cover, Lawgiver ready to fire.

"Don't move or I shoot!" she commanded.

Stammers looked up and grimaced. "Ahh, stomm!"

Miller moved into the clearing but kept a safe distance from him. "Is that all you've got to say? I've just watched you gun down two juves in cold blood."

"They were responsible for the arson attack on Robert Hatch. They planted the incendiary device that killed thousands of aliens."

"And we both know how much you care about off-worlders, right?" Miller sneered. "You gave them the incendiary device, you probably told them the best place to plant it. Those juves were no innocents, but you're just as guilty as them."

Stammers let go of the corpse and straightened up. "So what are you going to do about it, Miller? Send a good Judge to Titan just because a few vultures got overcooked?"

"You don't honestly think I can overlook this, do you?"

He shrugged. "I could make it worth your while."

"Adding bribery and corruption to your crimes won't help, Stammers."

"Maybe not, but I'd be more worried about my own future if I were you."

Miller frowned. "What do you mean by that?"

Something blunt and heavy smashed against the back of Miller's helmet, sending her sprawling. She narrowly avoided falling into the chem pit but her Lawgiver was not so fortunate: it disappeared into the bubbling liquid. Miller rolled over to see Riley looming above her, a Widowmaker rifle clutched in his hands. "Riley? Not you too…"

"Sorry, Lynn," he said, reaching down to snap off the microphone from her helmet radio. "You shouldn't have come here."

Miller could feel the darkness overwhelming her. Concussion, possibly a fractured skull, she decided. Got to stay conscious.

She tried to focus on the moon overhead but it had disappeared behind clouds. In the distance she could hear a pathetic gurgling sound and realised it was her own voice, trying to form words. Something warm and metallic filled her mouth, salty to taste – her blood, no doubt. Miller's legs had gone numb and she felt cold, far too cold.

Going into shock now.

Stupid way to die, so stupid–

02:00

Dredd had searched in vain for Maltin, determined to learn more about what had happened earlier outside Oswald Mosley. But the reporter had gone to ground, ignoring Dredd's command to stay put. The Judge began travelling back to Sector House 87 on his Lawmaster, the route still requiring a lengthy diversion while the Anton Diffring Overzoom was cleared of debris. En route Dredd called Control for Miller's whereabouts.

"She went off-radio twenty minutes ago. Said she was following a lead."

"Did she specify further?"

"Negative."

Dredd pulled into the sector house garage to find Tek-Judge Brady waiting for him. "I was wondering when you'd come back here," the mechanic said, holding out a small silver disc. "I've got a vid-message for you from Miller. She told me to deliver it personally. You can use the tri-D screen in my office."

After closing the door to the office, Dredd slipped the disc into the tri-D player. A mechanical voice announced the message had previously been played zero times, then a holographic image of Miller appeared in the air. She spoke quickly, her voice just a whisper but her features full of concern.

"Hey, partner. Sorry I'm not there but something's come up I couldn't broadcast over the radio. Seems Stammers 'borrowed' an incendiary device from the

Armoury matching the sort used to torch Robert Hatch. Stammers and Riley have gone to the local dust zone so I'm going off-radio to find them, see if this hunch plays out. To be honest, it could be something or nothing. I don't know if Stammers is behind the fire and, even if he is, I've got nothing linking Riley to it. If I haven't reported in by three, you'll know where to find me. Miller out."

The holograph turned to a blizzard of static before the tri-D player switched off, ejecting the disc. Brady knocked on the office door before entering.

"Anything interesting?" he asked.

"Time will tell," Dredd replied. "Thanks for the use of your office."

Conchita Maguire woke with a start. She had been dozing on her bed, with the lights still on. The last thing she remembered was hearing the front door opening and closing, and thinking it was Ramone and Dermot returning home. But she had heard nothing more since then, certainly not the usual late night jumble of noise she associated with her sons stumbling in. Conchita rolled over and realised Kasey was not in bed. Then she remembered the thrashing she had given her. Grud, that temper... She had better check Kasey was all right.

Conchita pulled on the khaki trousers and vest from her Citi-Def uniform before venturing out into the main room. She turned on the light but could see no sign of Kasey or the boys. Fighting back a rising wave of panic, Conchita hurriedly began checking the other rooms. But it was a tiny con-apt and there were only so many places the little girl could be. Conchita searched again and again without result. A chilling thought occurred. The noise of the front door earlier; maybe that had been Kasey going out, not the boys coming back in.

"Oh my Grud," Conchita whispered, the hairs on the back of her neck standing up. She pulled open the front door and peered out into the corridor, hoping and praying to see her daughter. But the hallway was empty. Only the erratic flicker of overhead lights provided any movement. Conchita went to the nearest con-apt and began pounding on the door, her spare hand pressing on the doorbell pad repeatedly. "Come on, open up! Please!"

Misch opened the front door of her family's new home and let Kasey inside. The R'qeen child was shocked by the new injuries Kasey had suffered since they first met. Why would anyone hurt their broodling like this? It didn't make any sense to Misch but there was much about the natives of this world she didn't understand. Metema might give you access to the thoughts and feelings of others, but it couldn't explain everything about them.

"Are you okay?" Misch whispered, keeping her voice quiet so she wouldn't wake her broodfather and brood-mother.

Kasey smiled. "I am now." She looked around the interior of the main living space, amazed at how large it was. The con-apt's lights were off, but the room was still illuminated by the night-time cityscape beyond the floor-to-ceiling window. "You live here? Just the three of you?"

"Only for tonight. Tomorrow the Judges will take us away again."

"Mom says we're supposed to be shifting to the top floor when it's ready."

Misch took Kasey's hand and reached her thoughts into the human girl's mind. *Let's talk in our heads – that way nobody else can hear us.*

Kasey nodded happily. *It'll be our secret!*

Misch tugged on her hand. *Come on, I'll show you the rest of the con-apt. If you're going to live here, you'll want to choose the best room.*

. . .

Evan Yablonsky was not having a good night. Since getting the anonymous tip-off about the incendiary device, Channel 27's news editor had been harassing his correspondents out on the skedways and pedways for proof so they could broadcast the story. All of them had come up empty, with the exception of Riff Maltin. The first-timer had sent back some great footage of a riot from outside Oswald Mosley with two Judges brutalising a crowd of residents (at least, that was how the footage looked to most viewers), and some nice comedy moments of Maltin being treated in the aftermath. But Riff had disappeared soon afterwards, with Yablonsky getting no reply from the rogue reporter and no signal from the hovercam.

When Riff finally did call in, the news editor was overjoyed and enraged at the same time. "Where the hell have you been?" Yablonsky demanded. "You're supposed to be impressing me with your professionalism. Not disappearing for hours at a time when you feel like it!"

Maltin protested his innocence. "I've already been threatened by one Judge, beaten by another and Dredd wants to interrogate me. So you'll have to excuse me if I decide to lay low for a while!"

"All right, all right," his boss conceded. "What's new? What have you got?"

"Nothing. I've been laying low."

Yablonsky rolled his eyes. "For the love of Grud, get back to Oswald Mosley. I think your hunch was right. That place is a tragedy waiting to happen and I want you on the inside, broadcasting every moment. You got that?"

"Got it."

"Do this right and you'll be famous overnight," the news editor said.

"Now you're speaking my language," Riff replied.

. . .

Conchita had roused all the residents on the seventy-second floor of Oswald Mosley, along with those on the floors immediately above and below. Each level had a representative on the block's Citi-Def squad. Conchita had her colleagues from seventy-one and seventy-three coordinate the search for 'Kasey on those floors, while she forced her way into the con-apts on her own level. Despite disturbing most of her neighbours, she had been unable to locate her missing daughter. Her sons were also absent but Conchita believed they would return soon.

Eventually she conceded defeat and decided to contact the Justice Department. It hurt her pride to ask for assistance from the same people that had helped those freaks move into the building – into her new home, for that matter – but they were best equipped to search for Kasey. Conchita made the call from the vid-phone in her con-apt. She had to ask a neighbour what number to dial, having never contacted the Judges herself. But when she got through to the Justice Department Hotline, it took her several minutes just to navigate the tortuous automated system. Finally, she was speaking to a human operator. A bored female Judge appeared on screen, rubbing the sleep from her eyes.

"Justice Department Hotline. What crime do you wish to report?"

"My daughter is missing!"

"Uh-huh. What's your name?"

"Maguire, Conchita Maguire."

The Judge began entering these details into a computer terminal. "And where do you live?"

"Con-apt 729, Oswald Mosley Block."

"How many people live at that location?"

"What the drokk does that matter?" Conchita exclaimed. "My daughter is missing! I need your help to find her."

"Citizen, we have a procedure we have to follow. If you deviate from that procedure, you will only exacerbate matters."

"Fine, whatever! Four people live here: myself, my daughter Kasey, and my two sons, Dermot and Ramone."

"How old are your sons?"

"What does that matter?" Conchita demanded.

"I am assessing the background circumstances, to ascertain whether a crime has actually been committed."

"My sons are both seventeen. Happy now?"

The Judge looked at Conchita with exasperation. "Citizen, I must ask you to desist with this aggressive, sarcastic tone, otherwise I shall have to report you for making abusive vidphone calls."

"For the love of Grud, my daughter is missing! I don't care if you make me dance naked in front of the Halls of Justice, I just want my daughter back!"

"I must ask you to calm down or I will be forced to terminate this call."

Conchita fought back the urge to smash her fist through the vidphone screen. "I'm sorry, I'm sorry – I'm just worried about Kasey, that's all."

"That's perfectly understandable. How old is your daughter?"

Conchita's mind went blank. "Eight? Or nine? I'm sorry, I'm so stressed I can't remember right now. I think she had a birthday recently…"

"Eight or nine, that's fine. I'll cross-check against our records. And how many days has she been missing?"

"Days? You think I'd wait days before reporting my own daughter missing? What kind of mother do you think I am?"

"Citizen, I must warn you again. Persist with that tone and I am required to recommend your arrest. Now, how many days has–"

"It's hours, she's been missing one or two hours."

The Judge sighed. "What about your sons, do you know where they are right now?"

"Not exactly," Conchita admitted. "They went out a few hours back. I'm expecting them home any time."

"But you haven't reported them missing?"

"Of course not! They're juves, they can look after themselves. Kasey is just a little girl."

"A girl who has been missing less than two hours." The Judge had stopped taking notes of what Conchita was saying. "I'm sorry but the Justice Department only investigates missing persons cases where the citizen has been absent for at least twenty-four hours."

"What?"

"Your daughter has been gone for less than two hours. For all you know, she may be with her brothers or her father."

"Her father is dead!"

"Nevertheless, the length of her absence is not sufficiently serious to warrant a response from the Justice Department at this time."

"Not sufficiently serious?" Conchita could not believe what she was hearing. "But she's gone and–"

The Judge was no longer listening to her. "In fact I would be within my rights to file a complaint against you for wasting our time with this call."

"No, you don't understand–"

"Bearing in mind the circumstances, I have decided not to do that."

"You've got to be drokking joking!"

"May I suggest contacting your daughter's friends to see if she has gone to visit them? Also, try getting in touch with any relatives nearby."

"We don't have any relatives in the city!" Conchita protested.

"Be that as it may, we cannot action your call until at least twenty-four hours have elapsed since you last saw your daughter. There are four hundred million citizens in the Big Meg. If we tried to investigate every person that had been missing for a few hours, we would never be doing anything else."

"But she could be dead by morning! Anything could have happened to her. It could be happening to her right now!"

"As I said, please wait–"

"No! I will not wait! If the high and mighty Justice Department is not willing to help one of its citizens, then I will have to help myself!"

"I must warn you against taking the Law into your own hands. The Department will not look kindly upon–"

"Drokk you and drokk your Department!" Conchita screamed, slamming her fist through the vid-phone screen. Sparks flew from the monitor and shards of glasseen embedded themselves in her raw knuckles but Conchita did not notice the blood dripping from her hand. She walked out of her con-apt to the corridor where the Citi-Def representatives from the levels directly above and below were waiting.

Kevin Amidou was from the seventy-third floor. A portly gun nut, he always dressed in camouflage with a black bandanna tied around his sweaty brow. "So what did they say?"

"Call back when she's been missing twenty-four hours," Conchita replied, her rage subsiding into a numb determination.

"But that's ridiculous! She could be anywhere by then."

Conchita nodded grimly. "We can't wait that long." She reached into the pocket of her trousers and pulled out a tiny red card encased in plastic. Conchita snapped the plastic in half, releasing the card from inside. "I'm mobilising the rest of the squad."

"Are you sure that's wise?" the other Citi-Def member asked. Mikell Fields was a cautious man in his fifties, pallid of skin and attitude. He wore old-fashioned metal glasses hooked over his prominent ears. "We're only supposed to be called out in the event of a city-wide emergency. After what happened outside the lobby–"

"I don't care about that!" Conchita hissed. "My daughter is missing and the Judges won't do a drokking thing to help. So we're going to find her ourselves."

She marched to a sign on the corridor wall marked CITI-DEF ALERT STATION. Beneath it was a slot in the wall just big enough to take the card in Conchita's hand. She rammed it inside and a red light began flashing overhead. "As leader of Oswald Mosley Citi-Def, I hereby summon the squad into action. We meet downstairs in ten minutes!"

The Med-Bay in Sector House 87 was at ground level, just below the check-in area where Judges brought perps for processing. Dredd was walking past the front desk on his way to the turbolift when a familiar voice called out. "Dredd? I didn't know you were working out of here!" He turned to see a black Judge entering the building, dragging an unconscious perp. The new arrival's name was clearly visible on his eagle badge: GIANT. The two Judges had known each other for more than a decade. Giant often worked undercover for the Wally Squad but tonight he was clad in a Street Judge's uniform.

"Pulling a graveyard shift," Dredd explained. "Who's your friend?"

Giant had reached the front desk and rested his perp against it. The unconscious prisoner was a muscular woman clad in strips of PVC with enough body piercings to set off every metal detector in the sector. Tattoos across the knuckles of her hands spelled the words BADD BLUD. "Her name's Big Bad Bertha, small-time muscle angling for a place in Jesus Bludd's crew."

"Not very talkative."

Giant smiled. "She popped a fistful of amp when I tried to arrest her. Took three of us just to beat her unconscious. The other two are still being treated at the scene by Med-Division."

"You getting anywhere infiltrating Bludd's crew?" Dredd asked.

"Nope. I've yet to find anyone who's even met Bludd, let alone someone who can tell us anything about him." The Big Meg's criminal underworld had been going though one of its bloodier phases with different gangs trying to assert their authority. The fall of crime boss Nero Narcos several years earlier had left a power vacuum and Jesus Bludd was among those who had emerged with plans to take Narcos's place. Unlike most of his competitors, Bludd was smart enough to keep a low profile, letting his crimes do the talking while others preferred to cultivate a cult of personality. As a result, getting an undercover operative close to Bludd was proving unusually difficult for the Judges.

"Stick with it," Dredd said. "Everyone makes mistakes. When Bludd makes his, you want to be ready."

"Natch. Heard you've been having problems with the Sector Chief here?"

Dredd grunted. "Word spreads fast."

"No secrets in this job," Giant replied with a smile. "Where you headed?"

"The sleep machines in Med-Bay. Been a long night and I don't think it's over yet. See you on the streets." Dredd strode towards the turbolifts, while Giant presented his captive to the Desk Judge.

"Let's make this snappy," Giant suggested. "You don't want my friend here waking up before we get her inside a cube."

Kasey and Misch had chosen a room with a large picture window looking out over the city. The interior was still unfinished, with discarded materials from the rest of the con-apt piled against a wall. The two girls used these to build a lean-to by the window, their playhouse hidden from the door by the rest of the building supplies. Misch pulled a small globe from her pocket. She carefully placed her right hand's three fingers in a triangular shape on the side of the globe. It began to glow, gentle lights coming alive inside.

"That's beautiful," Kasey gasped.

"It's the only toy I saved from our old con-apt," the R'qeen girl explained. "Now watch this!" She whispered a few words in her native tongue and the globe began to float in the air, shooting beams of coloured light around them.

Kasey watched, entranced. "I wish I had a toy like that," she said wistfully.

"You can keep it, if you want."

"I'd like to," Kasey admitted, "but it's your only one. Anyway, my mom would never let me have anything like that." The human girl looked away, ashamed. "She doesn't like aliens."

"I know. She seems so angry."

Kasey shivered, remembering the earlier beating. "Let's talk about something else, okay?"

Misch nodded hurriedly. "Why don't we–"

A hammering at the front door silenced her. "Open up!" an angry voice shouted from outside.

"Who's that?" Kasey wondered.

The banging resumed, with more shouting. The two girls could hear movement and a voice from another room in the con-apt. "That's my broodfather," Misch said, standing up. "You better stay in here. I'll see what's going on." She went to the doorway and peered out into the main room.

Nyon was pulling a robe on as he walked to the front door, the broken arm hampering his movements. After tying the robe together, Nyon opened the door. Three humans clad in Citi-Def uniforms pushed past him, storming into the con-apt. "What are you doing?" Nyon protested in Allspeak. "You have no right to come in here!"

One of the squad members, a wiry man clutching a laser-blade, pushed Nyon back against the door. "Shut your hole, ya alien freak! We got every right! My name's Billy-Bob Jolie and I'm the Citi-Def representative for the ninety-ninth floor of this block. Now you aliens may be too dumb to know any better, but Citi-Def members like us can go pretty much wherever we please. Ain't that right, boys?" The other two nodded their agreement. Satisfied, the leader sneered at the R'qeen patriarch. "Now, where is she? And speak English this time – none of your offworld mumbo-jumbo, blue boy!"

"Where is who?" Nyon asked in halting English, struggling to understand what the intruders were saying.

"Where's the girl? Not one of your vultures either. She's a human girl! Her name's Kasey Maguire and she was seen coming up here!"

"There are no human girls here," Nyon protested. "There is just myself, my pairling Lleccas and our broodling, Misch. Now, leave before I call the Judges!"

Billy-Bob punched Nyon in the midriff, winding the R'qeen. As he slumped to his knees, Lleccas emerged from the bedroom, still pulling on her clothes. "Nyon? What is happening here?"

"Lleccas! Go back inside!" Nyon shouted.

But one of the other humans had already grabbed the R'qeen woman and pushed her back into the bedroom. "Let's see what you've got hidden in here, you blue-skinned slitch!"

"Lleccas! No!" Nyon shouted. He tried moving towards the bedroom but Billy-Bob thrust the laser-knife under his throat.

"One more move and I'll take great pleasure in gutting you, boy!" Billy-Bob jerked his head at the remaining human in the main room. "Aaron, you check out the other rooms in this place."

Misch hurried back to the lean-to where Kasey was shivering with fear. "Three men. They're looking for you!"

The red-haired girl nodded. "Don't let them find me. If my mom knows I've been visiting you, she'll–"

"Shhh, it'll be okay," Misch said, giving Kasey a hug. "I'll send them away."

"How?"

The R'qeen child remembered what her broodmother had said before, about being able to push weaker minds. "I think I know a way."

Dredd was growing visibly frustrated. He had come to the Med-Bay for ten minutes on a sleep machine, but had spent fifteen minutes answering questions from a pedantic droid. It was now examining his medical records, having got his permission to download them from Justice Central. "Good, good," the mechanoid said as it studied the files. "Glad to see you haven't been overusing the sleep machines. Some Judges abuse the system. Just because a short stint is equivalent to a good night's bed rest, doesn't mean you should substitute one for the other. The human mind is a tricky creature, it needs to dream just as much as it needs rest. Take the case of–"

"Are we done with the preliminaries?" Dredd demanded.

"Well, yes, I suppose so," the droid replied petulantly. "But there's no need to snap. These procedures exist for a reason. You're new to this sector house, so I am obliged to go through the–"

"I said, are we done?"

"Yes, we're done. Machine six is waiting for you," the robot said, gesturing down the corridor. "Just place all non-essential items into the holder so they don't interfere with the–"

"I know the drill," Dredd growled, stomping away.

The droid sighed. "No pleasing some people!"

Dredd sat on the edge of the sleep machine, a long silver bench with a matching cover hanging in the air above it. He removed his utility belt, boot knife and Lawgiver, dropping them into a bin beside the machine. Finally, Dredd took off his helmet and rested it atop the other items. He swung his legs up on to the bench and then lay down full length, resting his head against a small pad. "I'm ready," Dredd called to the droid. "Activate the–"

"Control to Dredd!" The metallic voice issued from a speaker above the sleep machine. "Please respond immediately. Control to Dredd, please respond immediately!"

Grumbling beneath his breath, Dredd sat up again and pulled on his helmet. "Dredd to Control, go ahead."

"Reports coming in that the Oswald Mosley Citi-Def has illegally mobilised itself and is harassing some of the residents in that block."

"Acknowledged. Haven't you got any units nearer the scene that can respond? I was about to have a sleep machine session."

"Sector Chief Caine requested you attend personally, says you have a particular interest in this block."

Dredd's shoulders sagged. "Terrif!" He collected his belongings from the bin beside the sleep machine and stood up, wrapping the belt around his waist again. "Am responding now. Should be on the scene within fifteen. Dredd out!"

He marched past the droid on his way back out of the Med-Bay. "Excuse me, Judge, will you be back later to complete your session?" the robot asked. Dredd continued on his way, an angry snarl his only reply.

"I'll take that as a maybe," the droid decided.

. . .

Aaron Pressland was not the brightest member of Oswald Mosley Citi-Def by any recognised method of measurement. A mighty bear of a man, his vocabulary was limited, his general intelligence was even less and his ability to think sadly underdeveloped. But Pressland did have two key qualities that made him a valuable member of the squad – he was utterly loyal to the block, especially his neighbours on the ninety-eighth floor, and he was not afraid to kill.

During the dark days of the Apocalypse War back in 2102 he had murdered three Sov-Block soldiers single-handedly while defending the honour of Oswald Mosley. The Chief Judge had pinned a medal on Pressland's chest and pronounced him one of the bravest civilians in the Big Meg. The fact that he was also one of the dumbest was neither here nor there. So Pressland was not afraid when he found an R'qeen girl blocking the entrance to an unfinished bedroom in the penthouse con-apt. "Step aside, freak!" he bellowed at her.

The alien child did not flinch. Instead she smiled, revealing row upon row of teeth hiding inside her mouth. Creepy, Pressland thought, it looks just like... *It looks empty inside this room.* The Citi-Def member shook his head. He thought he could hear a voice inside his mind, talking to him. But it wasn't his own voice, it was somebody else's.

That's right, the voice replied. *I'm your guardian angel.*

"What the drokk?" Pressland said, banging a fist against the side of his head. "What are you talking about?"

You remember during the war? So many times you could have been killed. I was there to save you.

"Who are you?"

I'm your guardian angel. You believe me, don't you? Misch pushed with all her might, trying to convince the slow-witted human.

Pressland shrugged. "I guess so."

Good. Now, let's have a look in here.

Misch stood aside and let the squad member step into the unfinished room. Pressland began to wander about the space, peering into corners and lifting building materials aside for his search. He was getting closer and closer to the lean-to. Misch touched Pressland's hand, startling him.

"Hey, what are you–"

Don't worry, there's nothing to be afraid of.

"I'm not afraid!"

Of course you aren't. You're big and brave. You fought in a war.

"That's right!"

Now, when you look inside that lean-to, all you will see is an alien girl.

"An alien girl?"

That's right. Are you ready?

"I guess so."

Then have a look.

Pressland bent over and peered through a gap at the inside of the lean-to. Kasey pushed herself away from him, terrified at being discovered. Pressland found himself smiling at the girl before standing up again.

Now, what did you see?

"Just an alien girl, like you said."

Exactly. And that's what you'll tell the other men, yes?

"Yes," Pressland replied, turning to leave the room. He stopped at the door. "Will I always have a guardian angel like you?"

If you want.

"Good." The war hero left the room, smiling to himself. Misch listened as he reported back to his leader. "Nobody in there but an alien girl."

"All right," Billy-Bob replied sourly. "Seems these freaks were telling the truth. We better move on. Plenty of other places to search."

As the men were leaving, Misch told Kasey to stay where she was. "I've got to see if my broodfather and broodmother are all right. I'll come back and play with you soon."

The human girl pointed at her friend's face. "You're bleeding."

Misch wiped a trickle of blood from beneath her nostrils. "I'd better not try pushing anybody else for a while."

Lynn Miller regained consciousness when a rat ran across her hands. Her head was pounding fit to burst, like a Heavy Metal Kid was trying to hammer its way out through her forehead. There was a dull pain at the back of her skull, but other than that she felt only the usual aches and muscle strains that came with being a Street Judge in the Big Meg. She was aware of two different movements nearby: the footfalls of a person in heavy boots, and the rat as it scampered across uneven ground. Metal bit into her wrists behind her back, suggesting she had been handcuffed. The vermin begin nibbling speculatively at her fingers with sharp incisors. Miller flicked the creature away, catching the ear of whoever was leaning close to her.

"You're a lucky girl," someone said near her face. Stammer's rank breath and deep voice were unmistakable. "I wanted to let you die but Riley insisted on putting a rapi-heal patch on your head wound." Stammers nudged her in the stomach with a boot. "Don't try and pretend you're still unconscious. Sit up."

Miller opened her eyes and shivered. It was a hot, sticky night but a cool breeze was wafting through the dust zone, chilling the sweat on her arms and chest. While she was out cold either Stammers or Riley had stripped away much of her uniform. Gone were the shoulder, elbow and knee pads. Also missing were her boots, gauntlets and utility belt, and she was without her Lawgiver and boot knife. Miller's bodysuit had been unzipped and rolled down to her waist, exposing the white sports bra underneath. She forced herself up into a sitting position, a task made difficult by the handcuffs restraining her.

"That's better. Let me take a good look at you." Stammers was standing in front of her, and the moonlight glinted off his shaved skull. His helmet was resting on the seat of a Lawmaster nearby. Miller's own helmet was a fractured shell on the ground nearby, large cracks visible in its reinforced casing. Riley must have hit her with tremendous force. Stammers noticed where her gaze had wandered. "I know. You've got a skull like rockcrete to have survived that."

"My weapons?" she asked.

"Dissolving at the bottom of a chem pit. I wanted to throw you in too but my bleeding heart partner said he could persuade you not to talk."

Miller glanced around. "Where is Riley?"

"Dealing with your Lawmaster. That's the first thing PSU will look for when the search begins." Stammers sighed. "Well, Lynn... I can call you Lynn, can't I? Seems less formal than Miller."

"Be my guest," she replied sarcastically.

"Well, Lynn, how are we going to kill some time until Riley gets back?"

"Let's play twenty questions. Why did you kill those two juves?"

Stammers shrugged. "You heard them, they were trying to blackmail me. They were useful once but they were starting to overreach themselves."

"That doesn't justify murder."

"Those two were responsible for the deaths of hundreds in that fire. Killing the juves was a summary execution. I call it justice."

"You don't have the right to use that word," Miller spat at him. "I always thought you were a dirty badge, Stammers. I'm just sorry you've dragged Riley down to your level."

"Really? But it was Riley who first suggested torching Robert Hatch with all the aliens still inside."

"You're lying."

"Am I? You know how much my partner hates off-worlders – especially the vultures. How far do you think he'd go to get revenge?"

"I don't believe you," Miller maintained.

Stammers chuckled. "Your words say one thing, but your face says another, Lynn, You're just not sure anymore, are you?"

"Drokk yourself sideways with a daystick."

"An interesting invitation, but I'm just as fond of using a blade as a bludgeon." Stammers bent over and extracted his boot knife from its sheath. "How about you and I get to know each other better? I've seen you naked often enough and I've always liked what I've seen."

"You're disgusting," Miller sneered.

Stammers dropped to one knee in front of Miller and flashed the blade through the air, neatly slicing through one of her bra straps. "I'd be careful what you say next, Lynn. You wouldn't want me to slip while I've got this knife in my hand, would you?" He rested the flat surface of the knife against her skin. The touch of cold metal made her jump. "Now, where was I? Oh yes, we are going to become friends. Good friends."

"Not if my life depended upon it," she said.

"We'll see about that," Stammers whispered. He drew the blade sideways and cut through the other bra strap. "I don't want to hurt you, Lynn. Not unless you ask me to."

Miller licked her lips and swallowed. "All right. What did you have in mind?"

"Well, you mentioned something about a daystick. It's surprising the uses I can find for one of those."

Miller arched an eyebrow and leaned closer to him. "Perhaps you'd like to surprise me," she whispered. Stammers grinned wolfishly and moved closer to her, one hand stretching out to touch her–

Miller lunged at Stammers, smashing her forehead into the bridge of his nose. He fell backwards, clutching at his face, blood gushing from his nostrils. His knife fell to one side. "You slitch! You drokking slitch!" Miller scrambled after him, one foot kicking the knife out of reach.

Stammers reached for the Lawgiver in his boot holster, but Miller was already on top of him. Stammers clawed at her with his hands, fingernails tearing into her flesh. "You fight like a girl, Stammers!" Miller shouted. "Let me show you how a real man is supposed to fight!" She lunged at him again with her head, smashing it against his broken nose. Stammers cried out in agony. She head-butted him in the face once more. A sick, wet sound echoed around the dust zone as bone fragments from Stammer's broken nose were forced backwards into his brain. He cried out, twitched once and then he was dead, blood oozing from the mashed pulp that had been his face.

Miller rolled away, struggling to wipe the crimson viscera from her face. She had to get these cuffs off before Riley came back. She twisted round so her back was to Stammers, enabling her hands to get at the pouches on his utility belt. The electronic key for the cuffs should be in–

"Move away from him please, Lynn." Riley stepped out of the shadows, his Lawgiver trained on her.

"Riley, I–"

"Move away!" Riley shouted.

Miller shuffled away, still on her knees. Once Stammers was out of her reach, Riley retrieved the electronic key for the cuffs. "Looking for this?"

She just nodded. "He was going to rape me."

"Maybe. But you'd say anything now to stay alive," Riley replied.

"It's the truth! Use your lie detector if you don't believe me."

Riley just stared at her for a while. "Grud, what a mess!" he sighed, staring at the corpse of his dead partner, the Lawgiver still aimed at Miller. "What are we going to do about this?"

The carnage on Anton Diffring Overzoom had finally been cleared away and traffic was moving smoothly through 87 once more. Dredd returned to Oswald Mosley, having raced across the sector. He strode inside, not noticing the furtive figure of Riff Maltin lurking in the shadows nearby. The street reporter sidled into the building after Dredd, followed by the hovercam.

Inside, the lobby was packed with disgruntled residents shouting at each other. Seeing a Judge arrive, they began directing their ire at him instead.

"One at a time, one at a time!" Dredd commanded, shouting to be heard above the babble of voices. An eldster emerged from the throng, his thinning white hair almost as frazzled as his expression.

"My name is John Pigott, con-apt 333. You've got to do something about those Citi-Def hooligans, Judge! They've been tearing this block apart searching for some missing child while decent citizens are trying to sleep. I thought there were regulations about how and when the Citi-Def could be mobilised!"

"There are," Dredd replied. "What about the rest of you? Can you back up what this eldster says?" Another babble of voices filled the air, confirming they shared similar complaints. "Enough!" Dredd shouted before going back to Pigott. "You! Where were these squad members seen last?"

"Heading for the basement, I think. They were mumbling about breaking open the armoury and issuing weapons. There ought to be a law against it!"

"There is," Dredd snarled before raising his voice again. "All of you – return to your homes immediately. Anyone still in this lobby when I return will spend the next six months in the cubes. Do I make myself clear?"

Maltin stepped into a turbolift headed for the upper floors, keeping the crowd of residents between himself and Dredd. The news editor was right – there were enough storeyies inside this one block to keep Channel 27 on air for a month, maybe longer. And all of them were going to be Riff Maltin exclusives...

In the basement, Conchita was pounding on the door of the Oswald Mosley armoury. Every block had a cache of weapons in an underground bunker, for use by the Citi-Def in the event of a significant threat to the Big Meg. But to prevent the armoury being raided by perps or rogue squads, entry could only be gained with the proper access codes. These were held at the local sector house and were only released with the authorisation of the Chief Judge. The entrance to the armoury was made up of six inches of reinforced steel and rockcrete, proof against almost any force. The thinking behind this was simplicity itself – if you had enough firepower to break into the armoury, you wouldn't need to break in.

Two-dozen squad members were waiting their turn to attack the door, while those who had already tried and failed were resting against the walls of the basement. "Drokk you, open up!" Conchita screamed at the doorway, her bloody fists flailing against its impervious surface.

"You're wasting your time," a low, gravely voice boomed. Conchita and the others looked at the staircase. Judge Dredd was walking down the steps, his Lawgiver drawn and ready to fire. "You'll never be able to open the Armoury."

"We need those weapons!" Billy-Bob Jolie shouted at the lawman.

"Why?"

"My daughter has been abducted," Conchita replied, "and your precious Justice Department won't lift a finger to help. So we're helping ourselves."

"Do you have any evidence your daughter has been abducted?"

"I don't need evidence!" Conchita fumed. "She's gone and somebody took her. That's all I need to know!"

Dredd moved through the squad members towards the leader. "I checked the files on your family while travelling here. Several times anonymous callers have accused you of beating your daughter. Perhaps she ran away to escape the violence. Or perhaps you finally went too far and beat her to death. So you panicked, disposed of the body and are now staging all of this as an alibi."

"How dare you!" she raged. "You have no evidence for those allegations!"

Dredd almost smiled. "But you just said you don't need evidence to know that your daughter has been abducted. Why should I need evidence to accuse you of beating or even killing her?"

"I'll kill you myself!" Conchita hissed, lunging at the Judge. Billy-Bob and other squad members held her back.

"Don't do it, Maguire. He's just trying to bait you!" Billy-Bob hissed.

"Threatening a Judge is a serious offence," Dredd noted. "I could arrest this citizen here and now."

"Do that and you'll have a riot on your hands," Conchita said. "You may be a Judge but you're just one man, surrounded by dozens of my squad members. The odds are too great, even for the great Judge Dredd!"

"Perhaps," he conceded. "But I'm the only one with a gun and that's the way it is going to stay. I want all of you to return to your con-apts and stay there until morning. Once the sun is up, I will personally lead a search for the missing child. But until then I don't want to hear another report of trouble from this block. If I do, I'll be back here to arrest each and every one of you. Consider this an informal curfew. Break it and I'll break you."

Dredd glared at the squad members, his face utterly implacable. No one spoke, no one challenged his authority.

"That's better," he said finally. "Now go back to your homes and your families. And remember what I said!"

The residents began filing out of the basement. Conchita stayed until all the others had gone. "This isn't over," she warned. "Not by a long way."

"Save it for your followers," Dredd snarled. "I'm not impressed."

Conchita walked out of the basement, followed by Dredd. As he returned to his Lawmaster a message came through from Control.

"Dredd, when did you last see Judge Lynn Miller?"

"In person? Outside Maurice Waldron Block, about two hours ago. Why?"

"She went off-radio more than an hour past and hasn't reported back in."

Dredd scowled. "Better list her as missing and alert all Judges in Sector 87 to be–" He stopped in midsentence.

"Control to Dredd, you still there?"

"Yeah. Just remembering something someone said to me. Forget what I was suggesting. Sector Chief Caine runs 87. Notify her that Miller has gone missing and let her decide what to do about it. I'm just a Street Judge here."

"That's a roj. Control out!"

Dredd activated his on-board computer. "Show me the quickest route from my present location to Sector 87's dust zone."

03:00

"You'll have to kill me," Miller said. "If you think logically about this, you'll know you have to kill me." She was sitting on one side of Stammers's corpse, her hands still cuffed behind her back. Opposite her Riley was perched on a rockcrete slab, his Lawgiver clasped in one hand. Overhead the moon was beginning to descend across the night sky; the light reflected from its surface threw strange shadows across the dust zone.

"Don't say that," Riley replied.

"It's the only logical course of action. I know Stammers supplied the incendiary device that torched Robert Hatch. You're his partner, you must have known about it. Stomm, he said it was your idea!"

"It wasn't."

"I know that," Miller said. "You might have looked the other way, but you never enjoyed killing like Stammers, never got the same thrill from it he did."

"I always told Eustace he'd go too far one day."

"And you were right. But you should have turned him in, told the SJS what he was doing while you had the chance – while your hands were still clean."

Riley slipped off his gauntlets and held up his hands. "These? They stopped being clean a long time ago, Lynn."

"Why? At the Academy you were Roll of Honor material–"

"That was before Danny died. Everything changed after that."

"I know," Miller said. "I was there, remember?"

Riley smiled. "You were my best friend for all those years while we were cadets. I loved you like the sister I never had. But then..."

"Then you heard about Danny." Miller could not help thinking back to that day. She and Riley had been out in the Cursed Earth, fifteen year-old cadets on their first Hot dog Run. A message pod reached them from the Big Meg about the death of Danny Riley during a battle on the R'qeen homeworld. Miller had watched her friend scream and sob, wanting to ease his suffering in any way possible. That night they were posted together on sentry duty. That was when it had happened; the incident that almost cost both of them their badges.

"You should never have kissed me," Riley said, staring at his partner's corpse. "I wouldn't have dared to kiss you."

"You were hurting. I wanted to make you feel better."

"You did – until Judge Hallvar found us."

Miller smiled. "The most embarrassing moment of my life..."

"I didn't mind getting sent back to the city in shame, or losing my place on the honours board or the black mark on my permanent record," Riley said. "What I couldn't stand was the way you were with me afterwards: distant, aloof, as if you didn't want to admit it had ever happened."

"That was how I felt."

"But you never asked how I felt, did you? You showed me a brief glimpse of what my life could be like – to be wanted, to be loved – and then you tore it away. You showed me I could break the rules, Lynn... and then nothing!"

"I'm sorry..." she stammered. "I never knew."

"No. And you never gave me the chance to tell you!"

"Grud, what a mess," Miller said to herself.

Riley stood up, still clutching his Lawgiver. "So I tried to forget it ever happened – but I couldn't. When I got transferred to Sector 87 I put in a request to become your partner but you refused. Do you have any idea how that made me feel? I had lost someone I loved, lost my best friend – and now you were rejecting me again. So Caine partnered me with Stammers, and look where that's led us! Congratulations, Lynn. You just wanted to make me feel better. How's that plan working out now?"

"I didn't know," she protested. "I couldn't have known..."

"Didn't know or just didn't want to know?" Riley raged. "Grud forbid anything should get in the way of your glorious career! I bet you've had to work twice as hard as everyone else to overcome that blemish on your record. So sorry that I've inconvenienced the rise and rise of Judge Lynn Miller!"

"Is that how you see me? Too ambitious to care about anybody but myself? Too driven to give a stomm what happens to you?" Miller struggled to her feet to confront Riley. "You've no idea, have you? How many times I've covered for you and your precious partner! How many times I've cleaned up the messes you two left behind! Just a few hours ago I was telling myself I could never believe you'd had any involvement in that fire. I came here, hoping against hope to find it was just Stammers, that you had nothing to do with it!"

"They killed my brother!" Riley bellowed. "The R'qeen gunned him down and then they took his body away and hung it on a hook for days and days and days. Finally, when the rotting flesh was hanging off his bones, they cut off one of his arms and they were eating it when the rescue squad found them. I saw the report from the

Med-Judges identifying Danny's body – or what was left of him!"

Miller shook her head. "You could never have seen a report like that! Such findings are confidential, never revealed to any family members. Who showed that to you? Stammers?"

Riley ignored her question, too involved with his memories to hear it. "Afterwards, all I wanted to do was watch those monsters burn. They butchered my brother. I wanted them to suffer just a fraction of what he suffered!"

"So you arranged for hundreds of innocents to be burned alive? Is that justice? Is that what your brother would have wanted?"

Riley aimed the Lawgiver at Miller's head. "Don't you dare try to tell me what Danny would have wanted! You didn't know him, you never met him. You haven't got the right to talk about him! Just shut your drokking mouth before I do it for you, slitch!"

"That's Stammers talking, not you."

"You think so?" Riley moved his finger to the trigger. "Let's see."

Riff had been working his way up Oswald Mosley Block, trying to coax information from the residents about the latest incidents. Few would talk and those that did gave accounts so heavily laced with expletives that any attempt to broadcast them would be pointless once the Justice Department auto-censor had done its job. But the reporter was able to glean enough facts to know what questions to ask when he reached con-apt 721.

It took several minutes of insistent knocking and bell ringing before Riff heard movement from inside. Another two minutes had elapsed when the front door opened to reveal the scowling face of Kurt Sivell. "What the drokk do you want? Do you know what time it is?"

"Sorry to disturb you, sir," Riff began, "but I'm interviewing residents about the missing child. What do you think has happened to her?"

"To who? What missing child?"

"I understand her name is Kasey Maguire. She's from this floor, actually. Did you know her at all?"

"Did I know her?" Sivell was mystified by the questions. "Why are you using the past tense? Is she dead?"

Riff admitted he didn't know, but that was one theory he had heard. "You seem unaware of Kasey's tragic disappearance. I've been told the Citi-Def squad had searched almost every con-apt in this building looking for her."

"When was this?"

"Just in the past few hours!"

Sivell ran a hand through his greasy, thinning hair. "The past few hours?" The resident shrugged. "Well, nobody searched my con-apt. But I've been out cold since I took those Double-Doze. I'm amazed you managed to wake me."

"Really? Well, that's fascinating." Riff was ready to move on, having had enough of this slow-witted, half-asleep simp. He almost missed out of the scoop of his fledgeling career – almost. But Sivell grabbed the reporter's shoulder, a look of revelation on his face.

"Did you say Kasey Maguire was missing?"

"Yes."

"But I saw her, just before I took the sleeping pills. She accidentally brushed against my doorbell and woke me up."

Now Riff was paying attention again. He activated the hovercam from its rest mode to record what Sivell was saying. "When was this? Can you remember when you saw Kasey Maguire, the missing girl?"

"Yes, it was just before two this morning. I recall the time because I looked at the clock when I was woken up.

I was going to give whoever rang the doorbell a piece of my mind!"

"But it was Kasey who rang the bell–"

"By mistake, yes. She must have leant against it on her way to the turbolift."

"You saw her get into a turbolift?" Riff was excited now, he could sense something important was about to happen.

"Yes, yes. But before that I asked Kasey where she was headed at that time of the morning. She said she was going to stay with a friend on a lower floor," Sivell explained. "Then I saw Kasey get into the turbolift and the doors closed behind her. That was the last I saw of her."

"Are you sure about this, citizen? The girl's mother has made no mention of such an arrangement."

"Yes, quite sure. The reason it stuck in my mind was I looked back to see what floor Kasey was going to – just being nosy I suppose. The turbolift went up, not down."

Riff felt the hairs on the back of his neck rising. "Do you know what floor the turbolift went to?"

"Yes, of course. It was the top, the one hundredth floor – where the aliens are." Sivell frowned, unaware his next set of words would set in motion a tragic series of events. "You say Kasey is missing? I hope those vultures on the top floor haven't got her – they eat human flesh you know!"

Riff thanked the citizen for his time and apologised again for disturbing him. Once Sivell had gone back to bed, Riff contacted his news editor. "Tell me you got all of that!"

"You better drokkin' believe it!" Yablonsky screamed into Riff's earpiece. "Give an intro to the hovercam and we'll cut it together here. You have five minutes before it gets broadcast. Get up to the top floor now and confront the aliens with what you know. We'll cut to you live when you're ready!"

Riff smiled. Fame and fortune, here I come…

Dredd rode into the dust zone, scanning his surroundings for any sign of Miller. A call to PSU had provided her point of entry but surveillance beyond the perimeter was almost non-existent. That made the dust zone a perfect rendezvous point for anyone wanting to meet in secret. Dredd slowed his motorcycle to a crawl and activated the bike's on-board computer while calling Brady at Sector House 87. "Miller's gone missing and I have reason to believe she's in the dust zone," Dredd said. "Is there any other way of tracking her besides PSU's spy-in-the-sky cameras?"

"You could try her transponder," the Tek-Judge suggested. "Justice Department vehicles have a transponder built into them. They transmit a constant homing signal, unless they are destroyed or tampered with."

"I thought only H-Wagons and flying vehicles had a transponder?"

"That was recently extended to Lawmasters and other ground-based transportation," Brady explained. "We've been fitting them over the past month. I put one into your bike when you arrived at the sector house."

"And Miller's Lawmaster also has one?"

"Yes. I've been recalling its data, in case anyone asked. Normally the PSU cameras are enough to track anyone within the city, but…"

"Can you upload that data to my bike's computer?" Dredd asked.

"That'll take a few seconds, but I don't know how much help it will be," Brady said. "Miller's transponder stopped an hour ago."

"Meaning?"

"Either her Lawmaster has been destroyed or the transponder was sabotaged. Okay, your on-board

computer should show Miller's last recorded location and
the route her Lawmaster took to get there."

A map of the dust zone appeared on Dredd's computer
screen with a red line leading into the area. The line
stopped not far from Dredd's position. "Thanks for that,
Brady."

"Don't mention it. I just hope you find her alive."

"One last thing. Who else knows about these
transponders?"

"Everyone in Tek-Division, some Street Judges, Sector
Chiefs, plenty of people at Justice Central. An announcement about them is due any day. Oh, and the external
company that supplied them – Summerbee Industries."

"Second time I've heard that name tonight. Dredd out."
He switched off his motorcycle and dismounted. If
Miller's ride had been sabotaged or destroyed nearby,
those responsible might still be in the area. Advancing on
foot could provide an element of surprise. Dredd crept
forwards on foot.

Getting anyone on the top floor of Oswald Mosley to
open their door proved even more difficult for Riff than
further down the building. His report suggesting aliens
were responsible for Kasey's disappearance was due for
broadcast any minute. It was doubtful the new arrival on
the hundredth floor would be watching Channel 27, but
some human residents below might be. When that quote
from Sivell went out, the trouble inside Oswald Mosley
could only escalate. This was Riff's last chance to get the
aliens' side of the story.

He had hammered on the doors of all the top floor con-
apts without success. Either those inside did not hear
him or they were refusing to answer. Eventually a fearsome R'qeen appeared. One of his arms was broken and
his head badly bruised. The reporter recognised him as
the offworlder who had fought the two Judges outside

Robert Hatch. Could abducting the girl be some kind of revenge for that incident? Riff kept his speculations to himself and smiled broadly.

"My apologies for disturbing you at this time of the night."

"What are you doing here?" Nyon demanded in All-speak.

The reporter hoped Channel 27 had access to auto-translators and asked his next question in halting Allspeak. "I understand there has been some commotion in Oswald Mosley Block tonight. Residents have complained about their con-apts being subjected to an unauthorised search by the building's Citi-Def squad."

"Are those the thugs who stormed in here and assaulted my pairling?"

"Yes, I believe so. I'm investigating this for Channel 27. Would you be willing to talk about what happened?"

Nyon smiled. "Yes! The truth about this must be told!"

"Perhaps I could come in?" Riff asked, smiling ingenuously.

The R'qeen stood aside, letting Maltin and the hover-cam enter. Once they were inside Nyon began ranting and raving about the methods used by the Citi-Def. "One of them threatened our broodling Misch. We have only been in this building a few hours and already we are accused of a crime!"

"What crime was this?"

"The humans claimed we had taken one of their young. They searched this and all the other con-apts, but could not find her because she is not here. They probably thought we planned to kill her and then eat her!"

Riff nodded. "There is a lot of misunderstanding about R'qeen ways."

"We have endured enough. No more humans should be allowed to set foot on this floor. Those that try will learn exactly what R'qeen do to their enemies!"

Lleccas emerged from one of the side rooms. "Nyon!" she said in R'qeen. "What have you been saying to this human?"

To Riff her alien speech sounded harsh and frightening. Perhaps now was a good time to make his way back to safer territory. He had no urge to end his days as a rotting corpse in an R'qeen charnel pit. The reporter began backing towards the front door. "Thanks for your time and hospitality," he said in Allspeak. "Perhaps we shall meet again soon."

Nyon marched towards him and threw open the door. "Go now and tell the others. None may come here anymore. We have suffered enough at the hands of the humans. We will defend ourselves – by any means necessary!"

Riff ran for the turbolift, the hovercam hurrying after him.

Misch closed the door, having witnessed the encounter between her broodfather and the human. Bringing Kasey here had seemed like a good idea. But now events were beginning to spiral out of control. Misch did not know what to do next. If she sent her new friend back home, Kasey would probably suffer another beating. But if the human girl stayed here, Misch felt certain some greater tragedy lay ahead of them of all.

The R'qeen child returned back to the hiding place beneath the lean-to. Kasey was fast asleep, her face happy and contented in contrast to the dark bruises on its surface.

I can't send her back, Misch decided. She's my friend. I have to protect her.

"For Grud's sake, Riley, put the Lawgiver down," Miller pleaded. "We both know you're not going to shoot me."

"Do we?" Riley asked.

"Maybe it's not too late for you. I could testify on your behalf, say Stammers had some hold over you. He was threatening to tell everyone about us, what we did on that hotdog run."

"One lie to solve another?"

"What are your alternatives?" she asked.

"Kill you and push your body in the same chem pit as your Lawmaster. Say Stammers attacked me when I discovered he was behind the fire at Robert Hatch and I killed him defending myself. I'll probably get a commendation."

"I wouldn't hold your breath," a voice growled from the shadows. Riley spun round to see Dredd walking towards him, with his Lawgiver ready to fire. "You might be able to get off a shot before I do. I'm getting old and some people think I'm slowing down. Maybe they're right and maybe they're wrong. But you better kill me with the first shot to be sure – you won't get a second chance."

Riley's glance flickered sideways to Miller. "How long have you known he was watching us?"

"Long enough," she said.

"So the offer to lie for me. That was another betrayal?"

"I had to keep you talking long enough for Dredd to get into a better position."

"Grud but you're a bitch, Miller!"

"No, I'm a Mega-City One Judge doing my job," she snarled, leaping at Riley. He tried to bring his Lawgiver round to fire but she was too fast. She knocked him to the ground and sent his helmet flying off. Dredd moved towards them, trying to get an angle for a clean shot, but the pair kept rolling over and over, the gun trapped between them. Then a single shot echoed around the dust zone.

"Miller! Are you all right?" Dredd shouted.

She rolled away from Riley, her chest covered in blood.

"No, no…" she sobbed. But it was Riley who lay dying, a gaping wound underlining his fate.

Dredd crouched beside the body, straining to hear any last words. "Have you a final confession to make?"

Riley nodded, blood welling in his mouth then running down either side of his face. He coughed a red mist before speaking. "They-they used us… Used me… Showed me a file–"

"Who used you?" Dredd hissed.

"Summ-Summerbee…" Riley whispered. Then his eyes rolled back into his skull and he was gone. Dredd leaned forward and brushed one hand over the dead man's eyes, closing them.

"Rest in peace," he murmured.

Miller was still sobbing on the ground between the corpses of Stammers and Riley. Dredd waited until the worst of it had passed before speaking again. "Looks like you've been in the wars."

"Is that a joke?" she asked.

"Simply stating a fact. You should know by now, I don't make jokes."

"Jovus, do I look that bad?" Miller staggered to the nearest chem pit to look at her reflection. "Yes, I do. How'd you find us?"

"A tip from Brady got me to the remains of your Lawmaster. Riley's ranting and raving was loud enough to bring me here." Dredd pulled an electronic key from his utility belt and undid the handcuffs behind her back. Miller winced as she tried to rub some life back into her arms, the wrists red and raw from where the metal had cut into her flesh. Dredd helped pull her bodysuit back up into place.

"Stammers wanted to get up close and personal," she said. "I persuaded him it was a bad idea, Mean Machine style."

"That explains your black eyes."

"What did Riley say before he died?"

"That he'd been used. Someone showed him a file."

"Who?"

"Summerbee." Dredd studied the dead Judges. "Miller, do you know anything about this file he mentioned?"

She zipped up the front of her bodysuit. "Riley saw a sealed report on how his brother was killed and eaten by the R'qeen during the Colony Wars. That's why Riley was willing to see Robert Hatch burn. But how would Summerbee Industries have access to that file?"

"A good question," Dredd replied. "I think it's high time I paid a visit to Werner Summerbee, to find out if he has the answer."

"You want me to come along as back-up?"

"I can handle anybody called Werner," Dredd said. "Besides, you need to have Med-Division check your injuries and get a fresh uniform. What's left of that one doesn't exactly meet regulations." He activated his helmet radio. "Dredd to Control: I've found Miller. Judges Stammers and Riley are dead – they were holding Miller prisoner in the Sector 87 dust zone and planned to execute her. Have you got a trace on my signal?"

"That's a roj," Control replied.

"Good. Send a meat wagon for the stiffs and an H-Wagon to take Miller back to the sector house."

"SJS will want to interview both of you."

"Stammers and Riley will still be dead at the end of my shift. Tell the SJS they can interview me then. Dredd out!" He switched frequency on his helmet radio. "Bike to me!" Within seconds his riderless motorcycle had rolled into the clearing, responding to his summons. Dredd removed emergency flares and a first aid kit from the motorcycle and threw them to Miller before riding off, calling, "See you on the streets!"

Conchita felt as if she were losing her mind. Frustration, anger and worry all fought for control of her feelings. Not only was Kasey still missing, but Dermot and Ramone had not returned from their rendezvous with Stammers. The Judge had been the investigating officer when Conchita's husband died. Stammers wanted to have the offworlder cubed for murder but was overruled by his superior officer, Judge Temple. Afterwards Stammers approached Conchita, expressing his dismay at how the case had gone. They had become lovers for a brief time but she broke off the relationship, not wanting to get Stammers into trouble with his superiors.

A week ago he had returned to her con-apt with a question – how would she like to get back at the alien who killed her husband? Conchita had been sceptical, fearing it was a Justice Department trap. But Stammers used his own lie detector to prove the offer was genuine. The R'qeen alien now lived in Robert Hatch Block. Stammers would supply an incendiary device to torch the building, something that couldn't easily be traced. He even suggested she organise the public meeting protesting about aliens in the sector as a way of creating an alibi for herself and other likely suspects. Conchita got Ramone and Dermot to plant the device while she was at the meeting.

The plan had worked perfectly – until Stammers and his partner arrived outside Oswald Mosley with a hoverbus full of aliens. To maintain the pretence of not knowing Stammers, Conchita had been obliged to start the brawl, leading her fellow Citi-Def squad members against the one person who had helped avenge her husband's death. All her children were now missing and aliens were living in the home her family was meant to be shifting into any day. Where had it all gone wrong?

Sick of pacing up and down inside her cramped con-apt, Conchita turned on the tri-D. At this time of the morning there would be nothing worth watching, but the programmes might bore her to sleep. She set the tri-D to scroll through the thousands of channels broadcast across the Big Meg. Hearing her daughter's name, Conchita stopped at Channel 27 and watched a report by Riff Maltin. The journalist was looking into the camera sternly, his face contorted in a parody of concern.

"Tonight, a mother fears for her missing daughter. In a city of four hundred million people, what is one life more or less? To the Maguire family of Oswald Mosley Block here in Sector 87, it means the world. Little Kasey Maguire has been missing for hours and the Justice Department refuses to help. When the building's Citi-Def squad instituted a search for the missing girl, they were told to stand down.

"But while the authorities stand idly by and leave a little girl to Grud knows what fate, I – Riff Maltin, roving reporter for Channel 27 – have found a vital clue to the whereabouts of this lost angel. Less than an hour ago I interviewed Kurt Sivell, a neighbour of the Maguire family on the seventy-second floor of Oswald Mosley. It seems he was the last person to see little Kasey alive, witnessing her getting into a turbolift. I asked him where that turbolift was going. Here, in a Channel 27 exclusive, is what he told me…"

The tri-D screen hissed static for a moment before cutting to footage of the citizen frowning in the doorway of his con-apt. "It was the top, the one hundredth floor, where the aliens are. I hope those vultures on the top floor haven't got her. They eat human flesh you know!"

The image cut back to Riff. "Just before Kasey went missing, the Judges moved six families of aliens into Oswald Mosley. Among those are several from R'qeen, an offworld species of carrion eaters, also known as vultures. The R'qeen kill their food, then let it rot before consuming it. After hearing what citizen Kurt Sivell had to say, I confronted the aliens, speaking to an R'qeen male. Here is what he had to say. Viewers not fluent in Allspeak or who do not wish to read subtitles should engage their auto-translators."

After another burst of static, Nyon appeared on screen, his face a terrifying visage. "The humans claimed we had taken one of their young. They searched but could not find her because she is not here. They probably thought we planned to kill her and then eat her!"

Riff reappeared, his face even more serious than before. "Chilling words there. This alien denies having any knowledge of little Kasey Maguire's location but is he telling the truth? I asked him what would happen if anyone tried to look for her on the top floor again…"

Nyon was back on screen, his features savage and severe. "We have had enough. Not one more human shall be allowed to set foot on this floor. Those that try will learn exactly what R'qeen do to their enemies!"

Channel 27 cut back to Riff for the last time. "After that I was forced to leave the top level of Oswald Mosley, the alien's threats still ringing in my ears. All of this leaves three vital questions to be answered: why have the Judges been so lax in investigating this case, a case that will horrify and frighten parents everywhere? Secondly, why are the aliens so unwilling to let anyone search their quarters on the top floor of Oswald Mosley – what do they have to hide? Thirdly, and most importantly, what has happened to little Kasey Maguire? Is she now in the possession of flesh-eating monsters from another world and who will save her? More on this story as we get it. This is Riff Maltin, handing you back to the studio!"

Conchita sank back into her seat, stunned at what she had just witnessed. Had her daughter fallen into the clutches of those monsters?

Then doorbell rang.

Choking back tears of rage, Conchita ran to the door and pulled it open. "Kasey? Is that you?"

Standing outside was Riff, his hovercam filming them both from just behind the reporter's right shoulder. "Conchita Maguire? My name is Riff Maltin from Channel 27. I was wondering if you could spare me a few words."

04:00

Caine was waiting on the landing pad when the H-Wagon arrived at Sector House 87. She helped Miller climb out of the vehicle before it flew back into the night sky. "How are you?" the Sector Chief asked, shouting to be heard over the H-Wagon's engines as it ascended.

"I've been better," Miller replied. "You heard what happened?"

Caine nodded as they entered the sector house. "I've always had my suspicions about Stammers, but Riley as well? This incident is not going to be good for 87's reputation. Where's Dredd?"

"Gone to interview a suspect, Werner Summerbee."

The Sector Chief reacted with surprise. "Of Summerbee Industries?"

"Before he died Riley suggested Summerbee had some peripheral involvement with the fire at Robert Hatch. Dredd's gone to follow that lead." Miller staggered, exhaustion from the night's events catching up with her. Caine grabbed the Street Judge's arm to stop her collapsing.

"You'd better get to Med-Bay, have them check you over. I've already lost two Judges tonight," Caine said. "I don't want you joining them." Miller started towards the turbo-lift. Her Sector Chief had a final remark for her: "The SJS will be here soon. They'll want to interview you and Dredd about what's happened."

. . .

Dredd stopped his Lawmaster outside the entrance to Ridley Estate. This ultra-secure enclosed community was home to the richest of the rich in the Big Meg. The waiting list to buy a home here was decades-long, with prospective purchasers required to pay a deposit of several million credits just to be considered for inclusion. Outside the estate, a city of four hundred millions citizens struggled to survive, crowded into towering citi-blocks and eking out a meagre existence on welfare handouts. For the precious few who could afford it, living on the Ridley Estate was like having your own private utopia, far from the madding crowd. The residents were almost untouchable – almost.

The Judge approached the perimeter, where five fearsome security droids blocked the entrance. "State your business," the lead robot grated.

"Judge Dredd, here to see Werner Summerbee."

"Do you have an appointment?"

"At four in the morning? Of course not!"

"Unless you have an appointment, I must ask you to leave – now." The droids began charging their weapons systems.

"Unless you let me in I'll have to disarm you. Permanently."

The droid was not giving in that easily. "You have ten seconds to comply with our request or there will be... trouble."

Dredd sighed wearily. "Have it your own way. Dredd to Control!"

"Beginning countdown to pre-emptive action," the robot said. "Ten."

"Control to Dredd, go ahead."

"Nine."

"Am outside Ridley Estate. Some tin-pot guard droid refuses to let me in."

"Eight."

"Is that it counting down in the background?"

"Seven."

"That's a roj. Request security override for Ridley Estate."

"Six."

"Could take a few seconds, Dredd."

"Five."

"The sooner the better, Control."

"Four."

"Just coming…"

"Three." The droids began moving into attack positions around Dredd.

"Running out of time, Control!"

"Two." The robots obtained target lock on the lone motorcyclist.

"Here it comes…"

"One." The lead droid raised its weapon to fire. "Please accept our sincere apologies for your imminent death. All units, open fi… " At that the robot fell silent, its silver limbs frozen in place. The other mechanoids were also still, the hum of their systems slowly dying away.

Dredd relaxed, letting his breath out again. "Thanks, Control. Try not to cut it so fine in future."

"Roj that. Opening gates for you – now."

The entrance to Ridley Estate swung open and the Judge rode his Lawmaster in, swerving between the statuesque security robots. Once past the perimeter it was easy to see why this was the Big Meg's most exclusive address. A long driveway curled through acres of real grass and trees, not the usual synthetic plants. Ahead, a series of palatial bungalows sprawled across the grounds, each with its own private hoverpad. In a city where each cubic millimetre of room came at a premium, devoting so much to gardens and open spaces was evidence of vast, almost incalculable wealth.

Dredd rode on towards the luxurious lodgings, intent on locating number fifteen. No doubt the security droid had sent an alarm to Summerbee before the override took hold, warning about the arrival of a Judge. It would be interesting to see how the wealthy industrialist reacted.

Riff had to hand it to his interview subject, she could take up crying for the Mega-Olympic team. Conchita had been sobbing her heart out ever since the hovercam entered her con-apt. Yes, she had seen the report on Channel 27, just a few minutes before. No, she had not given her daughter permission to go out or to visit any friends. Conchita had forbidden Kasey from having any contact with the aliens, especially after the incident earlier.

"What incident was this?" Riff asked, looking back over his shoulder to smile at the hovercam. A winking red light on the side of the silver globe told him the interview was being broadcast direct to air. After this Channel 27 could not help but give him a permanent job.

"I staged a peaceful protest, here on the seventy-second floor, when the Judges were escorting the aliens up to the top of the building. While I was distracted one of those creatures lured my daughter away and was... doing things... to her."

Riff did his best to be soothing. "I know this is difficult and painful. But could you tell us what... things... this alien was doing to your little girl?"

Conchita's face contorted with disgust. "It was... touching her."

"And what did you do when you discovered this?"

"I dragged my daughter away. I thought I'd saved her. But now..."

Riff stroked his chin thoughtfully. "Which of the alien species was it that you saw with your daughter?"

"R'qeen," Conchita snarled. "One of those filthy vultures!" She collapsed into hysterics again, tears flooding down her face. "It was a vulture that killed my husband, that murdered Kasey's father!"

"This is shocking, Ms Maguire, absolutely shocking!"

It's also great tri-D, Riff thought, but kept that to himself. The woman looked at him, a new horror of realisation creeping across her face.

"You don't think when the freak... touched Kasey earlier, that it put some sort of influence on her? I've heard some of these R'qeen have mental powers, like Psi-Judges, only much stronger."

"It's possible, I suppose," Riff agreed. "That might explain how the R'qeen were able to lure your daughter to the top floor – if that is what has happened to her. Right now, the details remain uncertain."

"They've got her, haven't they?" Conchita cried out. "Those offworld freaks have taken my daughter, put her under their spell. Kasey may already be dead and rotting in one of their charnel pits, just waiting to be eaten..." She was falling apart now, her words panted out between sobs. "Kasey, my poor, sweet, innocent Kasey. What are they doing to you? Those drokkers, those devious, murderous, alien drokkers."

Riff decided Conchita could take no more of this. He turned round to the camera and delivered a few closing remarks. "There you have it – the terrible torment of a mother who knows not where her child is. Has Kasey been abducted by carrion-eating creatures now living in the luxurious new con-apts atop this terrified block? Is this beloved child already dead and being subjected to some unknown horrors? Why have the Judges refused to step in and relieve the suffering of this poor woman? Only one thing is certain – the battle lines are being drawn between human and alien, and it seems nothing can stop this situation from descending into bloody and brutal conflict. This is Riff Maltin for Channel 27, handing you back to the studio with this final thought: do you know where your children are right now? Goodnight."

The red light on the hovercam blinked off, the transmission at an end.

"Is that it?" Conchita said between sobs.

"Yes, it's over now. Thank you so much, you were so brave," Riff said.

"Save the stomm for your viewers," she replied, wiping the tears from her face. All trace of hysteria was gone, hatred and grim determination the only emotions remaining. "I've got a fighting force to mobilise."

"But you were... you were..." Riff stammered.

"Falling apart before your eyes? Weeping my little heart out?"

"Well, yes–"

Conchita held open her hands to reveal two halves of a synthi-onion inside. "Rub these into your eyes and you'll weep your heart out too."

"Sweet Jovus! Then all of that was just an act," Riff realised.

"I want those scum out of Oswald Mosley, one way or another. Once everyone else sees that performance, they'll be ready to burn or butcher each and every one of those freaks on the top floor. And I'll be there to lead the mob!"

Deputy Sector Chief Temple was sorting reports on screen when Caine strolled into his office. "Ahh, Patrick. Glad to find you still here," she said.

"The sector never sleeps," Temple replied.

"Yes, I often feel the same." Caine leaned on the edge of her deputy's desk. "Look, I know we've had our differences in the past. You were probably expecting to be promoted to my position before I arrived and that didn't help matters. But if there's anything that's troubling you, I'm always available. You know that, don't you?"

"Yes, ma'am. Of course, ma'am."

"Good, good. Well, that was all I wanted to say. You've seemed a bit preoccupied lately, so I just thought..."

Temple smiled at her. "Everything's fine. There have been a lot of rumours flying around about the future of this sector house and its senior staff, but I've always had total confidence in you, ma'am. If there's ever anything I can do for you, just ask."

"Excellent! Well, I must be getting on," Caine said cheerfully, making her way out of the office.

She paused at the doorway. "I've just remembered, there was something else. Psi-Division precogs foresee more difficulties at Oswald Mosley. That place is like a magnet for trouble tonight. Perhaps you could take a few helmets down there and sort things out, once and for all?"

"Of course, ma'am. That shouldn't be a problem," Temple replied.

"Good, good. Well, carry on!"

With that she was gone, leaving her deputy trembling with fear at his desk. It was years since he'd seen active duty. He was now being volunteered to quell a potential riot! Temple held back the vomit just long enough to reach the nearest bathroom cubicle.

Miller emerged from the Med-Bay to find three SJS Judges waiting for her. She recognised their leader, a fearsome black woman called Jefferson. "Let me guess – the Special Judicial Squad wants to congratulate me on killing two dirty helmets and sparing your blushes for not having caught them in the act?"

"We need to see you," Jefferson replied, her face utterly emotionless. "Interrogation Room Eight, now!"

"Why do we need to go to an interrogation room? Are you three shy?" Miller's joke got no response from the trio. She looked down at the remains of her uniform. "Could I at least get changed first?"

"Interrogation Room Eight. Now."

"What can I say? You're really sweeping me off my feet. Tell you what, let's all go to Interrogation Room Eight and you can impress me further with this witty banter of yours." Miller began strolling towards the turbolift, the SJS trio following close behind her.

Werner Summerbee was an ugly man, both physically and emotionally. His face was pitted and scarred from a childhood infection of the deadly hybrid disease Rubellaria, his body left utterly hairless by the wasting illness. Few survived the contagion and Summerbee had spent long years quarantined until every trace of the disease was eradicated from his body. In that time he had only robots and books for company. His parents were mildly wealthy and were able to afford the exorbitant treatments necessary to save their son's life, but they believed lavishing presents upon him avoided the need of loving Werner.

By the age of ten he was recognised as having the intellect of a genius. What the tests did not quantify were his character flaws. Love and friendship meant nothing to him. He just wanted more. By twenty-five he had seized control of his parents'' business in a hostile takeover. By thirty-five he diversified into a dozen different areas such as terraforming planets for colonisation, developing new technology for the Justice Department and helping revitalise derelict sectors of the Big Meg. Summerbee Construction became Summerbee Industries, one of the world's richest companies. Soon its leader's wealth was such that he had to live in tax exile on the Moon; accountants only let him visit Mega-City One for thirty-seven hours a year.

Now, at the age of forty-one, Werner Summerbee was all but untouchable. His actions affected the lives of millions and his opinion could make or break almost any venture. But what he wanted most of all was a challenge. Just how far could be go before getting caught? Were there any limits left to him? So Summerbee was quietly delighted when woken with news of Dredd's imminent arrival. He dressed in a robe of pure black silk and dabbed a few drops of exquisite scent behind his ears. Satisfied with the foppish effect, Summerbee sauntered into the lounge to meet Dredd.

The room was a sprawling, open plan space with a central area delineated by capacious sofas. The Judge was standing beside one of them, his back ramrod straight, a house droid keeping him company.

"Mr Summerbee," the robot said. "This gentleman insists on seeing you."

"Very well, Giles. You may go for now." Summerbee waited until his house droid had retired from the room before approaching the new arrival. "You must be the legendary Judge Dredd. I've heard so much about you!" Summerbee pulled a slim silver case from his robe pocket and flipped it open to reveal a row of cigarettes inside. "Smoke?"

"The consumption or burning of tobacco is illegal outside authorised smokatoria," Dredd snapped, "as you well know."

"Of course." Summerbee strolled to one of the sofas and flopped down upon it. "I just wanted to see how you would react. Please, take a seat."

"I prefer to stand."

"Have it your own way." The businessman smiled warmly. "Now, how can I help you at this time of the morning? I suppose this isn't a social call."

"Hardly. Werner Summerbee, I have reason to believe you are an accomplice to a serious crime."

"Goodness! Me, involved with a crime? This shall be interesting."

"Less than an hour ago, Judge Riley from Sector House 87 died. Did you know him?" Dredd asked sternly.

"Can't say that I do, but then I meet so many people."

"You don't seem concerned that he's dead."

"In a city this large I'm sure tens of thousands, even

hundreds of thousands must die every day. It's a shame this poor fellow has passed away, but these things happen – even to Judges."

"Is that a threat, Summerbee?"

"Merely an observation."

"Before dying, Riley named you as a co-conspirator in the arson attack on Robert Hatch Block, an attack that killed hundreds of residents."

Summerbee looked idly at the ceiling. "I do believe I may have seen something about that on tri-D before going to bed. But I certainly know no more about it than that. How can I possibly be a co-conspirator, as you so quaintly put it?"

"Riley said you used him."

"Could you be more specific, Dredd? I've 'used' many people in my time, but that doesn't make me an accomplice to mass murder."

"Riley said you had shown him a file, a confidential Justice Department report about the circumstances surrounding the death of Riley's brother during the colony wars."

"Really? Well, this is a fascinating story but it's all news to me."

"You deny showing Riley this file?"

"I've already told you, I never met this unfortunate so I certainly couldn't have shown him any file. Besides, you say this was a confidential Justice Department document. How could I have access to such data?"

"Your company was the driving force behind efforts to terraform the R'qeen moon, triggering the colony wars. It's not impossible for Summerbee Industries to have obtained such files through bribery and corruption."

The genial smile faded from Summerbee's face. "I would choose your next words very carefully, Dredd. I employ the best lawyers on this planet and a successful slander suit against you could bankrupt this city."

"Is it true one of your companies supplies the new transponders that are being installed on all Justice Department vehicles, including Lawmaster motorcycles?"

"It may well be. Summerbee Industries is an umbrella organisation for dozens of smaller companies. Frankly, I am only aware of a fraction of the business we do. Why do you ask?"

"Before he died Riley disabled the transponder on a Lawmaster with ease – despite the fact most Street Judges are unaware their motorcycles even have such devices fitted."

Summerbee shrugged. "I'm terribly sorry, but I still can't see what that has to do with me."

"Last night a construction droid operated by one of your companies went amok at the corner of Merrison and Currie. Dozens, perhaps hundreds, of casualties were averted thanks to the quick action of my partner."

"Well, you must make sure they get a medal for that."

"Why does your company use notoriously unreliable Heavy Metal Kid robots when other construction droids are available?"

Summerbee stood up abruptly. "You'll have to ask the appropriate manager that question, Judge. Now I think I've been more than patient, especially considering the timing of this unannounced visit, but unless you plan to formally arrest me I must ask you to leave. I only have a few hours before my business here is concluded and I fly back to Luna-City."

"So you deny all involvement with the arson attack?"

"Absolutely. Use your birdie on me if you doubt my word."

Dredd grimaced and held up the lie detector concealed in his hand. "I already have. It confirms everything you have said. But that's no surprise, since the device is built and supplied to the department by Summerbee Industries. No doubt you have countermeasures fitted in this building to negate the effectiveness of my birdie."

"Less charitable minds might consider that to be a rather paranoid conclusion," Summerbee said. "Now I must insist you leave. So far I have been most tolerant but that time is past. You have made serious allegations based upon the slightest of circumstantial evidence." Werner smiled. "It must be unusual for you to find someone who cannot be easily intimidated or browbeaten into a confession. Most perps probably give up hope when they see the name on your badge. But I wonder what would happen if you encountered a criminal equal or superior to you?"

"Like you, Summerbee?"

"There you go again – another unfounded allegation! If you had any rockcrete evidence you would arrest me, instead of simply making snide remarks." The billionaire called to his house droid that bustled into the room. "Please escort our visitor to the front door. He is leaving now."

"I don't think so," Dredd replied, pulling handcuffs from his utility belt. "Werner Summerbee, I am arresting you on suspicion of conspiracy to commit murder."

"I'm sorry sir, but I cannot allow you to threaten my master," the droid announced. One of its mechanical hands fell away to reveal a gun barrel inside the arm. "Leave now or I will be forced to terminate you."

Keno had been watching the news broadcasts from Channel 27 with increasing trepidation. She had come to Oswald Mosley with her three broodlings, hoping for a fresh start like the other survivors from the fire. The violent welcome soon put paid to that hope. That fool Nyon seemed intent on stirring up more trouble. They were all stuck here on the top floor, and the only way out was by passing the human residents. Challenge enough people to a fight and some of them will oblige you, or so Keno had been taught by her broodmother. If only Nyon had listened to the same lesson.

It was Conchita's performance that convinced Keno it was time to get out while they still could. The human female seemed to be crying but she had madness and hate in her eyes. Keno went into the next room and roused her three broodlings, Coya, Aldre and Selmak. "Come on, wake up. We're going away on an adventure!" The young R'qeen grumbled about getting up so early but the eldest, Coya, soon took charge of his siblings.

Keno gathered what few belongings they had rescued from their old home at Robert Hatch and pushed these into a carryall. After making sure her offspring were warmly dressed, she opened the front door and led them out into the hall. The nearest turbolift was just round the corner but Nyon was already standing beside it, clamping an electronic pad over the doors.

"What are you doing?" Keno demanded.

"Sealing off the turbolift access," her sibling replied. "From now on nobody but us will be allowed up here. It's for our own safety."

"What happens if there's an emergency?"

"We use the stairs like everyone else." Nyon finished his task, only then noticing Keno and her brood were dressed to leave. "Where are you going?"

"I don't know," she admitted, "but anywhere else has to be safer than this place. The humans want blood and your outburst only provoked them further." Keno stretched out her long blue arms to hug her brood closer to her. "Come away with us, Nyon. Don't stay here."

But he shook his head, face set into a frown.

"Then let me take Lleccas and Misch somewhere safe," Keno pleaded. "You might be willing to die here but don't condemn the rest of your family to the same fate!"

"They stay with me. We stay together," Nyon insisted.

"Fine. Be stubborn, like you always are. At least reopen the turbolift so I can get my own brood out."

Nyon pressed a button on the pad he had clamped over the turbolift. The doors sealed themselves together, metal fusing with metal. "You'll have to take the stairs," he said, no hint of apology in his voice.

Keno sighed. "Nyon, when will you learn it's just as brave to walk away from a battle as it is to join one? To fight fools is to let them drag you down to their level." Her sibling did not reply, folding his arms. "Fine, on your own head be it," Keno snapped. "Coya, take Aldre and Selmak round to the emergency stairs. I'll be with you in a moment."

She watched as her eldest son led the other broodlings away before she turned to Nyon for the last time. "Farewell, Nyon. I hope I see you again." Keno kissed him on the cheek before hurrying away. Her brood were waiting at the top of the stairs, a hundred flights spiralling down through the centre of Oswald Mosley. "Coya, you lead the way. Aldre, hold on to Selmak's hand. I'll be right behind you." Keno and her family began the long descent.

"Let's go over your story again."

Jefferson loomed over Miller, who was sat at a table inside the interrogation room. The other SJS Judges were standing either side of the locked door, their faces devoid of emotion.

"It isn't a story, it's the truth, and I've been through it three times already!" Miller protested. "If you don't believe me, go ask Dredd. He should be back from interviewing Summerbee by now."

"Summerbee?" The leader of the SJS trio glanced at her colleagues. "Werner Summerbee?"

"Yes. Dredd said Riley had named Summerbee just before dying."

"Stomm! Why didn't you mention this before?"

Miller rolled her eyes. "Evidence gained by hearsay isn't admissible as a defence against SJS investigation, you should know that by now. Or don't they teach you that at goon squad training school?"

Jefferson turned away, cursing under her breath. "Jefferson to Control, put me through to Dredd." After a few seconds she swore again. "Well if you can't get him, contact SJS HQ. Tell them Operation Werner has been compromised. Send in the troops right away!"

"This is very interesting," Miller said with a smile. "So Summerbee is involved with judicial corruption? I think it's time you started talking yourself, Jefferson."

Billy-Bob was visiting the eighty-second floor for an impromptu meeting of the Citi-Def squad's upper levels representatives. As most con-apts in Oswald Mosley were cramped, it was impractical to gather all one hundred squad members in one place. Instead they divided into four teams of twenty-five. Billy-Bob was leader of the 76-100 team until a new representative from the top floor could be found. Being chosen to lead these two dozen men and women was a proud achievement for Billy-Bob, who had failed to excel in every other aspect of his life. Citi-Def had consumed him, driving away his wife and children; it had taken up every waking moment.

Billy-Bob had called the meeting after hearing about the broadcasts on Channel 27, gathering everyone outside the turbolifts on the eighty-second floor. "By now you've all seen the news about little Kasey Maguire being abducted by those alien freaks on the top floor," he began, to murmurs of assent from the others. "We don't know if she's still alive up there. If she is, I plan to rescue her personally and Grud help the alien who gets in my way. If she ain't alive, Grud help them all up there."

"Billy-Bob?" A long voice spoke out from the others. Aaron shuffled forward, his right hand in the air.

"Aaron, I done told you there's no need to raise your hand. Just say what you want to say – we're listening."

That brought a laugh from the others. Pressland might be the biggest among them physically, but he was not the brightest of men. Aaron smiled with them, not realising the joke was at his expense.

"Well, you and Sam and me all searched the top floor and we didn't find no humans up there. Plenty of those blue aliens and some other kinds, but no sign of this missing girl. And that was after she was supposed to have gone up there already. Where can she have been?"

"That's a good question," Billy-Bob conceded. "But those aliens, I've heard tell they can do fancy mind tricks, stranger than any Psi-Judge. So maybe they pulled a swift one on us, to make us think Kasey wasn't there when she was."

The others murmured in their agreement. Who knew what things those offworlders could do to you? "I say we go up there and search the top floor again," Billy-Bob announced, raising his voice over the hubbub. "I say we make those aliens surrender little Kasey Maguire. I say it's time we stopped talking and started fighting back. Are you with me?"

The squad members were nodding and clapping.

"I said, *are you with me?*" Billy-Bob demanded, raising his voice to a shout. The others shouted back their agreement. "All right, that's better!" their leader yelled. "Now, Aaron tells me those sneaky freaks have locked off turbolift access to the one hundredth floor, so we'll have to find another way up. I want half of you to go up the emergency stairs. The rest of us will go up to ninety-nine in turbolifts and meet you there. Let's do it!"

Keno and her brood had reached the eighty-fifth floor on their long trek down the emergency stairs when shouting voices began to drift up from below. "Sssh, listen!" Coya hissed, stopping his siblings' descent. The voices were calling out in the human language, the words strange but the violent emotions behind them all too evident. "They're coming up towards us," Coya realised.

Keno peered over the edge of the metal banister, down the circular stairwell. Below she could see human faces looking up, their features contorted with anger and hatred. One of them pointed at her and screamed to the others. The humans began running up the stairs, some clutching laser blades and other weapons. Keno shrank back, her worst fears confirmed.

"What do we do?" Coya asked, his face full of concern.

"We go back to the top floor. We'll be safe there," his broodmother decided. "Come, we must hurry!" She picked up Selmak and began carrying him up the stairs, Coya following with Aldre.

But they had only ascended two floors when more human voices could be heard echoing down the stairwell from above, getting ever closer. "We're too late," Keno gasped. "They're above us and below us. We can't get back to the top floor – we're trapped!"

Coya shook his head. "Not yet!" He opened the door to the eighty-seventh floor. "We can go in here and get the turbolift down. Come on!" The R'qeen boy grabbed his sibling and hurried through the doorway to the hallway beyond.

Keno shook her head in dismay. They should have walked down one flights of stairs and then taken the turbolift the rest of the way; she just hadn't thought of it. She prayed that mistake did not cost them dear. Still carrying Selmak, Keno followed her other broodlings. Coya was already running along the hallway. "The turbolifts are just down here!" he shouted.

Billy-Bob had taken the turbolift up to the ninety-ninth floor only to discover the aliens had also barricaded the emergency stairs leading up to the top level. But a shout from below soon erased that disappointment. "We got 'em!" Aaron shouted from below. "They're on the stairs above us!"

"Where are you?" Billy-Bob bellowed back.

"Just passing eighty-three!"

"Keep coming. Drive them up to us!" Billy-Bob sent the others down ahead of himself. He was about to follow when a thought occurred. What was to stop those freaks leaving the stairs and trying to escape by turbolift? He grinned as the answer came in a flash – he was going to stop them. Gripping his laser-blade tightly, Billy-Bob rushed back to the ninety-ninth floor. The Judges had deemed him too mentally unstable to see active duty in the colony wars. Well, this was his chance to prove them wrong.

Summerbee hurried back into the lounge, now dressed in a business suit and clasping a hastily packed suitcase. "So sorry to keep you waiting," he said to Dredd, "but I hadn't planned on leaving for the Moon until midday. Your intervention has forced my hand, bringing forward my departure from this city."

The Judge was still standing in the same place, but now he had his hands clasped behind his helmet. The house droid kept its weapon trained on him, ready to fire. "You won't get far," Dredd replied. "Control knows where I am. If I don't report in soon, back-up will be despatched to this address."

"Not in time to save you."

"Werner Summerbee!" a voice shouted from outside. "Your residence is surrounded by Justice Department forces. Surrender now or suffer the consequences!"

"You were saying?" Dredd asked, resting his hands on his helmet.

His captor moved to the window and peered out. "Not regular Judges; those look like SJS insignia. How tiresome."

"Take their advice, creep. Give yourself up and you might live long enough to swap this place for an iso-cube."

"A tempting offer but one I must decline," Summerbee replied. "Droid, keep Dredd busy here while I take my leave."

The droid turned to acknowledge its master's command. "Yes, Mr–"

Dredd ripped the helmet from his head and threw it at the robot's gun arm in one smooth movement, but the droid was already firing back.

Keno found Coya jabbing the buttons beside the turbolift, still waiting for one to arrive. The other broodlings were frightened, too terrified to speak. Keno thought about knocking on a con-apt door to ask for help, but decided it was too risky. What little she had seen of the human residents told her they were on their own in this building. Nobody wanted them here.

"This one's coming!" Coya shouted, pointing at one of the turbolifts.

Keno set down her youngest broodling. "Coya, keep hold of Aldre and Selmak. We have to stay together. Do you understand?"

The eldest of her brood nodded.

"The same goes for you two," Keno said, her back to the turbolift. Behind her the doors began to open and she swung round to check if it was safe. Keno never saw the weapon that killed her.

The first shot punched through the top of Dredd's shoulder pad, narrowly missing his head. The second creased his side, slicing through the Kevlar-reinforced uniform and punching a hole just below his ribs before exiting his back. The third hit the flying helmet and ricocheted away.

Dredd was already diving sideways behind one of the sofas, drawing his Lawgiver from its holster. "Armour piercing!" he shouted, activating the handgun's ammunition selection and drawing the requiring round into the barrel. The Judge was firing before his body hit the floor, the shots piercing the sofa in front of him and thudding into the house droid. It fell backwards with a metallic squawk, still firing into the air. By the time Dredd hit the carpet the droid was permanently disabled, its systems shutting down.

The entire sequence took less than five heartbeats.

Billy-Bob found himself confronted by one of the freaks. Instinctively he lashed out with the laser blade, slicing the monster's head clean off in a single movement. As the creature collapsed to the floor three more of its kind began screaming, their strange alien noises scratching the inside of Billy-Bob's mind. "I got one!" he shouted delightedly. "I got me one of these freaks!"

Two of the aliens ran off down the corridor but one stood over the still twitching body. It shouted something at Billy-Bob. The words were unknown but the meaning was clear – this little freak wanted to fight.

"Now you're talking my language," Billy-Bob said, blue light from the laser blade illuminating his face. He stepped out of the turbolift and advanced on the alien child.

Dredd was crouching by Summerbee when the SJS Judges burst into the luxury bungalow. Subsequent forensic investigation would prove the shot that killed the billionaire had been fired by the house droid. The internal security cams showed Summerbee being more than a little surprised when hit by the shot that ricocheted off Dredd's flying helmet. He had fallen backwards over his case and collapsed in a heap on the floor, blood pooling out from beneath him and soaking into an antique sheepskin rug.

"Why?" Dredd hissed in the dying man's ear. "Why did you show Riley that report about his brother?"

"Needed him… to help Stammers… The incendiary…"

"But why torch those aliens? What did you hope to gain?"

"Not the aliens… The building…" Summerbee gasped, then lay still.

The SJS Judges swarmed into the building but their quarry had eluded them. "What did he say?" their leader demanded.

Dredd put his helmet back on before replying. "What's it to you?"

"Summerbee Industries has been worrying the Special Judicial Squad for some time," Jefferson told Miller in the interrogation room. "The many companies that make up the Summerbee empire have their tentacles into far too many areas of the Justice Department for our liking: weapons research and development, supplying crucial equipment, even taking over construction of new department buildings. We began to hear whispers about Summerbee's underlings using bribery and corruption to win contracts. After what happened with the Mark Elevens, we didn't want a rerun."

Crime boss Nero Narcos had begun supplying the department with a new model of Lawgiver, through a legitimate company. The Mark Eleven had been a big improvement on the old handgun and thousands were issued to Street Judges as their standard issue weapon. But Narcos had installed a modification of his own. When he decided to seize control of the Big Meg, the crime boss sent a signal that meant each Mark Eleven would explode when fired. The result temporarily crippled many Street Judges and made the new Lawgivers unusable. It was a masterstroke and one the department was keen to avoid happening again.

"So you launched an investigation into Summerbee Industries," Miller said. "But Dredd and I stumbled upon something you didn't know about."

"We knew Summerbee was close to winning the contract to build a new Grand Hall of Justice. That's why he came back to Earth. He was due to sign the deal today. The new site is being announced at midday. Our sources suggest it was going to be here, in Sector 87."

"But that's not possible," Miller replied. "There's nowhere central enough that could be used for such a large..." Her voice trailed off as realisation dawned on her face. "Of course – Robert Hatch!"

Jefferson was one step behind her. "The alien ghetto that burned down?"

"That's what the fire was about. It had nothing to do with anti-alien xenophobia. It was to clear a site big enough for the new building!"

Jefferson nodded. "Yes, you're right. That must be it." The SJS Judge stopped, concentrating on a message being relayed to her helmet radio. "That's a roj – Jefferson out."

"What is it? Is Dredd all right?" Miller asked.

"Yes, just a flesh wound. Summerbee is dead." Jefferson took off her helmet and threw it against a wall in frustration. "Drokk it! Six months of investigative work down the drain!"

"But if Summerbee is dead, isn't the threat dead too?"

"Maybe," Jefferson told Miller. "But what about the corrupt Judges that were helping him? They're still hidden within the system!"

Aldre and Selmak were huddled against a door, trying not to listen to the screams of Coya dying. A jumble of humans burst into the corridor from the emergency stairs. One of them spotted the two R'qeen children and shouted to the others. They surrounded Aldre and Selmak, a selection of weapons in their hands. Aldre hugged Selmak to her chest so he couldn't see what was coming and then closed her own eyes for the last time.

05:00

Dredd was returning to Sector House 87 after agreeing to keep details of the SJS's investigation secret for now. He was travelling via the Anton Diffring Overzoom when a call came through from Control. "Request you divert to Oswald Mosley. Deputy Sector Chief Temple is taking a dozen Judges there to quell a new disturbance and Caine wants you there as back-up."

"I've had about enough of this," Dredd said. "Control, put me through to Sector Chief Caine. It's time I had words with her." Dredd pulled into a Judges-only stop while waiting for the Sector Chief to call him back.

"Caine to Dredd – I understand you wish to speak with me?"

"That's a roj."

"Make it snappy. I haven't got all night to be dealing with the complaints of a single Street Judge."

"Fine by me," Dredd replied. "What I have to say won't take long. Tell me this – what the hell is going on, Caine?"

"Could you be more precise?"

"You've had me running from pillar to post since I set foot in this sector, traipsing back and forth to Oswald Mosley."

"Are you challenging my right to choose which Judges receive which assignments?"

"No, but I–"

"Perhaps you think the problems at Oswald Mosley are beneath you?"

"No, that isn't–"

"Then what the drokk is your problem, Dredd?" Caine snarled. "I said you'd be trouble and that's exactly what you are. You and Miller caused a riot on Anton Diffring, shutting that overzoom down for several hours."

"It had already been closed by a multi-vehicle pile-up–"

"You've flooded the holding cubes with a hundred religious kooks, all thanks to your grandstanding tactics!"

"I was not–"

"Rather than talk them down, you let them jump off Maurice Waldron and then you jumped off after them! If that isn't grandstanding, I don't know what is! You called the Chief Judge's office to lodge a complaint about me. When I asked you to defuse the situation at Oswald Mosley you bungled that too."

"The Citi-Def squad was forced to stand down. It was a final warning that the whole block would be placed under curfew if trouble started again," Dredd replied, finally getting to finish a sentence. "What more was I supposed to do?"

"Don't you try to deny your mistakes! We've got pre-cogs saying there will be a riot in that block within an hour and a reporter called Riff Maltin's broadcasting inciteful footage from inside the building."

"I said Maltin should be–"

"Don't interrupt me either! I'm still your superior, despite your best efforts to steal my job! Last but by no means least I learn you've been involved in the killing of two of my Street Judges. Perhaps you'd care to explain that?"

"Stammers and Riley were dirty badges," Dredd snarled. "You should have known that and acted against them sooner! But you've let your own paranoia and insecurities blind you to what's been going on under your nose!"

"It's always somebody else's fault with you, isn't it, Dredd? Well, not anymore! I'm recommending the SJS launch a full investigation into your behaviour. I'm going to have them so far up your ass you'll need a teleporter to take a dump!"

"My conscience is clear," Dredd maintained.

"Really?" Caine said, laughing bitterly. "Well, since you helped Miller kill two of my best Street Judges, I suggest you go to Oswald Mosley and try to take their places. Unless that's beneath you?"

"No, but I–"

"No buts, Dredd. Just do what you're told for once! Caine out!"

Temple didn't know whether to be excited or terrified. It was years since he had seen active duty. A dozen Judges were now waiting for his order to move into Oswald Mosley. They had erected a cordon around the building so all the skedways and pedways nearby were empty – for now. Keeping bystanders out was easy at this time of the morning. When the sun rose and the city awoke it would get considerably more difficult.

Jumbled reports were emerging from inside the building, with residents on the eighty-fifth calling the department about a bloody incident in the hallway. At least three aliens were dead, apparently butchered by vigilantes. More worrying were the pictures being broadcast by Channel 27.

Reporter Riff Maltin had been chosen by the Oswald Mosley Citi-Def as its official war correspondent. Dressed in camouflage with his own flak jacket and helmet, Riff was now providing a running commentary on events within the block. While Tek-Division tried to jam the signal and prevent anti-alien violence from spreading to other parts of the city, Temple watched the live pictures in an H-Wagon parked outside the building.

"Breaking news from inside strife-torn Oswald Mosley Block!" Riff announced. "The Citi-Def squad has accepted my credentials as a journalist and agreed to me being embedded with them. That means I will be able to provide live and exclusive coverage of this crisis as it unfolds. We already know the Justice Department has surrounded the building and is letting nobody in or out. I don't know how long these broadcasts can continue before they are jammed or censored, but everything that happens here will be recorded. Even if this signal is not escaping the building, my footage shall be released at a later date exclusively on Channel 27! Now, back to the studio."

Temple switched off the tri-D and left the H-Wagon. His squad gathered around him. "What do you want us to do?" a black female Judge called Washington asked. She had travelled to the scene on her Lawmaster after being diverted there from other duties. "It'll be dawn soon. Once residents in the surrounding blocks wake up and discover what's happening, the trouble will only spread."

"Tek-Division will soon have that signal jammed," Temple replied. He refused to countenance the use of immediate force. "If we could just gain access to the top floor and prove the missing girl isn't there; that would take the heat out of the situation."

"And how do you suggest we do that, sir?" Washington said. "The aliens have sealed off the emergency stairs and all turbolift access."

Temple realised the solution was just behind him. "Simple! I'll go up in the H-Wagon and talk some sense into these offworlders. Once they see I mean them no harm, they're bound to let me in."

Washington shifted uneasily at this, glancing at some of the other Judges. "Are you sure about this, sir?"

Temple nodded happily. "Yes, definitely. If we can resolve this situation peacefully, it will be quite a feather

in my cap!" He got back into the H-Wagon, his uncer-
tainties banished. "Washington, you'd best stay here and
keep an eye on things from the ground. The rest of you
are coming with me."

The other Judges reluctantly clambered in after Temple.
Washington closed the side door of the vehicle once they
were inside. "I've got a bad feeling about this," she
muttered under her breath.

The H-Wagon lifted into the air as Dredd arrived on his
Lawmaster. "Where are they going?" he asked.

"On a fool's errand," Washington replied. "Temple
thinks he can talk the aliens into surrendering."

Dredd used his helmet radio to call the deputy Sector
Chief. "I've just arrived as back-up. Where do you want
me?"

"Stay where you are and take no action," Temple
replied. "That's a direct order, Dredd. Caine's told me
what you're like. Temple out!"

Riff was admiring himself in a mirror when the hunting
party arrived with its trophy. The reporter decided he
looked good in camouflage, and he adjusted his combat
helmet to a jauntier angle. He was due back on air in a
few minutes with an update. Yablonsky had been full of
praise for Riff's work so far but reminded him that most
viewers were still asleep. The big ratings would not kick
in until after dawn when the slumbering citizens woke to
what was happening at Oswald Mosley. Already the feed
was that Channel 27 was being picked up on a dozen
larger stations in other sectors. It was only a matter of
time before the broadcast spread citywide. Riff smiled at
that – only a matter of time.

"Where's that dang fool with the hovercam?" a gruff
voice demanded outside the bathroom. Riff emerged to
find Conchita's con-apt filled with Citi-Def squad
members. The person speaking was a thin, wiry man

clutching a heavy carryall. "There he is! My name's Jolie, Billy-Bob Jolie. I'm head of the 76-100 team. Boy, have we got a story for you! Do you like hunting at all?"

"Can't say I've ever–"

"Get your hovercam rolling and feast your eyes on this little beauty," Billy-Bob said, digging his hands into the carryall. He struggled to get the contents out, shaking the bag vigorously until it fell free. Billy-Bob proudly help up the severed head of an R'qeen female. "Cut it off myself, only took one swipe. Used a laser blade, so that it cauterised the wound and stopped the blood getting everywhere. What do think? Is this newsworthy or what?"

Riff could feel his insides pulsating. It had been hours since he last ate but what little remained in his stomach was in a sudden hurry to leave again. "Oh my Grud," he gurgled, clamping one hand over his mouth.

Billy-Bob jerked a thumb towards the door. "We got the rest of the body outside if you'd like to film that too. I'm thinking of getting this one stuffed and mounted when all this is over. You know any good taxidermists?"

Riff couldn't hold back any longer. He ran back into the bathroom, vomit already spilling out between his fingers. "Excuse me!" he shouted.

"That's all right, we can wait," Billy-Bob said. "I'd have shown you the three little alien critters we killed too, but the boys got over-excited and made a real mess of them. Not much left to see, if you know what I mean. Besides, they were so small we should have just thrown them back."

Riff wretched again and again.

Billy-Bob grabbed hold of the hovercam. "Say, this red light just came on. Does that mean I'm on the air?"

Nyon was leaning against the doorway to the emergency stairs, listening intently. He had sealed it like the turbolift doors but still feared the humans would find a way through. Most of the other aliens were asleep and unaware of what was happening. Nyon did not like to think what their reaction would be to his actions, but he would deal with them when the time came. For now he was more worried about the safety of Lleccas and Misch.

His pairling called from the doorway of their con-apt. "Come away from there, Nyon! You need to sleep – we all do."

She was right, of course. Nyon couldn't recall the last time he had rested or eaten. The fire at Robert Hatch seemed like a lifetime ago instead of just a few hours. He returned to the con-apt. The first glints of dawn had begun to lighten the skyline outside the floor-to-ceiling windows. But there was something else out there, a dark shape moving towards them...

"My name is Deputy Sector Chief Temple!" an amplified voice bellowed from beyond the window. A spotlight swung round to illuminate the interior of the con-apt from outside, dazzling Nyon and Lleccas. "I need to talk to you!" the voice continued in Allspeak. "Can you understand me?"

Nyon peered between gaps in his fingers, trying to see what was outside the window. He could just discern the shape of an H-Wagon, hovering near the top of the building. The R'qeen leader went to the glasseen wall and opened one of the windows. "Get that light away from us!" he bellowed, raising his voice to be heard above the H-Wagon's engines.

"Move that light!" the voice outside commanded. The dazzling spotlight shifted sideways, enabling Nyon to see who was speaking. A human in the uniform of a Judge was clinging to a walkway extended from the H-Wagon.

"What do you want?" Nyon asked.

"We need access to the top floor of your building. A girl is missing and we need to prove to the other residents she is not in there with you."

Nyon almost laughed. "The humans have searched here already. Once was enough. No more!"

"I understand you have barricaded yourselves inside."

"That was for our own safety. Two humans set fire to Robert Hatch; my broodling saw it in their minds. Hundreds of our own kind died in that fire but no more will die this night."

"If you let us in, we can protect you," Temple offered.

Nyon heard Lleccas gasp behind him. She was watching the con-apt's tri-D set, a luxury their previous home had not afforded them. Nyon looked at the images being broadcast. The same human who had threatened him earlier was appearing on the tri-D now, proudly holding up the severed head of Keno.

Nyon flew into a rage, hurling objects at the tri-D until it exploded. Lleccas tried to comfort him but Nyon pushed her away. Instead he returned to the open window and screamed at the H-Wagon about what he had just seen. "No human sets foot on this floor while we still have life!" Nyon vowed.

"You are being foolish!" Temple retorted. "What if there is another fire?"

"Then we will burn and it will be on your conscience, human!" Nyon pulled the window shut and locked it. He found Lleccas standing beside him, sadness and regret in her eyes. Neither of them noticed Misch watching them from the doorway of her room.

"They killed Keno, butchered her," Nyon snarled, his face risen with anger and sorrow. "What have those monsters done to her brood?"

Misch closed the door quietly and realised Kasey was standing nearby. "I thought you were asleep," the R'qeen girl whispered.

"Loud voices outside woke me. What did they say?"

"The humans want to search the top floor again." Her voice trailed off.

"For me?" Kasey asked. "Then I must go back."

"You can't."

"I know my mom will hit me again, but that's–"

"No, I mean you can't go back, even if you wanted to. My father has barricaded us all in on the top floor. We're stuck here."

"Oh," Kasey said.

Misch gave her a hug. They needed each other more than ever now.

Temple retreated into the belly of the H-Wagon, unsure what to do next. They could try and storm the top floor, but that would not be easy. If the aliens were holding the girl hostage, she would certainly be dead before Judges could rescue her and that would turn the block into a war-zone. Anti-alien hysteria could spread and engulf the sector, perhaps the entire city. No, he would not be responsible for starting that. If the aliens would not budge, perhaps the human residents could be persuaded to take a step back.

The Deputy Sector Chief called Control on his helmet radio. "Get me in contact with the leader of Oswald Mosley Citi-Def. I don't care how you do it, but I need to talk to them right away!"

Conchita returned to her con-apt to find Billy-Bob and his cronies from the 76-100 team holding an impromptu news conference, using the hovercam to film each other. "What the drokk are you doing?" she demanded. "Where's Riff?"

"In your bathroom, puking his guts out," Billy-Bob said with a smile. "Where the hell have you been?"

"Working with the other team leaders to develop a strategy for reclaiming the top floor – a meeting you should have been at!"

He held up Keno's severed head. "Yeah? Well, while you were busy talking, we were taking action. Got us a count of four so far, including this one."

"Get that out of my sight," Conchita warned. "I lead the Citi-Def squad, not you, and I decide when we take action. Is that clear?"

Billy-Bob winked at his team members. "Well, I'm not so sure about that anymore. Seems to me that we've just–" His next words were cut off by a sharp intake of breath as Conchita grabbed his testicles in her right fist and began squeezing them together.

"Now, you were saying?" she asked, smiling sweetly.

"Nothing…" Billy-Bob gasped. "I wasn't saying nothing."

"That's better. Now, who's in charge of this Citi-Def squad?" She gave his testicles a violent twist, enticing a shriek of pain from him.

"Y–you are!"

"And don't you forget it, drokker!" she growled in his ear. Conchita abruptly released Billy-Bob and stepped clear as he collapsed to the floor, whimpering in pain. "Anybody else want to challenge my authority?" The rest of the 76-100 team quickly denied any such ambitions. "Good. Now get the drokk out of my con-apt and take this rat-weasel with you."

They were all gone when Riff emerged from the bathroom, still wiping his mouth clean. "Conchita, you're back – thank Grud! Those goons that were in here before…"

"I got rid of them," she replied. "I've been talking with the–"

The reporter pressed a hand to his earpiece. "Hold it, I'm getting a message from Channel 27. Have you got a vidphone here?"

Conchita grimaced. "No, I smashed it earlier, Why?"

"Seems the Justice Department want to talk to you.

Also my news editor has a message for you from some-one called Stummers?"

"Stammers?" she suggested.

"Could be. He's got something you want. After that, the message is just gibberish, a bunch of numbers and letters all jumbled together."

Conchita was perplexed. "Something I want?" she wondered, before her eyes widened. "The code. That must be the override code! What is it?"

Riff relayed the rest of the message to her. "What about the Justice Department? My news editor says a Judge called Temple still wants to talk."

"They can wait. I've got more important things to do right now." Conchita strode purposely from her con-apt. Riff and his hovercam followed.

Dredd and Washington were still in position outside Oswald Mosley, looking up at the H-Wagon. It had hung in the air for several minutes without changing position or taking any visible action. "For Grud's sake, what is Temple doing up there?" Dredd growled.

"He hasn't been out from behind a desk in years," Washington said. "I don't know why the chief sent him to sort this mess out. We should be inside now, rounding up the ring leaders and imposing discipline before the rest of the block wakes and things get out of hand."

They were interrupted by a high-pitched screeching from above, then the sound of Temple clearing his throat. "Testing, testing, one, two, testing."

"What the drokk is he doing?" Washington wondered. "He'll wake up the whole block if he uses the H-Wagon's public address system!"

"I think that's the idea," Dredd replied, scowling with dismay.

"This is a message for all residents of Oswald Mosley Block. My name is Patrick Temple and I am Deputy Chief of Sector 87. As of now your block is being placed under curfew. No citizen may enter or leave the building without permission of the Justice Department. Furthermore, no resident may leave his or her con-apt without permission until the curfew is lifted. That is all!"

After another ear-piercing squeal of static the speakers shut down again. Washington and Dredd exchanged an unhappy look. "The precogs predicted there'd be a riot and Temple has just ensured that prophecy comes true," Washington said. "Now the stomm really hits the fan."

In the basement of Oswald Mosley, Conchita punched the code supplied by Stammers into a keypad. The reinforced steel and rockcrete door to the armoury swung open, revealing a vast array of weapons and ammunition stored inside. Conchita turned to the other Citi-Def squad members crowding the basement. "I want only six people in the armoury at a time. There's no need to fight each other for the best weapons, there's plenty for everybody. All of you take a gas mask. The Judges have already used stumm against us once tonight, they'll probably try it again."

Riff was standing near her, his hovercam capturing every moment. As the squad members began raiding the armoury's contents, he pulled Conchita aside for a quick interview. "Ms Maguire, you're the leader of Oswald Mosley Citi-Def. Why have you raided the block's cache of weapons, in clear breach of Justice Department guidelines?"

She stared directly into hovercam. "We no longer recognise the authority of the Justice Department. It was not willing to intervene and save my daughter from the alien scum on the top floor of our block. But one Judge, a true patriot, was ready to break the rules and give us the code for this armoury. Now, armed and ready, we will take the Law into our own hands!"

In the garage at Sector House 87, Brady was watching the live Channel 27 transmission from Oswald Mosley. What Judge would be foolish enough to give the armoury code to those trigger-happy kooks? His thoughts were interrupted by a call from outside the sector house. "Brady, I need your help again," Dredd said. "PSU has been monitoring a broadcast–"

"About Oswald Mosley Citi-Def getting the judicial code for the armoury? I was wondering when you'd call," the Tek-Judge replied. "I'll start a trace on all incoming calls and messages to that block."

"If a Judge did send that code to Maguire, it's doubtful they did it directly," Dredd suggested. "Try to identify any third parties who could have helped."

"I'll contact Channel 27, see if they have been passing on messages via their reporter inside," Brady offered. "But what if they refuse to help?"

"Remind them they live in Mega-City One, where freedom of the press is a privilege, not a right. They give you full cooperation or I'll extract it from them personally – with my daystick."

"That's a roj, Dredd. I'll get back to you."

Ken Amidou was the first Citi-Def squad member to emerge from the armoury. While his colleagues were selecting bat-glider suits and body armour, Amidou was content just to grab a gas mask and a shoulder-mounted rocket launcher. The portly citizen shoved three missiles into the belt of his camouflage trousers, hitching the elasticised waistband up above his ample belly. "Let's see how the Judges like a taste of their own medicine," he muttered.

A quick trip in the turbolift took Amidou back to his con-apt on the seventy-third floor. Once inside he ripped the seal off the rocket launcher and began reading the simple instructions printed on its side: PLACE MISSILE INSIDE LAUNCHER – TAKE AIM – PULL TRIGGER – BOOM! It all seemed simple enough. Amidou plucked one of the missiles from his belt and dropped it into the launcher's long barrel. It fit snugly inside, clicking into place.

The Citi-Def member carried the launcher to his living room window and looked out. Yes, the H-Wagon was still hovering outside, but it had moved sideways. To get a better shot Amidou needed to fire from the bedroom. He marched into the next room and clambered over the bed, startling his obese wife, Gerta.

"Ken! Where are you going with that thing?"

"Just a little target practice, my beloved," Amidou replied soothingly. "You go back to sleep, nothing to be alarmed about."

"Nothing to be alarmed about? It's five in the morning!"

"Hush now, sweetness. I've got a job to do." He pushed open the window and pointed the rocket launcher out into the cool early morning air.

"Come back to bed," Gerta urged. "I'll give you a job to do."

"Not just now, dear." Amidou closed one eye and took aim, sighting down the barrel at the bulky profile of the H-Wagon. He closed his finger around the trigger, ready to pull. "Be with you in a minute…" Amidou pulled the trigger. The missile flew out of the launcher and through the opposite wall of the bedroom. It continued through five more walls before exploding in a con-apt on the far side of the block, incinerating the residents of 737.

Amidou opened both his eyes again and looked out of the window. The H-Wagon was still intact, no damage visible on it in the blue light of near dawn. "Strange. I followed all the instructions – that should have worked." A podgy finger tapped him on the shoulder. Amidou turned in time to see the fist his unhappy wife threw at him, but not soon enough to avoid it. He sunk to the floor, quite unconscious from the mighty blow.

Gerta picked up the rocket launcher and took one of the remaining missiles. "You want a job done properly, get a woman to do it," she said, slotting the rocket into place. Making sure she had the arrows labelled AIM THIS WAY facing out the window, Gerta got a bead on the H-Wagon and closed her finger around the trigger.

"What do you mean, you don't know what caused that explosion?" Temple demanded. "A con-apt inside Oswald Mosley just got incinerated and I want to know why!" He was shouting at three Tek-Judges manning consoles inside the H-Wagon, but his words were lost among many others on various channels.

"Temple, this is Dredd," a familiar voice shouted into helmet radios. "What the drokk are you doing? Did you just open fire on Oswald Mosley?"

"Dredd, this is Temple. No, we did not open fire! Now get off this line—"

"Sir, I think you ought to see this," one of the Tek-Judges interrupted.

"Will you be quiet?" the Deputy Sector Chief demanded. "I am trying to maintain discipline here and I will not be interrupted."

"But sir, there's a woman on the seventy-third floor. She seems to be—"

"I don't care what she seems to be doing. I only want to know what caused that explosion!" Temple replied.

"Looks like a missile went off inside one of the con-apts, origin unknown," another Tek-Judge shouted. "No heat trail leading into the building."

"Well, that's something," Temple said. "We don't want another block getting involved with this. We've got enough problems—"

"Sir, this woman: she's got a rocket launcher. She's about to fire at us!"

"What?" That got Temple's attention. "Why didn't you say so earlier? Control, this is Temple. We are under attack fr-"

But his next words were never uttered. The rocket punched a hole through one of the H-Wagon's windows and exploded inside the cabin, killing everyone inside almost instantly. The fireball blew out the windows, spraying glasseen and other shrapnel across five blocks nearby. Its engines destroyed, the H-Wagon began to fall from the sky.

Gerta smiled in satisfaction as the rocket penetrated the H-Wagon. As she bent down to remonstrate with her husband, she missed the fireball blossoming outwards from the exploding vehicle towards their con-apt. "See? All you had to do was point this thing the right way and you-"

Her next words were lost as the flames scorched the skin from her flesh, then the flesh from her bones, and then Gerta Amidou and her husband were no more.

Dredd and Washington were right underneath the H-Wagon when it was hit. Washington stared at the spectacle, mesmerised by the fireball exploding outwards from the vehicle overhead. "Sweet Jovus..."

Dredd gunned his Lawmaster into life. "Come on, Washington – we've got to move!" But the other Judge remained where she was, transfixed.

"But it's... it's impossible..." she whispered.

Dredd leaned across and activated the engine on Washington's bike before yelling at her. "We've got to move! Go!" He tore away, the tyres on his motorcycle squealing in protest. The noise finally jolted Washington into life and she accelerated after him, just clearing the deserted skedway before the burning remains rained down upon her.

A fresh explosion tore the H-Wagon apart as it hit the ground, fragments flying out in all directions. A shard of metal sliced through the rear tyre of Washington's Lawmaster, sending the bike careering out from under her. The Judge skidded along the ground at high speed before slamming headfirst into a rockcrete wall with a sickening thud. Dredd slammed on his brakes and ran back to Washington with a med-kit, the scene lit brighter than day as the ammunition inside the crashed H-Wagon exploded. But Washington's helmet had cracked open like an egg, a crimson pool forming beneath her.

"Dredd to Control, all hell's just broken loose at Oswald Mosley. We lost the H-Wagon and everyone inside. Looked like it was hit by a rocket fired from inside the block. The vehicle has crashed in front of the building, killing another badge on the ground in the process. I'm the only Judge left alive on the scene! I need everything – Meds, Teks and back-up – and I need it now!"

"Roj that, Dredd. Units already on their way!"

He looked at the carnage around him. "Send more," Dredd growled. "And tell Sector Chief Caine I'm assuming control of this crime scene. If she wants to argue with me about it, she'll have to come down here herself. Dredd out!"

The detonation on the seventy-third floor of Oswald Mosley had woken most people inside the building, as the shockwave had sent shudders throughout the structure. The explosion that incinerated the H-Wagon woke up the rest of the residents. Those on the eastern side of the block hurried to their windows in time to see the Justice Department vehicle slowly tumble downwards, turning end over end as it fell to the deserted skedway below. Few who witnessed this terrible spectacle would forget the image of the burning H-Wagon's descent.

On the top floor Misch and Kasey ran out into the central room of the con-apt, terrified by what they were witnessing. Lleccas embraced her broodling while Nyon stared in dismay at the human child. "Who is this?" he demanded.

"Kasey," Misch said. "I hid her when the men came."

Nyon sunk to the floor, his head in his hands. "Oh no…"

"She's my friend," Misch explained. "Her broodmother hurts her. I could feel how unhappy Kasey was, so I told her to come up here."

Lleccas put her broodling down. "Do you realise what you've done? We told the humans she was not here. Your broodfather has…" Her voice trailed off, as she realised the enormity of what they faced. "We cannot go back now. Even if we wanted to, we cannot send her back. And if we did, it would just prove the humans were right and we were liars."

Misch began crying, her unhappiness setting Kasey off too, even though the human girl had understood nothing of the R'qeen words. "I'm sorry, I didn't mean to…" Misch sobbed, her emotions overwhelming her words. "I'm sorry."

Lleccas embraced her daughter and then drew Kasey to her as well. "It's all right, it will be all right," the broodmother said soothingly.

Nyon looked up at her from the floor. "Will it?"

Riff was still in the basement with Conchita as the last weapons were removed from the armoury, so he didn't see the H-Wagon get hit. A slight tremor ran through the building's superstructure as the vehicle exploded but it was little more than a twitch.

"What was–" Riff began, but his question was cut short by the scream of metal and rockcrete when the H-Wagon crashed outside.

"Sweet Jovus, what's going on out there?" Conchita wondered. Mikell Fields ran down into the basement, pointing behind himself.

"Somebody just took out an H-Wagon! It's crash-landed outside the lobby. No survivors!" he gibbered.

"Terrif," Conchita hissed as she strapped a flame-thrower to her back. "They couldn't maintain discipline, could they? Our fight is with the aliens, not the Judges! Now the whole department will come down on us."

Riff picked up a discarded gas mask and looped it over his head. "What are you going to do?" he asked the Citi-Def leader.

She noticed the hovercam was still watching her. "In every battle there are casualties. But our war with the aliens is just beginning. Let's go!" Conchita ran up the stairs, a gas mask in one hand and a heavily laden carryall in the other. Riff went after her, determined not to lose his place on the front line.

Miller was changing into a fresh uniform when the news about the H-Wagon reached Sector House 87. She ran to the briefing room where all available Judges were being assembled at Caine's request. The Sector Chief was visibly shaken by what had happened but warned against retaliatory action. "As far as we know, the attack on the H-Wagon was an isolated incident by a single individual from the Oswald Mosley Citi-Def. Make no mistake, they will be made to pay for what they have done. But our first priority is to restore law and order in that block. Punishments will be handed after that is achieved, not before or during. Do I make myself clear?"

"Yes ma'am!" the gathered Judges yelled back at her.

Caine nodded her approval. "All right, now Dredd's the only helmet still alive on the scene. Others nearby are scrambling to his position. But we need a cohesive strategy to retake control of Oswald Mosley. Miller?"

"Yes ma'am?"

"I want you to form a strike team. Choose two dozen of your colleagues and get suited up. The Citi-Def members have obtained access to the block armoury, so they've got enough weaponry to start a small war. Your job is to stop them. Prepare for the worst. Got it?"

"Yes ma'am!"

"Everyone else, listen up. If this lawlessness spreads, we can kiss this sector goodbye. Miller and her squad will be fighting it at the source. Your job is making sure nobody else takes this incident as a sign that we're fair game or that the Law has forsaken 87. Crush all resistance, be utterly ruthless. At least a dozen Judges have already died tonight. Don't let those deaths be in vain. Show the people of this sector and this city who is in charge. Dismissed!"

Dredd emptied Washington's utility belt to replenish his own supplies of extra ammunition, stumm gas grenades and other equipment. Using a tool from his bike he disabled the palm recognition unit on her Lawgiver so anyone could fire it safely. He then added a fresh clip of ammunition. After switching his motorcycle to voice-activated remote control, Dredd lowered the respirator on his helmet. He rolled three canisters of stumm gas into the lobby of Oswald Mosley, the interior quickly filling with the noxious yellow gas. No doubt the Citi-Def members were wearing masks but the canisters' contents would still obscure the vision of those guarding the entrance.

"Dredd to bike," he snarled into his helmet radio, "Enter the lobby – now!"

The Lawmaster revved its engine and roared into the gas cloud. A hail of bullets blazed past the motorcycle, uselessly passing through the air where its rider should be. But their direction gave a good clue to the location of those inside. After letting his bike draw the enemy out, Dredd ran into lobby, both Lawgivers blazing. His remorseless advance was rewarded with the screams of men and women dying. Dredd was taking no prisoners.

Conchita and Riff had already reached the fiftieth floor when Dredd launched his attack on the lobby. The Citi-Def leader received a brief progress report from Fields, who was guarding the ground floor entrance with half a dozen others.

"Maguire, we're under attack! At least two Judges, maybe more. We can't hold them back, we–arghhhh!" The radio cut to static, then the sound of heavy boots approaching. Someone picked up Field's discarded radio.

"This is Judge Dredd. Who am I speaking to?"

"Conchita Maguire, leader of Oswald Mosley Citi-Def. We have taken control of this block and are ready–"

"Listen to me, Maguire. Stand down your teams or you will all suffer the consequences. A dozen Judges have just been murdered by a rocket attack launched from within this building. The penalty for killing a Judge is death. Surrender now, all of you, and I'll commute that sentence to life in the cubes. Otherwise I shoot to kill. What's your decision?"

"You're just one man, Dredd."

"But dozens of other Judges are on their way here now. You've got two minutes at most before Oswald Mosley is surrounded and your precious block becomes your tomb. I'm giving you one last chance. What do you say?"

Riff could hear Dredd's words, utterly implacable. The Judge would kill them all if necessary. Riff willed Conchita to listen to reason, but she was already shaking her head.

"This is our block now. The Justice Department refused to help rescue my daughter, so Oswald Mosley no longer recognises your authority!"

"Wrong answer," Dredd replied. "You just signed your death warrant."

The radio cut to static. Conchita switched frequencies. "Maguire to Citi-Def members. Judge Dredd has entered the building and is threatening to kill all of us. The solution is simple – kill him before he kills us. Maguire out!"

"Are you sure that's wise?" Riff asked.

Conchita drew a pistol and aimed it at Riff's head. "Are you questioning my judgement, Maltin?"

"No, no! I just–"

"Then you better take this." She threw the handgun to him. "You're going to need it to get out of here alive. Now come on: we're going to the one hundredth floor and nothing is going to stop us!"

Having cleared the lobby, Dredd broke open the Oswald Mosley environmental control box. Inside were all the building's failsafe systems, including secondary power, air conditioning and the anti-suicide nets.

"Dredd to Control, I need the judicial override invoked for air conditioning within Oswald Mosley."

"Roj that. Overriding system now."

"Got it. Dredd out." He was now able to vary the contents of the air being pumped into each con-apt and corridor. After the anarchy of Block Mania more than two decades before, the department had installed concussion gas cylinders in each citi-block. The contents could render every citizen inside a building unconscious for hours. Dredd began flooding each floor with the gas. Those Citi-Def members who kept on their masks would not be affected, but it should keep all the other residents out of the way while the block was subdued.

On the top floor of the building Nyon was arguing with the other alien families: two R'qeen, one from Wolfren and Gruchar the arthropod. The explosions had woken and frightened them all. But when they tried to leave they were dismayed to find themselves barricaded in, trapped on the one hundredth floor by Nyon's conflict with the human residents.

The argument had raged for many minutes and showed no signs of abating. It was only the gas seeping in from the ventilation shaft that stopped it. Gruchar was the first to react, his head lolling forward and his limbs sagging sleepily. Eventually the arthropod rolled over to his back and stayed there, snoring loudly. Nyon realised what was going on.

"Something in the air!" he shouted. "The humans are trying to gas us all! Quickly, use your respiratory bypasses." All R'qeen had the ability to breathe by two distinct methods: taking air into their lungs like humans or by filtering air through the fat tendrils of flesh that hung from the back of their heads. The latter method required much more concentration and was only used in environments where the atmosphere was close to poisonous.

The family of creatures from Wolfren had no such capacity and quickly succumbed to the concussion gas seeping onto the top floor. Nyon returned to his con-apt to find Kasey also out cold, being nursed by Misch and Lleccas. They had realised what was happening and were breathing via their tendrils. "Who is doing all this?" Misch asked.

It was then that the first wave of bat-gliders began attacking the top floor.

06:00

Billy-Bob had volunteered to lead the bat-glider attack on the one hundredth floor, hoping to redeem himself after the incident in Conchita's con-apt. That slitch might believe he was a redneck who liked to kill first and think later, but he wanted to show the others he was the right person to take her place. Billy-Bob had his doubts Conchita was getting out of this mess alive, especially if he got the chance to take her out amidst all the confusion. Being leader of the 76-100 team wasn't enough anymore; he had higher ambitions.

Bat-gliders were cumbersome pieces of aerial equipment that looked much like they sounded, transforming the person inside the suit into a cross between a bat and a glider. Put one on, jump off a high building and extend your wings to fly – it was that simple in theory. In reality becoming proficient at bat-gliding required years of practice to learn how best to use the up-drifts and air currents around every citi-block. Prospective Citi-Def members were required to take a proficiency test with the equipment before being admitted to the squad.

Billy-Bob's second-in-command Aaron had passed the test with flying colours. The only problem was somebody else had snatched Aaron's specially enlarged bat-glider from the armoury before he arrived. The big man now found himself wedged inside a suit made for someone much smaller. It was all Aaron could do to keep the wings out level.

Once snug inside his own suit, Billy-Bob led the two dozen bat-gliders up to the ninetieth floor which had a special launching area built into a public balcony. The first wave of twelve flung themselves off the balcony, Billy-Bob at the front. They let the warm up-draft catch their wings and send them soaring towards the higher floors. The second wave was Aaron's responsibility but he fell like a stone after leaving the balcony, dropping twenty storeys until he got control of the under-sized suit.

"Aaron, what the hell are you doing?" Billy-Bob demanded. Each suit's flying helmet included a tiny receiver, transmitter and microphone for ease of communication.

"Just... coming," Aaron gasped, his breath stifled by the tortuously tight harness. He didn't have any children and Pressland doubted he would still be able to after this, such was the pressure applied by the crotch straps.

"I'm going in," Billy-Bob announced to the others. "First attack wave, follow me down!" He flipped one wing of his suit up and went into a steep dive, flinging himself towards the windows of the top floor con-apts. To the east the sun was just appearing over the horizon, light rising from beyond the Black Atlantic in the distance. Morning was breaking over Mega-City One.

In the lobby Dredd had used his judicial override to lock down Oswald Mosley's turbolifts, restricting the Citi-Def squad's movements. But solving one problem created another; how was he to gain access to the aliens on the top floor? Getting them out of the building would help defuse the situation, the sooner the better. "Dredd to Tek-Judge Brady, can you hear me?"

"Brady receiving. No answer yet about who supplied the armoury code."

"Acknowledged. I need a fast alternate route to the top of Oswald Mosley. Turbolifts are locked down and the stairs are perfect ambush territory."

"Hold on – I'll call up the building's blueprints." Seconds later Brady offered a solution. "Try the cleaning probe. It's a small platform that scuds up and down a tube at the side of the block, scouring the ventilation shaft. I'm sending a visual to your bike computer now."

Dredd strode to his Lawmaster, activating the small screen positioned behind the handlebars. It showed a tiny circle rising and falling just inside an exterior wall of Oswald Mosley. "Doesn't look very big," Dredd noted.

"It's not," Brady agreed. "Just over half a metre in diameter. You'll have to shed your shoulder pads, probably your elbow pads too to squeeze yourself in. When the probe reaches the top or bottom of the shaft, it pauses for six seconds before moving again. Makes the trip up and down once a minute, travelling at about ten metres a second."

"Sounds like being stuck inside a bullet," Dredd said.

"That's not a bad analogy. You wanted a fast alternate route – you never mentioned comfort."

"Roj that. Dredd to Control: where's my back-up?"

"It'll be there soon," Control replied. "However Sector Chief Caine has imposed a no-fly zone around Oswald Mosley. Says she doesn't want to lose any more H-Wagons to rocket attacks. So your back-up is coming by road, not by air."

"Well, I can't wait any longer. Dredd out!"

Lleccas screamed when the first bat-glider thudded against the floor-to-ceiling window. Billy-Bob used the suction pads on his knees and elbow pads to cling to the exterior, his wings a frightening silhouette in the dawn's early light. With his hands free, Billy-Bob pulled a laser-drill from his belt and began slicing through the glasseen of the window. More and more of the bat-gliders landed beside him, swarming over the outside of the building.

The other R'qeen families ran into the con-apt, looking for Nyon. "You brought this upon us," one of the brood-fathers said accusingly. "What do you suggest we do now?"

Nyon looked at his pairling who was still hugging Misch and the human child to herself. "We fight back!" he vowed. 'Lleccas, take all the broodlings into one room and keep them there. We will stop the humans as long as we can."

She nodded hurriedly and began ushering all the off-spring away. Nyon followed her, pressing a laser-knife into her hand. "You saw what they did to Keno. If we can't keep them out…"

Lleccas took the laser-knife and kissed her pairling. "I understand."

Dredd pulled open an access hatch to the cleaning probe. Inside was a smooth circular shaft, cool air rushing out-wards from it. Dredd leaned in to peer upwards but hastily withdrew his head. The probe was racing down the shaft towards him. It paused briefly in front of the Judge then shot back up again. Brady had been right, the interior was just only large enough to accommodate a human passenger. Dredd hastily began shedding the bulkier elements of his uniform, aware he only had one minute before the probe returned.

Fifty seconds later the air began whistling past Dredd again, indicating the probe was returning. He stepped back two paces and prepared to throw himself into the space. The probe arrived and Dredd flung himself at it, just pulling his arms and legs inside before he was shooting up the inside of the shaft, metal screaming past him in a blur.

. . .

Billy-Bob smashed in the section of window he had been cutting, the glasseen dropping into the con-apt's main room. The aliens had retreated to other parts of the top floor but they would soon be found, Billy-Bob was confident of that. He punched the clasp on his chest, letting the wings of his now redundant bat-glider fall away. Billy-Bob drew a bulging Deathbringer machine pistol from the holster at his waist and signalled the others around him. "I'm going in. Follow me!" He lowered both his legs inside the hole and dropped to the floor of the con-apt before scuttling across the main room like a beetle. More and more of the Citi-Def bat-glider squad dropped in behind him.

A shape raced past the front door of the con-apt, a blue blur of movement. Billy-Bob began firing, his Deathbringer spraying the doorway and the wall beyond it with bullets. Others joined in the shooting, happy to have the chance of using their training for once.

"Cease firing!" Billy-Bob shouted. By now nearly a dozen of the Citi-Def had joined him inside. Billy-Bob could see Aaron and the second attack wave circling overhead, awaiting the order to come in.

"Aaron, you and your boys hang back for the minute. We don't know how much resistance we're dealing with here."

"Affirmative," Aaron replied.

Billy-Bob sent half his men up one wall of the con-apt and the rest up the other side. As they reached a doorway two of the Citi-Def would burst in, guns blazing. But the con-apt had been evacuated, with no targets emerging so far. Billy-Bob stood up, relaxing his grip on the Deathbringer. "All right, everybody knows the drill. We secure the floor room by room, going two by two. Check all the corners and watch each other's backs. I don't want any nasty surprises!"

Billy-Bob stopped as a long drip of mucus fell on the barrel of his weapon. "What the drokk?" He looked up in

time to see Nyon and the other R'qeen clinging to the
high ceiling of the con-apt, their three-fingered hands
adhering to the surface above them, razor-sharp talons
growing from each finger like knives. "Sweet baby
Jovus…"

Nyon screamed an attack cry and the R'qeen dropped
on their prey.

Dredd checked the clips in his two Lawgivers as the
probe hurtled upwards, the g-force pulling at his facial
muscles. Then the air-piercing noise began dropping
pitch as the probe's upwards momentum decreased.
When it reached the top, there would be only seconds to
get out or die trying. Abruptly the probe stopped, throwing
Dredd up into the roof.

Five seconds. He slumped back down to the floor, still
trying to get his bearings. Four. Dredd kicked out with his
boots, smashing away the exterior access hatch. Three.
The probe would slice him in two if he wasn't all the way
out when it began descending. Two. Dredd had one leg
and one shoulder out, but his twin Lawgivers were
caught on the side of the access hatch. One. Wrenching
his weapons clear, the Judge threw himself away from
the probe. Zero. The probe flung itself downwards again,
wind whistling past Dredd as he lay gasping for breath on
the floor.

Once the probe was gone, he could hear screaming and
gunfire nearby. The Citi-Def must have found its own way
up to the top floor. Dredd was too late – the
slaughter had already begun. Pulling himself to his feet,
Dredd ran towards the sounds of death, both guns ready to
fire.

Aaron watched in horror as the aliens attacked his friends,
tearing at the Citi-Def members' protective clothing, slicing
through metal and flesh. As the first gout of blood coloured

the air, Billy-Bob's bellowed command almost overloaded Aaron's helmet radio.

"Get them!"

The 76-100 leader began firing randomly, his Death-bringer swinging through the air, bullets indiscriminately puncturing R'qeen and human. The others began shooting too, screams and gunfire filling air already crowded with cries of pain and death.

The other bat-gliders still in the air were also watching, unsure how to react. "What do we do, Aaron?" one of them asked.

The big man floated above the melee. He had never wanted this, never expected to see active duty. For him the Citi-Def was a way of making friends. "Stand down," he said. "We can't help them now."

"But you can't leave them!"

"Watch me," Aaron replied and let one wing dip. He glided away in a slow spiral, descending to the deserted skedway one hundred storeys below. A few stayed above the battle scene watching impotently, but the rest followed Aaron's example. They might not like having aliens in the block but it wasn't a cause worth dying for.

Billy-Bob had lost his Deathbringer and was now down to just a kitchen laser. He passed it back and forth between his hands as he retreated towards the glasseen window. The alien leader was closing in on him, its lips pulled back in a cruel mockery of a smile to reveal row upon row of teeth.

"Stay back!" Billy-Bob warned. "I know how to use this thing!"

"So do I," Nyon replied in halting English. "My brood shall feast on your remains for many weeks, human."

"Drokk you!" Billy-Bob screamed and threw himself at the alien.

. . .

When Dredd reached the con-apt the floor was soaked red with blood. The walls were studded with bullet holes and scorch marks, while the room was strewn with severed limbs and corpses. One of the R'qeen was still alive, just. It gestured to Dredd who approached, stepping carefully through the carnage. "Too... late..." Nyon gasped. "You're... too late... human..." Then he said no more.

The Judge activated his helmet radio. "Dredd to Control, I've reached the top floor of Oswald Mosley. Citi-Def got in here, looks like they came by bat-glider. There was a pitched battle – plenty of casualties on both sides. I'll investigate the rest of the rooms for survivors. Where's that back-up?"

"Just arriving now."

Miller had the transporter stop just short of Oswald Mosley. "We go the rest of the way on foot," she told her strike team. They were all clad in a double-layer of body armour, with Widowmaker assault rifles at the ready. "No point giving these Citi-Def bozos any big targets to fire at. Spread out and move in."

The Judges jumped out of the vehicle and began advancing on their target. Miller had the three best long-range shots stay at the perimeter of the nearest building, Enoch Powell Block. "I want you scanning the windows for snipers. If you see anyone firing from inside, take them out. Shoot to kill." The trio nodded grimly and moved off to find the best vantage points. "The rest of you: keep it tight but don't get bunched up. I'll lead."

Miller emerged from cover and started running towards Oswald Mosley, zigzagging from side to side as she did. Shots began ringing out from the upper floors, but the snipers were soon eliminated by Miller's sharp-shooters. She was across the open space in thirty seconds, the remainder of her strike team following.

Within a minute all twenty-two Judges were in the lobby.

"Turbolifts are locked down so we take the stairs, two by two," their leader said. "This is going to get bloody but we're not taking any prisoners. If it moves, shoot it. Last one to the ninety-ninth floor has to help carry out the bodies. Let's move!"

Dredd found five unconscious aliens in the hundredth floor's central circular corridor. He recognised one of them as an arthropod, no doubt from Andromeda IV. The others were all from another species, their bodies covered in thick hair, prominent ridges running down the centre of their faces.

"Dredd to Control, I've located five alien survivors in Oswald Mosley. Looks like the concussion gas kept them out of the fighting. Am continuing my search of the top floor."

The Judge began moving cautiously onward when a gasp from nearby stopped him. Somebody else was alive up here.

Misch could feel the intruder getting closer. She was leaning against the door of the dark chamber. Behind her Lleccas, still clutching the laser-knife, was guarding the other broodlings and Kasey. Misch concentrated herself on the approaching human.

She had sensed her broodfather's death and the loss of so many others, both R'qeen and human. It was an ugly thing that had happened. Misch did not know if she would even recover from the shock of what she had felt. But her gift was important, it could help keep the rest of them alive.

The human who was approaching was ready to kill, she could sense that, but there was something else clouding his thoughts. Unable to easily discern them, Misch reached out with her senses.

Too many dead already – wasted lives.

Need to find the others.

That sound – is the girl here after all?

Wait, something else – something in my head!

Get out! Get out of my mind!

Misch fell backwards, as if she had been punched. She cried out as her head hit the ground with a thump. No, no, she thought, I've given us away! The door was ripped open, and light flooded in, temporarily blinding those inside. Standing over them was an imposing figure, weapon drawn and ready to fire.

Lleccas stood up, brandishing the laser-knife. "You shall not take them," she screeched in R'qeen. "I will die killing you before that happens!"

The human took a step forwards to confront Lleccas.

"No, wait!" Misch cried out in Allspeak. Her broodmother and the human stopped. "He's here to help us, I can feel it!"

Dredd touched a hand to his helmet. "You were the one in my head."

The R'qeen girl approached him. "Yes. I had to know whether you wanted to hurt us." She took his hand in her own, the green gauntlet dwarfing her three small fingers. "Thank you for rescuing us."

Dredd looked around the room. "Are there any more elsewhere?"

"No," Lleccas replied in Allspeak. "We are the last." She rested a kindly hand on her broodling's head. "Misch told us what happened to my pairling Nyon and the others."

The Judge began to usher them out into the circular corridor. "We need to evacuate all of you, the sooner the better. The Citi-Def has already launched one attack on this floor and failed, their leader will be getting desperate. There's no telling what she'll try to do next." He reactivated his helmet radio. "Dredd to Control, I've located the last of the aliens. Immediate evac required!"

"No can do, Dredd. Caine is keeping the no-fly zone in place."

"Put me through to her!"

Conchita and Riff had reached the ninety-ninth floor, the reporter left breathless by the long climb. Conchita had gathered a dozen Citi-Def members on the way up, ordering the rest to defend the stairwell below. She was dismayed to discover the emergency access door to the top floor was still impassable.

"I had hoped Billy-Bob and his bat-gliders would take care of this for me," Conchita scowled. She tried to contact them but the aerial wing's radio channel remained silent. "Typical, have to do everything myself. Pass me that carryall." From inside the bag Conchita pulled out a rubbery grey brick and a fistful of wires. She clamped the brick to the side of the door near the hinges and began plunging wires into it.

"What's that?" Riff asked, aware his hovercam was still recording events, even if his earpiece had long since fallen silent.

"An incendiary device, not unlike the one my boys planted in Robert Hatch. Blow the door in and burn out the top floor of this block," Conchita said.

"But if your daughter is still alive up there, won't the fire kill her too?"

"She chose to be with the aliens instead of me," Conchita replied. "She has to face the consequences."

"But you told me she'd been abducted!" Riff protested. "That was the reason you mobilised the Citi-Def!"

"She chose to be with those alien freaks. She has to pay for that!"

"With her life? And what about all those from your Citi-Def squad who have sacrificed themselves for your crusade?" Riff turned to those gathered behind him. "How do you feel about this?"

"We didn't know," the nearest one admitted. "We thought this was a righteous cause, defending our block against–"

He was cut short by a bullet through the brain. Riff was sprayed with the dead man's blood. When he had wiped it away from his eyes, he found Conchita pointing her gun at him. "You're drokking insane!" he whispered.

"No, I'm a mother and I love my daughter. If she won't listen to me then she has to be punished," Conchita insisted. "Now, I suggest you all leave. This is between me and the aliens."

The remaining squad members were already retreating down the stairs but Riff stayed for one last question. "I've still got that pistol you gave me. What's to stop me shooting you?"

Conchita smiled. "It isn't loaded. If you're leaving, you better hurry. This is going to blow in the next few minutes."

"No, Control, I do not wish to speak with Dredd," Sector Chief Caine said. "I'm rather busy. Tell him to be patient. Caine out!" She returned to deleting files from her office computer system as someone knocked on her office door. "Come in." Brady opened the door and entered. "Close the door behind you, we don't want to be disturbed." Brady did as he was bid and then stood in front of Caine's desk.

"You sent for me, ma'am."

"That's right. I understand you've been giving Dredd a lot of help during this graveyard shift."

"Yes, ma'am. He helped me become a Tek-Judge instead of just another perp, so I wanted to repay a little of that debt."

"Commendable sentiments. However there is little room for sentiment within the department." Caine pulled open a drawer in her desk and reached inside it with both hands. "I notice you've been making particular enquiries about the armoury code for Oswald Mosley Block, trying to find out who leaked it to the Citi-Def. What progress have you made?"

"Well, it's proving to be something of a mystery. Channel 27 eventually admitted to acting as a conduit for the code's transmission into Oswald Mosley, but the news editor claimed he had been sent it by Judge Stammers."

"That fits Stammers's profile," Caine said. "Rabidly anti-alien and just stupid enough to do something like this. So where's the mystery?"

Brady's face lit up. "The message was sent to Channel 27 just after five this morning. But Stammers was reported dead two hours earlier!"

"So he recorded the message before he died and arranged for it to be transmitted later. I still don't see–"

"That's just it. Channel 27's system shows the message was sent as a live text-only message, not as a recording. And there's something else. It wasn't sent from any public vidphone booth, it came from inside this building! So someone here leaked the code to the Citi-Def squad. Whoever did that is culpable for the rocket attack on the H-Wagon that killed Deputy Sector Chief Temple and eleven other Judges."

"This is shocking news," Caine said. "Have you told anybody else about this yet? I wouldn't want word leaking out. The culprit might hear and take flight."

"Nobody else knows except you and I," the Tek-Judge said.

"Let's keep it that way, shall we?" Caine pulled a Law-giver from inside the drawer of her desk, a silencer fitted snugly over the end of the barrel. She fired twice, both bullets thudding into Brady's chest. He tumbled back-wards to the floor, still reacting with surprise. Caine stood up and walked round the desk to examine the dying Tek-Judge. "After all, we wouldn't want to create a panic. *Sector Chief Escalates Anti-Alien Conflict* doesn't make a very good headline for the department, does it?"

Brady coughed up blood, his hands feebly trying to staunch the bleeding from his wounds. "W–why?" he gasped.

"You and Dredd have forced my hand," Caine replied. "I had hoped to slip away quietly, with nobody else getting hurt. But your private investigation triggered the alarms I had built into the sector house comms systems. So you had to die. Sorry about that, but these things happen. Now, if you'll excuse me, I have one or two little chores to complete before I depart this sector. Goodbye, Brady." She snapped the microphone from his helmet radio and switched off the computer screen on her desk before leaving, locking the door on her way out.

Brady tried to drag himself across the floor towards the desk, but his strength was fading fast. A coughing fit gripped his body, blood spread outwards across the floor beneath him, and his spasming legs kicked splashes against the side of the desk. The Tek-Judge looked up at the picture window. The sun was over the horizon now, lighting up the cityscape once more. Despite the absence of Weather Control, it was going to be a glorious day. But Brady's eyes could no longer see the brilliance of the blue sky. Brady's eyes could no longer see anything.

Miller and her strike team had met surprisingly little resistance as they climbed the stairs inside Oswald Mosley. A cluster of hardcore Citi-Def members had attempted to lay an ambush at the twenty-seventh floor but it only required a mixture of ricochet and heatseeker bullets to kill the ringleaders. Those left alive quickly surrendered, grateful to have met someone other than Dredd. "He says he's gonna kill us all if he finds us," one squad member said, her face full of fear.

Miller shoved her Widowmaker assault rifle under the woman's chin. "Get on your frequency and tell the others. If they surrender now they might get out of here alive. If they don't, we'll let Dredd have them. It's their choice."

After that the charge up the stairs passed with little incident. Each new group of Citi-Def fighters they encountered were more than happy to lay down their weapons and surrender. Miller's biggest problem was having to assign two of her team to supervising the removal of each group of prisoners. Still, the concussion gas had done its job and kept the other residents sedated and out of danger. The remnants of Miller's team were passing the sixtieth floor when another cluster of Citi-Def members appeared, all with their hands behind their heads. "We surrender, we surrender!" the man nearest the front cried out.

"How many of you left?" Miller demanded.

"There's just Conchita Maguire. She's still up on the ninety-ninth floor," another voice replied. Riff Maltin appeared from among the squad members and approached the Judges, his hovercam just behind him as always. "She's got an incendiary device like the one used at Robert Hatch. She plans to burn out the aliens on the top floor."

"You're the one who's been inciting these idiots to riot!" Miller snarled at the reporter. Her first punch broke Riff's nose, sending blood gushing down his face. Her second punch broke his jaw, the bone smashing beneath her gauntlet's steel-capped knuckles. The reporter collapsed to the stairs, his hovercam moving in for a close-up of his injuries. "Without your inflammatory reports, the Citi-Def would have seen sense and backed down hours ago. But you kept turning up the heat, until Conchita and her

cronies didn't dare lose face. I'll be holding you personally responsible for every death that's taken place here!"

She swung the hovercam round so it was filming her
face. "The same goes for everyone at Channel 27 and
anybody still watching this. Turn yourself in to the nearest sector house. This transmission ends right now!"

Miller smashed the hovercam against a rockcrete wall
repeatedly until few fragments bigger than her fist
remained. She assigned half of her remaining team to
escort Riff and the other prisoners down the stairs, while
she pressed on with three other Judges. There was just
the ringleader left to subdue, but Conchita was always
going to be the most difficult. It was her missing daughter
that had been one of the catalysts for all of this. This
wasn't just about hating aliens, this was personal.

Conchita finished wiring the incendiary device
together and set the timer for sixty seconds. That
would give her enough time to retreat a safe distance
down the stairs and get her flame-thrower ready. Any
aliens that survived the initial explosion were going to
be burnt to a crisp, one way or another.

Caine emerged from the turbolift into the sector
house's registration area, a smile playing about her
lips. The Judge behind 87's check-in desk saw her and
called out. Caine stopped, sighed and walked towards
him. "Yes, what it is? I'm running late for an early
meeting at Justice Central."

"It's just that Dredd's been trying to contact you for
some time. Apparently he's very unhappy about something."

"Well, that's no great surprise. I've got a hover pod
waiting for me outside. Tell Dredd I'll give him a call
en route to my destination. Anything else?"

"No, ma'am, just that."

Caine smiled. "Very well. Oh, could you tell Tek-Division that Brady is fixing a fault in my office and is not to be disturbed under any circumstances. He tells me it may take several hours. Is that quite clear?"

"Yes, ma'am!"

"Excellent. Well, see you on the streets." She marched from the sector house, never to return. Once outside she stepped into a waiting hover pod. "The spaceport and make it snappy," Caine told the droid driver before activating her helmet radio. "Control, this is Caine. Patch me through to Dredd."

Dredd sealed off the air vents, stopping the flow of concussion gas into the top floor. It didn't take long for Gruchar or the Wolfren family to revive, no doubt thanks to their alien physiognomy. But the Judge was having less luck undoing the damage Nyon had wrought on the turbolift doors, which remained fused shut. He would have to find a way to reopen access to the emergency stairs, unless an H-Wagon could be brought in to evacuate the aliens. A voice from his helmet radio offered new hope. "Miller to Dredd, can you hear me?"

"Loud and clear. What's been happening?"

"I brought in a strike team and we've cleared most of the hostiles. Just Conchita Maguire left."

"Do you know where she is?"

"According to the others she's about to detonate an incendiary device on the emergency access door to your floor. It could blow at any time and we're still forty storeys below you!"

Dredd shouted at Misch and the other aliens to start running. "Get as far from here as you can!" He pulled open a door and crouched behind it, using the metal rectangle as a shield.

"Caine to Dredd: you wanted to talk to me?"

"Not now! This place could–"

The explosion cut off his transmission.

Caine pulled off her helmet, the radio a frenzy of white noise. "How very rude."

The emergency access door exploded into the top floor of Oswald Mosley. It sliced neatly through three walls and out of a large glasseen window. It took nearly a minute for the crumpled and charred rectangle of metal to hit the ground below, burying itself into the deserted skedway.

The fireball from the explosion expanded into the circular corridor and split into halves, each flying out sideways. The door Dredd was crouching behind buckled and boiled, but the reinforced metal core held firm, protecting him from the flames. The twin fireballs scorched round the corridor, splaying sideways through any open doors and incinerating everything in its path. Fortunately Kasey, Misch and all the other aliens had retreated to the far side of Oswald Mosley, closing the doors behind them. By the time the fireball had reached the final barrier, the flames were burning themselves out.

Dredd stood up and looked along the corridor. The walls and floor were still burning but the immediate danger was past. But smoke inhalation or fire could still claim everyone alive on this level. The need to evacuate was now more urgent than ever.

"Where is she?" a woman's voice screeched. "Where's the little monster that caused all of this?" Conchita Maguire stepped through the now empty doorway to the emergency stairs, a lit flame-thrower clasped in her hands, twin fuel tanks mounted on her back.

"Are you talking about your daughter or yourself?" Dredd asked from behind the protection of his door.

Conchita whirled round, sending a fresh ball of flame at the wilting rectangle. "I'm talking about Kasey! My darling little Kasey, the waste of skin and bones that has shamed me from the moment she was born!"

"Not what I call motherly love," Dredd replied, his words goading Conchita still further. He was rewarded with another dose of flame.

"What would you know about it? Did you ever have a mother?"

"The Law is my family!" Dredd shouted. "Look what's happened to yours!"

"My family loves me!" Conchita screamed.

"Your daughter ran away, she'd rather be with aliens than with you."

"Not that little slitch! She was a mistake. I'm talking about my sons!"

"Ramone and Dermot?"

"That's them. Two of the finest boys a mother ever had."

Dredd was backing slowly away from Conchita, always keeping the door between himself and her. "If they're so fine, why haven't you heard from them?"

"How did you know that?"

"Because they died last night. Judge Stammers gunned them down in cold blood and pushed their bodies into a chem pit." He listened carefully to her reply, using it to determine her position and take aim.

"No, you're lying!" Conchita raged.

"You'll never know – I just wanted you to think about that as you died. Armour piercing!" Dredd fired six times in succession, each bullet piercing the door and travelling on through Conchita's body. As they spat out her back the bullets punctured the tanks of the flame-thrower, releasing jets of flammable gas into the air. It mingled with the flames from the nozzle of her weapon. Conchita was toast.

Miller was running up the stairs past the ninety-fifth floor when the second fireball exploded. It flung itself out of the doorway five storeys up and surged down the stairwell, roasting everything in its path. "Take cover!" Miller screamed.

Dredd rolled over and over, trying to extinguish the flames that had engulfed him, but their grip on his uniform was too strong. He was being burned alive. It was the aliens that saved him; Lleccas and Gruchar dragged him out of the corridor and doused him with water. Misch and Kasey had closed the door behind them so now all the survivors were trapped in one room.

Once the flames were extinguished, Dredd reactivated his helmet radio. "Miller, can you still hear me?"

"Just," came the coughing reply. "What was that second explosion?"

Dredd noticed Kasey, her face still showing the bruises and scars inflicted by her mother. "Conchita Maguire won't be hurting anyone anymore."

"Well, that's good news," Miller said. "The bad news is we can't get close to you. The fire has cut off all access from below. What's your status?"

"Not good. All the survivors are in one room with me, but we're cut off by the flames. There is no escape except the window. We need evac and now!" A burst of static indicated another voice cutting into the conversation.

"Control to Dredd: Chief Judge Hershey has overruled the no-fly zone imposed by Sector Chief Caine. H-Wagons should be with you any minute."

"Thank Grud for that. Dredd out!" He let himself slump against a wall, exhaustion catching up with him.

Misch whispered something in her broodmother's ear. Lleccas smiled and nodded. Then the R'qeen child ventured over to the Judge and cleared her throat.

"Excuse me," she said in perfect English. "Would you like me to make you feel better?"

Dredd opened his eyes and looked down at the broodling. "Why? Have you got a med-kit stashed about here somewhere?"

"No, but I do have the gift of metema. It can ease away your weariness."

Kasey stood beside her friend. "She makes everyone feel better."

Dredd shrugged. "Give it a try, kid."

Misch rested her hand inside that of Dredd and closed her eyes, reaching out to drive away his fatigue. After a few moments she staggered and took her hand away, Kasey helping the R'qeen girl to stay upright. Dredd straightened. His muscles and joints were not as stiff as before, and his back was slowly unbending.

"What's your name?"

"Misch."

"Thank you, Misch. If there's ever anything I can do for you..."

She beckoned him to bend over and whispered something into his helmet.

Dredd frowned slightly, before nodding. "I'll see what I can arrange."

Then the H-Wagon appeared out of the dawn sky, the sunlight glinting off its metal panels and glasseen windows.

07:00

Caine emerged from the spaceport restrooms a different woman. Gone was the close-cropped mass of black curls; a copper bob replaced them. Shed was the Sector Chief's uniform, supplanted by a stylish catsuit of black leathereen that gripped her in all the right places. She wore matching stiletto boots. Her eyes looked different: dark green contact lenses in place of the usual hazel pupils. Even her travel documents were a lie; she now assumed the fresh identity of galactic bounty hunter Dakota Biggs. The new persona helped explain the small but deadly weapon concealed in her hip pocket.

The flight to Luna-1 and then onwards to the Eden colony on Mars, had already being called. Caine presented her documents to the Judge on Customs, careful to keep her smile friendly while idly leaning forwards to give him an eyeful of her cleavage. Law enforcers might not be permitted sexual or romantic liaisons, but they didn't stop them looking, in her experience. Sure enough, he waved her through to the first class waiting room after admiring the view for a few moments longer than were strictly necessary.

The waiting room had been an agonising experience. Caine's eyes constantly darted to the doorway, expecting a Judge to burst in at any time looking for her. But the expectation went unmet. After several minutes the first class passengers were called through to take their seats on the flight. There were only three others joining her on this jaunt, all of them frequent flyers judging by their bored expressions.

Even while being strapped into a seat for lift-off, Caine found herself waiting for a gauntlet-clad hand to rest itself on her shoulder, a quiet word in her ear as a Lawgiver was pressed into her back. But the pre-flight procedures passed without incident and the engines were engaged. At last Caine let herself relax. She ordered a champagne cocktail from the robotic steward and closed her eyes. Now, this was the life! No more reports to read, no more bureaucracy to tangle with, no more responsibility. She was looking forward to being a rich, dangerous civ...

"Your champagne, ma'am," a voice growled.

Caine looked up to find Dredd standing over her, Lawgiver in one hand, a glass of bubbling liquid in the other. His uniform was a charred mess, his face blackened and burnt. Caine took the glass and sipped at the contents. "This is warm," she protested.

"So was the top floor of Oswald Mosley. Get over it."

"Fair point," Caine agreed and took another sip. "How did you find me?"

"The Desk Judge at the sector house got suspicious after you said 'See you on the streets' as you left. you'd never been that nice to him. They found Brady's body in your office. He had written CAINE = KILLER in his own blood. Seems the SJS have been watching you and Summerbee for months."

"I've had my suspicions of that," Caine conceded. "When you turned up, I was convinced Hershey had sent you in to find evidence against me."

"That's why you reacted so strongly to my arrival."

"It seemed the best strategy – keep you off-balance, moving from one end of the sector to the other and you wouldn't have time to investigate me. None of it would have been necessary if the Heavy Metal Kid had done its job properly."

"That was meant for me?"

"Just like you should have died inside Oswald Mosley. Grud knows, I put enough obstacles in your way." Caine finished her champagne. "Well, what's the plan now? Shoot me here or ship me to Titan for a long slow death there?"

"I'm asking the questions," Dredd snapped. "The fire at Robert Hatch; you used Stammers and Riley to torch the building so Summerbee could get the contract to construct the new Grand Halls of Justice there. What was your cut of the deal? Half? A quarter?"

"I don't know why you bother asking me questions if you're going to answer them yourself," Caine said, shoving her hands petulantly into her pockets. "Summerbee and I were going halves, my nest egg for retirement."

"Judges don't retire. They die in the line of duty or take the Long Walk."

"That's where you're wrong, Dredd. The department was about to retire me. Except they called it a sideways promotion. I was a rising star once, destined for big things. I thought I'd be heading up a division of my own by now, perhaps have a seat on the Council of Five, maybe even be Chief Judge one day. Instead I was to be shuffled sideways, pushed out for someone younger so Hershey can make her mark on the department! Well what about me? What about my contribution? Twenty years a Judge and what did I have to show for it? Nothing, except a synthetic lung and bionic eye implants. I was getting put out to pasture, past my prime, out of date. Well not this Judge!" Caine pulled her hands from her pockets, a tiny pistol in her grasp, one finger on the trigger.

"You can't escape," Dredd said wearily. "Every Judge between here and Pluto has your new identity by now. Fire that and you'll be dead in moments."

"How right you are," Caine replied, lifting the pistol up to her mouth. She pulled the trigger before Dredd could wrench the weapon from her grasp.

"She would have killed herself sooner or later," Miller said when Dredd walked out of the spaceship. "Least this ways the department doesn't have to pay for her to be shipped to the judicial prison on Titan."

The two Judges strolled through the spaceport as a forensic team from Tek-Division moved in to clean up the mess. Overhead a robotic tannoy regretfully announced a delay in the departure of the morning flight to Luna-1 and Mars, due to "technical difficulties."

Miller smiled at the euphemism. "Technical difficulties must mean how hard it is to get fresh brains out of such plush upholstery."

Chief Judge Hershey was waiting for them outside. "I hear she's dead."

"Killed herself rather than go to Titan," Dredd said. "How long have you known about Caine?"

"Known? Only for the past hour or so. Suspected? More than a year. That's why I sent you in, Dredd. Thought it might make Caine show her hand."

"It did. You could have told me I was acting as bait for your trap."

"Better to keep you ignorant and Caine guessing at your motives," Hershey said.

"What about the plans to build a new Grand Hall of Justice in Sector 87? Was that just another lure for Caine and Summerbee?" Miller asked.

"Yes. It was the only way to draw out as big a fish as Summerbee. And it worked."

"Just a shame so many good people had to die to prove it," Dredd said.

Hershey nodded. "You know, with Caine and Temple dead, there's a vacancy for a new Sector Chief in 87..."

Dredd didn't want to know. "I did my time in the Pit. I like being out on the streets, not stuck behind some desk."

"Actually, I was making the offer to Judge Miller," the Chief Judge said.

"Oh." Dredd cleared his throat. "Good choice."

"That's what I thought," Hershey agreed. "Well, Lynn, how about it?"

"I didn't think I'd get a shot at the big chair, in view of my record."

"A dozen exemplary years on the streets, good leadership skills and a willingness to confront corruption in the force – even from old friends. I think that outweighs one youthful indiscretion," the Chief Judge said. "We've all made mistakes in our time, haven't we, Dredd?"

"Some more than others," he replied, prompting a smile from Hershey.

"It will still have to go before the Council of Five," she said. "But if you're willing to take the post it could be yours."

Miller nodded happily. "I'll do it!"

"Good. Well, if that's everything settled–"

Dredd held up a hand to interrupt the Chief Judge. "There's one other matter arising from the incidents at Oswald Mosley."

"I suspect Tek-Division will condemn the building. Those residents not going to the cubes for their part in the lawlessness will have to be rehoused until the block can be rebuilt."

"No, it was something else," Dredd said. "I have a request to pass on."

EPILOGUE
08:00

"You can open your eyes," Lleccas said. Kasey and Misch pulled their hands away from their faces and gasped. They were standing in the middle of a palatial bungalow, the open plan lounge sprawling out before them, large sofas and luxurious furnishings spread around the huge space.

"What is this place?" Misch asked.

"It used to belong to a rich man called Summerbee," Dredd said. "When he died he left all his residences to the city. The Chief Judge has said Summerbee's properties can be used to house all the alien families who lost their homes in the fire at Robert Hatch. Lleccas and Misch will be living here from now on, with several other R'qeen families."

"Oh," said Kasey sadly. "Where will I go?"

"That's up to you," Lleccas replied. "All your family are dead but the Judge says you can stay with us, if you want."

The human girl turned to Dredd, her face full of hope. "Can I? Really?"

"If you want. It may not be as easy as you think. Most of the R'qeen cannot speak English like Misch and many do not know Allspeak either."

"Misch will help me," Kasey announced.

The R'qeen broodling nodded. While Lleccas, Kasey and the others went off to explore the rest of their new home, Misch stayed behind with Dredd.

"I wanted to thank you, for making my wish happen," she said.

"Your broodfather is dead, you've been burnt out of two homes in twelve hours. Not what I'd call a happy ending."

Misch smiled. "It would have been worse, without you. Thanks."

Dredd nodded, watching the alien child run off to be with the others. The Judge walked back out of the luxurious home to his Lawmaster motorcycle. "Dredd to Control, you got anything for me?"

"Nothing at this time."

"In that case I'm done for this graveyard shift. Sign me off."

"Where will you be if needed?"

"On a sleep machine. I'll be back on call at nine. Dredd out!"

ABOUT THE AUTHOR

David Bishop was born and raised in New Zealand, becoming a daily newspaper journalist at eighteen years old. He emigrated to Britain in 1990 and became sub-editor of the *Judge Dredd Megazine*. He was editor from 1992-1995, a period when the title was voted Britain's best comic every year. He edited *2000 AD* weekly from 1996 to 2000 before becoming a freelance writer. His previous novels include three starring *Judge Dredd* (for Virgin Books) and four featuring *Doctor Who* (for Virgin and the BBC). He also writes non-fiction books and articles, audio dramas, comics and has been a creative consultant on three forthcoming video games. If you see Bishop in public, do not approach him, alert the nearest editor and then stand well back.

THE BIG MEG GLOSSARY

Allspeak: A language favoured by aliens throughout the galaxy.

Bat-Glider: A bodysuit with wings that allows its user to soar over the city by utilising the air currents.

Birdie: A hand-held lie detector.

Block: Giant skyscrapers that make up most of Mega-City One. The inhabitants of blocks are known as blockers. Sometimes the pressures of living in such cramped high-rise conditions lead to block mania, which may spark a block war.

Brit-Cit: British counterpart of Mega-City One.

Citi-Def: A civilian militia, the City Defence Force: a voluntary civilian army organised on a block basis that saw action against the Sov-Bloc invaders of the Apocalypse War in 2104.

Con-Apt: Connecting apartment, usually small and modest.

Control: The nerve centre of Mega-City One, relaying information to Judges on the streets.

Council of Five: The central ruling council of Judges, including Chief Judge Hershey.

Cursed Earth: A vast radioactive wasteland that stretches across North America, populated by mutants, freaks and wild creatures.

Daystick: The Judge's favoured truncheon.

Dust Zone: Sector in the city dedicated to industrial use.

Graveyard Shift: A term coined by the Judges for the late night/early morning period of duty.

H-Wagon: A heavy Justice Department hover vehicle, usually well armoured and armed.

Hotdog run: An expedition into the Cursed Earth for trainee Judges.

Indo-Cit: Indian counterpart of Mega-City One.

Iso-Cube: The standard imprisonment for criminals; a huge block full of very small isolation cubes.

Lawgiver: The weapon of choice for the Judge; an automatic multi-shell gun whose ammunition ranges from armour piercing to ricochet rounds.

Lawmaster: The Judge's computer controlled motorbike – extremely powerful, intelligent and heavily armed.

Luna-City: Counterpart of Mega-City One located on the Moon, aka Luna-1.

Med-Judge: A medic specialist usually in support of a meat wagon; very much like an ambulance. Med-Judges work within a Med-Squad, for Med-Division.

Offworlder: Alien.

Pedway: A pedestrian-only pathway, often motorised.

Perp: A criminal.

Pre-Cog: A special type of Psi-Judge with precognitive powers, able to predict the future to a limited degree.

Psi-Judge: A Judge with psychic abilities, a psyker, from the Justice Department's Psi-Division.

Psycho Cubes: A prison cell for psychological disturbed and highly dangerous citizens. Also known as the Kook Cube.

R'qeen: An alien race that once fought a war with humans. R'qeen are carrion eaters who prefer to eat rotting flesh and a number live within Mega-City One. Some R'qeen are blessed with metema, the ability to read the minds of humans.

Shoppera: A block constructed into a huge shopping centre, aka dhoplex.

SJS: The Special Judicial Squad act as the Judge's police; they seek out corruption and crime within the Law with extreme prejudice.

Skedway: A minor roadway; smaller than a megway but larger than an overzoom.

Sleep Machine: A cubicle for Street Judges who can rest for ten minutes and gain a whole night's sleep.

Smokatorium: A huge, block-sized building dedicated to legal tobacco smoking. To smoke tobacco outside the building is deemed illegal and can warrant a six-month iso-cube sentence.

Street Judge: A Judge on the beat who tackles crime and issues sentences.

Tek-Judge: A technical and engineering specialist whose skills range from advanced forensic analysis to the repairing of vehicles, weapons, etc.

Titan: A small moon orbiting Saturn, used as a dedicated maximum-security prison for Mega-City One's most dangerous criminals, where they spend their days breaking rocks.

Tri-D: Also known as holovision; there are over 312 channels in Mega-City One.

Weather Control: A Justice Department dedicated to artificially maintaining the weather over Mega-City One as well as being able to rain upon an illegal demonstration, etc. If the Weather Control should fail, the temperature within parts of Mega-City One becomes incredibly humid that can entice rioting.

ATTENTION MEGA-CITY!

JUDGE DREDD

DREDD VS DEATH

GORDON RENNIE

BY GORDON RENNIE

DEATH IS BACK AND HE'S
JUDGING THE CITIZENS OF
MEGA-CITY ONE!

The Butterfly Effect

CHANGE ONE THING. CHANGE EVERYTHING.

...van Treborn devises a technique of traveling back in time to inhabit his childhood body. But ...th his past in tatters and his future just as bleak, he soon realises that some things are better left untouched!

Based on the awesome New Line Cinema release starring Ashton Kutcher.

WWW.BLACKFLAME.COM

LET THE GALAXY BURN!